I0536945

Echoes from the Past

TAYO EMMANUEL

Published in 2018 by Total Word Publishers, United Kingdom

Copyright © Tayo Emmanuel 2018

ISBN: 978-0-9565259-2-5

Tayo Emmanuel has asserted her right under the Copyright, Designs and Patents Act, 1988 as the author of this book.

A CIP catalogue record for this book is available from the British Library.

For the life so inspiring, though brief
For the smile that cuts through the deepest grief
For the legacy of love like showers of rain
For things that happen, that we can't explain

To the memory of Funmilayo Ajimo Williams

*Those who cannot forgive others break the bridge
over which they themselves must pass*
Confucius

PROLOGUE

Fourteen Years Earlier

As a child, she hated the smell of hospitals despite having visited several, since her mother was a nurse. Every time she entered a new one, she always wondered why they all smelt alike. She felt no consolation even when she grew older and realised it was the caustic scent of disinfectants that usually assaulted her senses at hospitals. This one was no different, perhaps worse, combined with the mixed emotions plaguing her.

She sat at the small reception room, fidgeting and glancing furtively at the wall clock as if she would rather be somewhere else. Every time someone came in, she wondered if they could guess why she was there and if they were there for the same reason, which might explain why they also came at such a time of the day. The reception was the worst of its kind she had ever seen of hospitals; floored with tattered and fading black

1

and white linoleum, with a tired looking nurse sitting behind an equally decrepit shelf containing brownish white files.

The nurse pretended to be detached from the Nollywood film on TV and focused on writing when she was not calling out the names of the people waiting to see the doctor. A large part of the fake leather covering the two benches was worn and faded.

Ordinarily, with his wherewithal, Tokunbo would not have been found anywhere near such a place, but this was the only referral she could extract from one of the girls in school. If she had a choice, she would disappear right now, but with Tokunbo beside her, holding her hand tightly, there was no way she could turn back. Even without him, she was realistic enough to know that going back home this way wasn't an option as she couldn't bring herself to face her mother's disappointment after all they'd both been through. He had agreed with her that this was the best decision. Except that now, she was not sure anymore, especially when she saw the young girl with an unpleasant scowl on her face return to the waiting room, clutching her stomach while trying to keep her profile upright.

She turned her face from staring at the girl towards Tokunbo. "Are you sure we should still go ahead? What if something goes wrong?" He did not respond at first, but continued stomping both his feet in slow rhythmic motion. Was it fear or impatience? She could not tell as his passive face did not reveal any emotion. She almost pitied him, but her own fears quickly obliterated any thought she could have spared for him.

He squeezed her hand gently, forcing a smile. "Don't worry, everything will be okay. The doctor has promised that it won't take long and you won't feel anything." A few minutes later, the nurse called her name after the buzzer. Tokunbo got up with her and released her hand gently as she dragged her feet to follow the other nurse who was waiting by the door. He looked on emptily, avoiding her eyes when she turned back to look at him. He continued to mutter under his breath until she disappeared with the nurse into the corridor, closing the door behind them.

To overcome the self-consciousness of revealing her nudity to the stranger, she forced her mind to drift to her mother, while the nurse mechanically strapped her legs to the stirrups and set a line for the drip. Could her mother really kill herself if she found out as she had often threatened? She doubted that, but she knew the shame of what people would say could break her mother's heart. Especially her grandmother, who would likely gloat and broadcast to whoever cared to listen, that her mother had reproduced after her own kind. No, she could not bear to be the hinderer to her mother's constant prayer point – affliction shall not arise a second time. It would be unfair to put her through such distress solely because at twenty-three, she had failed to apply her senses at the appropriate time.

The doctor came in and she shifted her eyes to meet his stern face. He looked rather young and she wondered if he was competent enough to execute the task. As if he heard her thought, he nodded and patted her hand with the nurse looking on without any show of emotion. "Just relax, it won't take long." The nurse passed on a syringe to him, and she closed her eyes to start praying for God's forgiveness, hoping that would get her to heaven in case anything went wrong and she woke up on the other side. She did not shake as she usually did when she felt the injection pierce through her shoulder muscle.

She started to see the people most precious to her forming around the bed; Tokunbo, gently stroking her hair with one hand while caressing her left hand with the other; her mother

3

with arms folded across her chest silently chanting a psalm under her infectious smile, yet accusing Tokunbo surreptitiously with her fiery eyes; and the other figure, the one wearing a scowl on his face was drifting into the background, shaking his head profusely and wagging his finger at her. She wanted to ask her mother not to let him go, but her mouth would not open as she glided into nothingness.

By the time Tara woke up, it was over, and in self-pity, she looked into the bedpan at what could have been her first child if she had waited another five months. She ignored the heaviness tugging at her heart and the mass building up behind her eyes, willing herself not to cry despite the excruciating pain below her stomach. She had heard it said that success was the achievement of a set goal, but what she felt now was an overwhelming sense of failure. Without any finesse, the nurse propped her up, and for now, she was grateful that she was alive, with a new zeal to live life right.

CHAPTER ONE

September 2012

Tara

Forty-seven, forty-eight, fort … a girl rushes past me like one chased by a predator, violently brushing my shoulder. The rude interruption of the metrical sound of my heels on the marble floor makes me almost lose grip of the wood-covered railing in the process. "Hey, watch it." She does not bother to stop and apologise, but the tiny snuffles escaping from her equally tiny frame as she continues down the flight of stairs hint me that she has something more important to deal with than a weary me struggling to climb seventy five steps to the office. It is not her business to care if she ruins my recent daily ritual, in my erratic bid to ward off the threatening weight to stay on size fourteen.

It seems the only way my body reacts to the fertility drugs I have to pump myself with is to pile on weights everywhere, except inside my womb. After changing almost all my wardrobe from size twelve to fourteen, I am very reluctant to move up another size. What or who could have caused that girl such distress this early Monday morning? Who is she? Definitely, not someone from my floor; I would have recognised her. I straighten my CK jacket after catching my breath and continue on my quest to reach my fifth floor office.

I love my job at the bank and the dynamism that comes with working in the legal department; meeting new people, discovering new places, uncovering new challenges, and sometimes, hearing about the most intimate details of my customers' lives assures me that my own existence is perhaps a little bit better. Any customer who ever has cause to interface with my department does so on the basis that their account has been classified and needs some form of almost impossible intervention. They usually start with a litany of their aspirations, then conquests, and then the woes, and finally they would start pleading, looking for unrealistic ways to salvage whatever asset they can on the assumption that the bank should be able to afford to write off a few millions here and now.

My work routine makes me forget troubles at home with my husband whenever he sets on that course. Nothing else matters much, once I can dip my head in the pile of paperwork, reviewing deals and transactions, and making recommendations, which my boss sometimes complains are too empathic towards customers. I don't blame him though; he is not the one that has to listen to all those customers' near-fictional miseries.

But some things conspire to make my job unattractive sometimes; the fact that my office is in Marina and I always have to resume unreasonably early and close perversely late, despite the fact that we live at Lekki Phase I, a mere distance of about ten kilometres. Sometimes I deliberately tarry to come to the office just to catch up with myself. Today, I left home at seven thirty and got downstairs on the dot of five minutes to nine, so it just never makes sense leaving home after seven, since a journey of thirty minutes then takes me almost two hours. Like Chico, the presenter on Classic FM describes it, that road whose name we dare not mention had better be completed on time, before the whole of the Lekki and Ajah working class falls into traffic-induced stress.

As usual with my office, multiple files are open on different desks and telephones are blaring unanswered, despite policy guideline that phones should not ring more than twice. The only difference is that nobody seems to be in working mood; only one person at his desk, violently chewing his pen. Others are converged in two groups, huddled at different sections of the massive open-plan office, in hushed and loud voices at the same time. Everyone lifts their heads to look at me when I walked in.

"Did you know?" Daisy Brisbe leaves the group which continues to console Kola David, bent over in the middle. Even Daisy's eyes are bloodshot, and her mascara and lashes have run down her now blotched face. Something must be terribly wrong today. "Did you know, is that why you came late today?" Without waiting for my answer, she continues in a low voice for only me to hear. "I've been calling your phone since and you switched off."

"Know what, what's happening, why is he crying, why are you not working, what's wrong with you?" I hope Kola's fiancée is not dead or suffered from something terrible because he is supposed to be getting married in three weeks.

"Because we've been sacked!" She drops into the swivel chair by the door as she starts to stifle a cry.

"Again? When? Who?" No one bothers to answer me.

Probably they all believe I knew, as Daisy insinuated. That is because they are privy to the fact that I got the job through the former Company Secretary, who himself has been relegated by being moved to a subsidiary company. I thought the bank had gotten rid of enough people after sacking over three thousand staff.

The cycle of mass retrenchment started in 2009 when the Central Bank Governor announced the takeover of five banks in one day and then another three banks sometime later. The boards were dissolved and most of the executive directors and top Management were either sacked or asked to resign unceremoniously when the new boards and managements were imposed, and the whole system was plunged into uncertainty. Will it never end? How many people this time? It usually happens on Monday mornings, which means HR and IT have been at work yesterday. No queries, no warnings, you only get to know when you cannot log into the system.

Oh, I have not powered on my computer. I scurry away from Daisy, drop my bag and switch on the computer. It feels prickly, all eyes staring at me while the computer decides to take forever to finish booting to get me to the log in screen. With my heart palpitating and my brow emitting a tiny flash of sweat, I manage to type my name and password, before my fingers totally stiffen. The alert message screams at me. 'This system has been disabled, contact Human Capital Development Group.'

I have been sacked too! I continue to stare at the screen, unable to stop the cloud above my head from darkening and enveloping me in. My head starts swelling and the blood drains from my face. Expectedly, the dormant throbbing behind my left eyeball sprouts like a fountain all inside my head and it feels as if my head is about to explode with the pulsating migraine which I have been managing for the past three days to avoid taking any medicines that can threaten a forming foetus. I ease myself into the chair.

"Are you okay? Did it affect you?" Daisy bolts to my desk. I can only nod as a mass of vapour obscures my sight. The groups disperse and two people begin to empty their drawers while the others continue to glare at me.

No one ever expects to get sacked. You always hope to be the last man standing, no matter what happens, so how can you prepare for it? What else is there to do? Go to Human Capital, and do what? Collect a letter that tells me my services are no longer needed with a terse explanation about my entitlements and what I should do next. I already know the routine.

Most of my colleagues who got sacked last year have not collected their entitlements. In fact, a whole lot of them especially those in Business Development, left owing the bank more money than their calculated entitlements, based on the continuous spurious debits passed to their accounts at the slightest notice that their overdraft customers have defaulted. A lot of them also had no recourse to any retrenchment benefit. Worse still, is the fact that many bank workers have numerous loans with various other banks and when the mass sack suddenly burbles, the story of their lives takes the most unpalatable turn as they become haunted in different loan recovery bids. Talk about double trouble!

"I guess that's it then." I look up at Daisy and the others as I massage my left temple with a finger. "How many of us?"

"With you, that makes us five." It is nothing about the law of average, five out of eighteen people in the department and I am one of them. I must have been worthless for them to let me go. Although, he would not say it aloud, that is what my husband would think. This is over a decade of my life over. Looking at my colleagues' faces, I don't have to ask who the other two are, apart from Daisy, Kola and I.

"What do we do now?" Daisy looks to me forlornly.

We? Who is we? To your tents O Israel. Well, we go back to wherever we came from this morning to lick our fresh wounds. I go back to my house, to face my life and my husband. Not a very good prospect to start the week. Five sullen faces hover around me as I start rummaging through my drawers, scanning and thrashing documents, business cards, greeting cards and mementoes.

"So sorry about this, we didn't see it coming. We don't know if it will be our turn tomorrow."

"Don't worry, you'll soon get a job, at least you're well qualified and you have years of experience. I'm sure something will come up soon."

"Please, let's keep in touch, don't let this affect our friendship."

"I'll mention you to my cousin at Fidelity Bank. Send me your CV as soon as you can."

"If I were you, I won't even go near a bank again. It's not like you need the money, so just take your time."

It is difficult not to cry. For over ten years, I have spent more time with these folks than with any member of my family and most of us have seen each other through thick and thin; and all of a sudden we are acting like total strangers for want of something appropriate to say. Even those who have not been sacked cannot openly express their gratitude for escaping the big knife. Life, a thin thread of hope and probabilities. On a regular day, apart from discussing our customers, we would have been catching up with one another's lives over the weekend, talking about families and friends, parties and different mundane affairs.

"Thank you, thanks." I pat the hand of one over my shoulder. "At least, now you know that I'm not as connected as you used to think. Have you gone to HR?" I turn to Daisy.

"I was there, it's a mad house, but I've picked my letter." Kola David stretches out the letter.

Daisy shakes her head. "I'm sure they can afford the extra postage fee it will cost them to mail the letter to my house. If you're ready to leave now, I'll come with you."

We, the five, gather the rest of our personal belongings and bid farewell to our former colleagues; who with all good intent would be secretly happy to be the ones remaining in the office, rather than heading out with overfilled files and bags right now. The elevator is filled with solemn people like us from different floors, and an awkward silence persists until we got downstairs. No one engages in any idle chatter after the initial nods and greetings unlike what it used to be.

"Where do you want to go?" I open the door of the new model Murano, after waving to the other three. I toss my LV bag in the back seat and change into my driving flip-flops. Now I wish I had not bought the bag last week.

"Anywhere you want to go, I need a clear head and I don't want to face my father until I decide what to do. What about you, do you want to go home now?"

Home? What will I do at home on a Monday morning? I thought driving Daisy home will give me a clear head, but she does not want to go home too. This is the first time in a long while I don't have any plan for a Monday morning and it is beginning to dawn on me that it may not be the last. "Maybe we should go somewhere and have breakfast. Things can't get worse than this."

"Anything you say. Maybe Shoprite. I should plump myself up with some ice cream to sweeten my life." Daisy attempts to infuse some cheerfulness in her voice as I start the car, heading towards Victoria Island. About time too, no need to carry a sorry face all over town. "You haven't called your husband."

Her comment sounds more like a query.

I can understand her concern. She, being unmarried assumes that high level of intimacy between couples that makes their minds pre-occupied with knowing every tiny detail about each other. Not that getting sacked should be a tiny detail, but Tokunbo is as unpredictable as the sea waves and one can never be sure of his reaction. I am not sure how I will feel if he dares tell me congratulations, which is a high possibility. He still managed to chip in that I could resign just earlier this month. Moreover, he should be airborne on his flight back from South Africa. As is his custom, he will go straight to his office and go to the club once he closes, before coming home.

"No. I can't reach him, because he should be over thirty thousand miles above sea level." It is also likely that he will hear about the mass sack before he gets home. How bad news flies fast. Well, good that one of us still has a source of livelihood. There was a case in the last sack that a couple working with different banks got sacked the same month. "That reminds me, will you please, get my phone from the bag." I forgot to switch on my phone when I got to the office. "Thanks." I collect the phone, but quickly hand it back to Daisy to switch it on, as the traffic light turns green. The phone start beeping as different messages pour in and then, it starts ringing endlessly too. I should have known that the news about the sack would be all over town by now and even people I have not spoken to in years would want to find out my position. "Please turn it off." It does not make sense to collect the phone from her. "What did you do to your phone? I haven't heard it ring since?"

"I put it on silent after I discovered I couldn't log on, you won't believe I have over fifty texts and BBMs."

"Tough luck, it's so bad we can't even get sacked with some level of privacy."

"I just pray no one calls my house to tell my father before I get home." Daisy laments.

"What we need to do is put ourselves in the right frame of mind to deal with this. Once today is over, it will become history." I veer into Shoprite. Ever since the massive shopping mall opened about six years ago, it seems the entire residents of Victoria Island and Lekki conveniently forgot they used to shop elsewhere before. As usual finding a space to park is a difficult task.

After driving in two full circles, Daisy notices a spot on her side and she points it to me. "There, that's a space."

I slow down to manoeuver into the parking spot. "Jesus Christ!" I jolt forward as the back of my car suddenly sways aside as if it wants to dismember itself from the body when a reversing car rams its rear into the trunk. "Oh, my God, what's the meaning of this?"

"What is this now?" Daisy bellows and hisses as she bolts out of the car.

I jump out of the car too. The driver of the other car takes his time to get out of his car as if what he did is of no consequence. I start walking towards him, ready to make him the receiver of the venom that has been brewing inside me from the office; but the car behind me starts honking, for me to get out of the road. How insensitive. I keep muttering incomprehensibly under my breath and run back to the car to get it off the road and into the parking spot. No need to create a scene. Why should this happen to me today of all days? I hop out of the car again.

"But you could have used your rear mirror to see that a car was right behind you. What do you want to do about this mess now?" Daisy's face is crumpled with her eyes snapping up and down as she asks the driver of the other car, who is bent over beside the trunk. He examine the dent he created, with his

Bluetooth earpiece still stuck to one of his ears.

The hunk of a man straightens up to face her, while one of his hands remains on the trunk. Probably because of his towering height against her diminutive body, Daisy's facial knots relax, bringing down her aggression as she lets out an almost inaudible gasp. "I'm sincerely sorry, I don't know what happened. I'll get your car fixed right away." It is difficult to reconcile the tiny voice to the tall figure talking to Daisy, but the voice does sound very familiar.

I know what happened, you were on the phone and not paying particular attention, as you ought to. "How do you intend to do that right away mister?" I interject angrily. "Do you think…?"

He turns, startles, and screams, "Tara! Omotara Gomez!"

"Fola! Oh my God. You, FG! I feel like slapping you right now." I make a weak fist, raising it up to him as a gush of hot fluid flows all over my body. For a moment, I feel like hugging him too. No wonder Daisy startled, Fola had that effect on girls.

"Come here, you." He envelopes me tightly and pulls my cheeks as he used to, but stops himself from going further.

"You two know each other?" Daisy looks from me to him. "Are you related?"

"Yes, yes, I do. But I'm sorry, truly sorry, Tara." He grabs my hand again, almost shaking me as his body jerks with excitement. "How are you? How have you been? It's been quite a while. You haven't changed at all, just more beautiful." A beam of smile forms on his face.

It is a great effort to suddenly transition from an angry mood to a pleasing one, but my fuzzy brain seems to be taking the lead on this. Surprise yes, but pleasing, which I should be for meeting Fola Gomez under normal circumstances is difficult at this moment. Somehow, I manage to squeeze out a smile. "This is so annoying. I need to kick someone for bashing my car."

"You can kick me all you want, although if I knew it was you I would have hit you harder." He looks at Daisy. "Sorry lady, this woman owes me plenty." Once again, but with some calmness, he stretches his sturdy hand to take mine and holds on a bit, smiling. "This is awkward, meeting you this way after such a long time."

"Daisy, this is Fola Gomez. FG, meet my friend Daisy Brisbe."

"If I tell you it's a pleasure to meet you, I'd be lying." Daisy's face struggles with holding a smile, but she shakes hands with him after he releases mine. "Are you related in any way?" We both jiggle our heads, while he retains the smile around the well-trimmed stubble below his jawline, like a clowning face. We make an effort not to make it obvious that we are sizing each other up.

"I can't say how sorry I am about your car. I'll get someone to pick it up later today or tomorrow, if it's okay with you, Tara. I was rushing off to an appointment, I would have loved to rile you some more. Let me have your card. From where should I pick it up?" He pokes his head into his car and brings out two business cards, sharing to Daisy and I.

"You need to focus on one thing at a time, because next time it won't be Tara's car you'll be reversing into." She collects the card with a pout and hurries back to her side of the car. I think I heard her hiss too. I cannot blame her. Like me, she must have wanted to lash out at someone all morning.

The gold plated metal card reads Chief Executive, Grand Holdings. "It seems like you're now a big boy." I try to tease him, tracing the card. He has always been as big a boy as they come. The texture of his business card, his checked cotton shirt, his white leather sandals and S-Class coupe all scream exclusive. "Unfortunately, I don't have any business card to give you. I just got sacked this morning and I didn't bother to pick up any." I did not mean to mention that.

"You just got sacked?" His eyes widen. "And then this. I'm so sorry dear. Please let me have your phone number, I have to make this up to you." He pokes his head into his car again to pick up his phone.

"It's not your fault I got laid off, so don't go feeling sorry for me. Give me your phone, let me key in my number." I collect his iPhone, type and dial my number so I can pick his number on my missed calls. Then I remember I may not be able to tell his number since I have had many missed calls. "It's better you send me a text, so I can save your number once I switch on my phone. But it will be odd calling to remind you that you need to fix my car, I'll get it fixed, don't worry about it."

"No, no, you won't do that. I insist, please let me handle it."

"Okay, Mr. Gomez, I'll talk to you later then. Make sure you don't reverse into another car." I am almost tempted to ask him to replace my car, but I dare not say it out, knowing he just might do that.

He smiles and pats me by the shoulder. "I won't, Mrs …"

"Akande."

"Akande?" He rolls his eyes to ponder for a bit and raises his brows. "Did you marry that man?" He makes a mischievous face.

"I couldn't find a better one. See you." I hurriedly head for my car to join Daisy, who is talking morosely on the phone. She reluctantly waves at Fola as he pulls out his car to zoom off. My day could not have been more interesting.

CHAPTER TWO

Even on a Monday afternoon, everything is predictably in its place. The coffee-tanned mahogany bookshelf indented into the wall is dusted, proudly housing the mostly hardcover volumes of law books. The limey green leather sofas are clean and smoothed; the gold trimmings on the two seater Louis XV Rococo sofa shine brightly beside the polished wooden console which stands regally, backing the wall, displaying some miniatures and our wedding picture.

The flowery damask curtains are partly drawn to let in the little sunlight that struggles to find its way in against the high walls. The sixty-inch TV is tuned to my favourite African Magic channel, buzzing on in low tones. The complementary mahogany table is perfectly centred on the exquisite verdant silky-haired rug and the flowers look alive and comfortable with the refill of fresh water in the crystal vase. My gaze remains on the translucent flower vase blankly, counting the green stalks, yet not counting.

Finally, I succumb to the subconscious prodding to find out

what his current status is after trying unsuccessfully to fill in the gap of what could have been and the past fourteen years of his life. Like someone on an urgent mission, I dart to the guest room to pick up the laptop and hurriedly log on to Facebook. His name in the search box turns up four matches, some with pictures. I carefully scan them one after the other, looking for the one that will be his profile, but none is the same person. I try Fola Gomez, FG, Gomez Fola, still no luck. Well, maybe people like FG don't do Facebook, where one million posers claiming to be friends can bombard them.

But everybody is on Facebook. Except Tokunbo, who rather than admit he is old-fashioned, declares it as a convergence of idle and lonely people trying to remind the world they still exist with some sort of relevance. I sight a GTB advert and Fola Adeola flashes through my mind. I impulsively type his name in the search box; interestingly, he is also not on Facebook, only a page linked from Wikipedia with over a thousand likes. If Fola Adeola is not on Facebook, what would FG be doing there? He has nothing to prove to anyone. I randomly browse through my wall to see what is trending; the mass sack, sympathy for the victims and mixed emotive comments about the CBN Governor's confusion regarding how to fix the economy by creating chaotic unemployment, and the different banks' insensitivity. With no intention to be part of that discussion from a victim's perspective, I log out and turn off the laptop.

Is he married now? Definitely, that should not be a question. Although, the last time I saw him in a soft sell magazine, he was listed as one of the ten most eligible bachelors in Lagos. That was a few years ago. Is she beautiful? Is he happy with her? He definitely did not look sad or tired. With how many children? I wonder. Fola Gomez! The muscular Mr. T's lookalike, but without the heavy chains. Every lady swooned over him, none of whom he wanted. We met in university when he sought me out at the library. According to him, people kept telling him he might have a pretty sister he never knew existed.

He was in for his MBA after getting a first degree abroad and I was in year three. Being one of the richest boys on campus, he was also one of the most popular. Then he became the captain of the basketball team, which endeared him more to a lot of girls, especially when the team won the *NUGA* cup for the first time.

There was something about the children of rich people that made others avoid them, naturally assuming they were boring, unintelligent, arrogant and sometimes undeserving of their wealth; but it was not so with Fola, who was an only child and heir apparent of a business dynasty. He never threw his weight around; rather, he was unpretentious to a fault, which was a put-off for some of the other rich kids in school, because he continually undermined their supposed VIP status by mixing with everyone.

He had a two bedroom flat to himself off-campus at Yaba, his own car and a help who came around once a week. He went on overseas trips with his mum whether school was in session or not, yet his grades did not suffer. Not that he needed the certificate like the rest of us. With his enigmatic profile in school, he could have gotten any lady he wanted. So it was a shock to many, especially me, when he started showing interest in plain, easy-going, somewhat brilliant Omotara Gomez, who had very few friends, paraded in second-hand clothes and hardly paid her school fees on time. Except for the Gomez, I could never figure out what else might have put me on his radar.

Due to his playful nature, everyone thought Fola was a flirt, but no one could say he had a particular girlfriend. Another reason girls continually threw themselves at him. Who would not want a piece of the rich, dark-skinned, muscular, six foot three, bearded, handsome FG, as he was popularly called? Except me! And that was not because I did not find him attractive too, I simply found his personae too intimidating, I always felt inadequate and I knew I was too reticent and inexperienced to fight all the ladies who wanted a piece of the action.

I made some enemies for attracting his attention in the first place and more, for seemingly playing hard to get. But, like a snail fated to its shell, FG stuck to me. He insisted he was drawn to my enterprising spirit, my seriousness with my studies, and my mixed personality of shyness and vivaciousness, even though I did not know all that about myself. Above all, he said I would not need to change my surname when we got married, which was what he expected to happen after school. I had not given any attention to dating, because I had sworn that my first boyfriend would be my husband. When FG continued talking about our future together, it took me only three months to be persuaded he was not joking about being with me. We became the most unlikely couple, but we loved each other as much as any pair could. He was extremely good to me, dedicated, protective, humorous and generous.

Like me, he was an only child with a single parent – his mother, having lost his father in a car accident. My father was a medical doctor who impregnated my mother, while he was married to someone else. I had never met my father then, because my mother assured me he would come looking for me when he was ready and with a caveat that I should never try to contact him and his family. She told me he moved back abroad anyway, so it was not a struggle keeping off.

As the story went, as told by one of my aunties, my mother

met him in the teaching hospital when she was schooling and training as a nurse and the man came in as a consultant on a research project. He was abroad when my mother discovered she was pregnant and he had advised her to abort because he could not afford his wife to find out about me. That was contrary to what he had earlier told my mother, who had been naively in love and believed that her lover was going to leave his wife for her. She had chosen to keep me, probably hoping my father would change his mind.

The last time my mother saw him was when he came to town to sort out some documentation and still insisted they could not be together anymore by which time I was about six months old in the womb. Neither of them had tried to contact each other since. Except for giving me his surname, I might as well not have had a father. But my mother did not have a choice over that since her own parents had warned her not to put their family name on her illegitimate child. She subsequently threw herself into church and did her best to raise me up by herself, without any bitter reference to my father in spite of my disillusionment about being able to ever meet him. The only bitterness I associated with my mother was with other men who tried unsuccessfully to make her break her unconscious oath of never being with another man.

I never felt comfortable enough to take FG to our ramshackle one-bedroom flat at Ketu. I knew he would not think less of me, but it was one thing to be poor and entirely another thing to be seen in a poor state. Nonetheless, FG found his way to my house, charming himself into my mother's heart, which was a pleasant surprise for me because my mother suspected anyone who vaguely had a streak of masculinity. I had nowhere to hide and he became a regular item in my house. Almost two years into our relationship when I was getting ready to graduate, he suggested promoting our relationship to the next level by inviting me to his family house to meet his Mum, but, I had my doubts.

I wanted to be sure that he would still be interested in me after school, so I pushed it till later. Luckily, he was able to influence my *NYSC* posting to Lagos and I went back to the law firm where I had been working for vacation jobs in Victoria Island, against his proposal to fix me up in one of his family businesses. He also moved into one of his family's properties at Victoria Island and went to work at Orchid Mills. The proximity made us grow closer together. It was during my fourth month in Law School that I eventually agreed to meet my much talked about adorable future mother-in-law.

FG's family was old money mixed with new. His father had been from a lineage of wealth with family investments in manufacturing, textile and mining. He had resigned from his high-flying job with an oil company to venture into a mining partnership. His mother was a representative for imported Swiss and Austrian lace with distribution channels all over Nigeria and multiple sales stores at Balogun Market.

I did not have to follow him home to be impressed; everything about him was naturally overwhelming for me, except his reassuring love. However, nothing prepared me for the kind of grandeur of the fairy-tale house, the remote-controlled gate, the well-manicured garden, the dainty huge dogs, the tennis court, the water fountain, the uniformed servants and the spotless concrete floors that felt like no one had ever stepped on them. The tiny one bedroom flat I shared with my mother could not even compare with the one-storey servants' quarters which stood a good distance behind the main house. I took it all in with graceful silence for fear of making a fool of myself as he led me into the house after we came out of his car and he greeted the uniformed gateman.

The big angled kitchen led into a dinning cum living room

that led further into a bigger living room via an arc-shaped doorway where I guessed the front door was. A good part of the living room was walled high, without ceiling. After FG briefly showed me the big living room with the all-white walls and life-size TV screen which, despite the fact that it was currently uninhabited, was brightly lit with beautiful dangling chandeliers and scented with a kind of air-freshener I had never perceived before, we returned to the small living room. The small living room maintained the classiness of deliberate furnishing.

There were two small side tables adorned with tiny pieces of antiques and photographs; on the lustrous white wall hung a big family painting from when FG was a child, probably about six or seven years old. It clearly revealed to me where he got his teddy face from – his father. A wide-screen TV stand compartmentalising books, photo albums and CDs created a little divide between the living and dining area.

"How often do you have visitors staying over?" He had told me there were six bedrooms in the house even though his Mum practically lived all alone.

"Do you think there's too much space or it's too clean? One of my aunties has practically taken over the guest room and you'll be shocked that mum has already started complaining that she's running out of space with her third room. I've warned her nobody should touch my rooms, so she won't venture there. Don't worry, you'll see when I show you the house. It's not as big as you think." I was amazed that he lived elsewhere, yet laying claim to two rooms in this big house. He went to a small table and picked the intercom. "Tony, afternoon, is there something to eat?" He paused for a moment and covered the mouthpiece. "Hold on, Tara, do you want rice or *asaro*?" I shook my head. "Snacks?" I nodded. "Yes, Tony, what snacks have you got?" He covers the mouthpiece again and whispers to me. "Meat pie?" I nodded. "Meat pie is fine. Yes, Thanks." He came to sit on the arm of the sofa, roughening my short weave. "Shouldn't you be hungry by now?"

I swallowed before I answered. "I was hungry until I got here. Your house looks too perfect, I don't want to soil anything until I leave, so you won't give me a bad name." The closest I had seen to the house had only been in movies.

"Better get used to it." He started unbuttoning his shirt and smiled mischievously. "It might do some good if you soiled the wall. That would give mum something to yell about and the cleaner would at least have real work to do."

"Thank you. That's not going to be me. When are you expecting her?" I had almost succeeded in quietening the flying butterflies in my stomach until he mentioned his Mum again.

"That woman is as unpredictable as you can imagine. She comes and goes anyhow. Sometimes, I think she likes to sneak up on the servants. Although, I've already told her you're coming with me, I'm not really expecting her anytime soon. If she comes, that would be your luck. It doesn't matter anyhow since you are staying the night." He said matter-of-factly, winking at me. I had let him cajole me into sleeping over on the condition that we would not let his mother know. One could never tell with Nigerian parents; she could label me a slut. Suddenly, staying overnight in the vertiginous perfect house did not look an exciting option. Except for campus and FG's apartment, I had never stayed in a house where children were not prancing about or adults bickering at one another or *okadas* and *danfos* competing with their loud speakers.

A uniformed diminutive elderly man – who I guessed was Tony, rolled in a gold-plated trolley with a tray of two bottles of different wines with glasses and two plates, one with two meat pies and the other filled with samosa and fried fish. "Good afternoon ma." He bowed to me and FG gestured to me to pick the wine I wanted. The man opened the wine, filled the glass cups and stayed with his trolley.

"Thank you sir." I muttered without thinking. Why would anyone ever defer to me as Ma?

"Thanks Tony." FG said. "We're okay."

"Okay sir." He took an almost unnoticeable bow before leaving the trolley behind, finally allowing me to breathe freely.

"Even when you come to this house, you don't do anything?" I shook my head and chuckled. "I'm not sure I can get used to this. Do you even lift a finger?"

"To bathe myself, at least." He laughed at the pretentious look of derision on my face. "You know it's not the fault of a fish that it was born in water, how can it imagine living anyhow else?"

"Hmm." He is definitely in his natural habitat. I am the one who has issues expanding my mind.

He gave me one glass and took the other one. "What shall we toast to?"

"You seem to have everything you need, what would you want?"

"Even the Queen of England would have something she's missing. Let's toast to a forever relationship."

I smiled, raising my glass to his. A forever relationship sounded good. I offered my own thoughts. "And to a brighter future."

"Together." He added and gulped down the wine. "I'm going to try and ..." His mother came in then. "Hello Mum." He went and hugged her.

* * *

My phone will simply not stop vibrating and is about to slip off the coffee table, so I pick it up. It is my mum, calling for about the hundredth time today. My first impulse is to ignore the call again, but then I have to tell her one way or the other. "Hello mother, how are you today? Sorry…"

"Keep your sorry to yourself." She will not let me get away with it easily as she yells angrily into the phone. "With what happened at your office today, shouldn't you have called to let me know what's happening, or don't you think I should be worried. What is all this about? Do you know how many times I've called you today? How busy can you be that you can't spare one minute to tell me you're okay and save me the anxiety?"

I wait a little to be sure she has finished before responding. "I'm truly sorry, *ema binu*. My phone has been on silent since morning and I need to avoid using the phone so I don't make my migraine worse. I need to save myself the headache of…"

She interrupts again. "Sorry, I understand you have headache, but is that enough reason to give me headache too? No problem, next time I won't bother."

"That's not what I mean. I needed time to myself to process what happened. I was also asked to leave." I decide to save her parrying around the reason for her call.

"Ha, *pele Arike* Omotara, I didn't expect to hear that. All the same, God is good. It is well with you. In no time, God will turn your story to joy." She goes on praying and concludes by reminding me that everything happens for good. For her and Daisy, it is always about God. "Is your husband back home or should I come tomorrow? I can close early and come to spend some time with you if…"

"Mother, no need for that. I won't be home tomorrow and Tokunbo will be back home today. I'm sure I'll find something soon and I'll be fine, don't worry." I assure her. Sometimes, being an only child makes me feel smothered, as my mum has nowhere else to channel her affection.

"That's what you'll say. All the same, I'll call you tomorrow."

"Thank you ma." I quickly cut the line before she says anything else.

CHAPTER THREE

Tokunbo

"Give me a bottle, and a big one for him." I nod at Mike MBA as I shout out the order to our regular waiter. I like my Guinness occasionally and although Tara goes on about how it is bad for me, I believe she is more afraid that hanging out with my friends will lead me to undesirable paths. But a man has to have at least one vice. One small bottle is just about okay for me tonight as my body is tired from jetlag. If I had gone home straight from the airport, I would have missed Big Sam who is on his way out of town tomorrow and I need that information from him badly. "And ask the *asun* boy to bring two plates. Anybody for *asun*?"

"It's extra *suya* night." Kunle Wright volunteers, pointing at the empty plates of *suya*. "No need paying for full when you can save half the money."

Mike Mba has been my best friend since university and I met Kunle and Big Sam, his brother-in-law through him, at

29

Ikoyi club. I turn to Big Sam. "Did you get to see the Commissioner?" Two of our solar panel containers arrived at the ports last month. Despite paying all the import duties and charges, somebody somewhere decided the containers will not be released unless we pay an un-receipted cash sum of four million naira. After two weeks of fruitlessly trying to resolve the issue, Big Sam, who is the only one that has the affinity to consort with politicians, offered to speak with a Commissioner friend of his. I have just one more week to get that container out of the ports, otherwise it will delay the delivery date promised to customers, which may also affect their contract performance.

"Oh, yes, but he wasn't of any help. Something about the man at the ports having allegiance to the other political party. I'd pay that money if I were you. Because those losers don't have anything at stake and no one is going to prosecute them since they all do whatever they like in their own kingdoms."

"Didn't I tell you what happened with our national computerisation bid?" Mike does not wait for anyone to answer. "They had already sent someone to procure the computer parts from India before they even asked us to submit our bid with a five hundred thousand naira deposit." The waiter brings the order and more drinks for everyone. "It was one of my former employees that advised me not to bother wasting my money. Of course, most of the equipment is there now, not useful for anyone. I've decided I'm never going to do business with any government agency again. It's a waste of everybody's time and too much money you can't account for."

With the tasty meat in my mouth, I continue to shake my head. "I don't see what else I can do now, except pay that money. As wrong as that may be."

"Pass on the cost to your customers." Kunle bellows, patting me on the thigh. He belches before reaching for his refilled cup. "You did your best under the circumstances, Pastor Tokunbo." He finishes with a sneer.

My family try to live by Christian moral values. We go to church and do our charitable bit, but it is very difficult to adhere to those moral values in this society. Sometimes, the challenges of the business make me wish I had not ventured into this line of business that requires so much hand greasing. If I had stayed with contracting out all our construction work, I would still make enough money with some of my integrity intact. But I had to step in to save the reputation of the company I have worked so hard to build when building contractors would end up delivering houses to sub-standards of finishing, different from what we agreed and what our clients expected to get. I discovered that the contractors would submit good quality samples of materials, but install the lower grade version and sometimes even mix different materials. Quality standardisation was the basic problem I was facing when I decided to start importing building materials myself.

We started with importing ceramic tiles and granites and later moved to sanitary wares. Two years ago, we added the option of equipping our developments with solar systems since the state of electricity supply still falls short of expectations in the country. Surprisingly, even with the extra millions to pay, clients embraced it and now we deliver over seventy percent of our buildings with solar energy. How can I pass on this additional cost to clients, after we have agreed prices over six months ago?

Since there is no way I can possibly walk away from a thriving business I have struggled to build thus far, I need to keep on sorting this mess of complicity against my conscience. It is easy for pastors to stand on the pulpit and preach against corruption when they are not exposed to the real world of business in Nigeria. When I started importing, I made sure to review all the relevant regulations before I placed the order, so I felt justified to ignore the request for bribe from a junior officer. I gathered all the necessary documents and records of payments and reported him to his boss, who assured me that the shipment would be released within the next three days.

By the third day, the officer and the boss had simply disappeared, with the documents I would need to refresh the process. The three containers were released after two weeks of demurrage, several emissaries, more money than the first request, and a bank loan that was waiting to be called in.

Of course, all the other ones suffered the same fate with the amounts solicited gradually increasing, except for a time when there was a hurried reshuffle at the ports amidst rumour that the government was serious about restoring sanity and another time when a new management team was introduced.

Tara never supported the idea of *settling* officers, insisting that those who gave bribes were as good as those who solicited. What she could not come up with however, is how to keep the business moving until I came up with the idea of outsourcing clearing of the goods to a contractor. That way, I could easily dissociate the company and myself from any corrupt activity.

However, in this instance, the contractor rang me up to complain that he could not accommodate four million naira from his budget. At this rate, I am also not entirely sure the contractor has not inflated the solicited amount. I think it is about time we started re-considering manufacturing. My head moves from left to right of its own volition.

"There has to be a way to stop this cycle of corruption in Nigeria. It's indirectly eating into everybody's pocket. Unfortunately, I can't go back to my clients to review prices since we've signed contracts."

"So you want to continue the war against corruption

because of four million naira? You need to research how many people have fought this battle and lost, bro. How far do you think you can go?" Big Sam snorts at me. "Anyway, about the mass sack today, I hope Tara wasn't affected."

I am speechless. The news was all over the radio and as soon as I got into the car, Ola, my driver mentioned he heard something happened in Tara's office. But I continued making business calls until we got to the club and I have not called her since. I hope she is still awake. Before I can respond, all eyes turn away from me in a unified motion to the inner bar right behind me. I turn my head too, to see a lady with gold and red dyed hair who has just stepped out from the inside bar, looking around guardedly.

Scanning the rows of people sitting or slouched over bottle-laden tables, she takes a step to one side, tilts her head and retreats. Big Sam follows my gaze, lifts himself up and hails her with a sway of his hand and she starts walking in short strides towards our table. He points her to pick a chair from the extras and makes room for her to join us. She is wearing a red lacy bra which only half covers her skin-bleached breasts, struggling for freedom from her tight white chiffon top. The sight of these mounds sends a current through my veins. After a moment, the picture of Big Sam's beautiful petite, modest wife flashes through my mind and I cannot rationalise what the attraction with this young lady is for him. His big arm goes round her waist, jamming her breasts to his face while she manages to spill out a 'good evening' to us all.

"Where are your friends?" Kunle nods at her.

"They'll soon be here, they are stuck somewhere in traffic." She pouts with her red outlined thick lips, clutching a small purse under her chest. The purse seems to assist her hands in supporting the weight of the breasts.

Mike coughs and it sounds like my prompt to stop starring

at her chest. Quietly ordering my member to stop every attempt at rousing itself, I drag my eyes to the table while Kunle leans forward and whispers in my ear. "I asked her to invite an extra girl for you, just in case."

For me? How? Why? When? I cannot remember having any discussion with Kunle about any girl. Or have I hinted about lack of activity in my bedroom to him? That is not possible. What does he want me to do with a girl? It is indeed true that the company you keep has a great influence on you. I glimpse at the young girl again, now seated, smiling and leaning sideways on Big Sam's abdominal protuberance. He keeps his arm around her as her breasts almost touch the table.

If I am truthful, I would not mind burying my head in between such inviting ridges. I discreetly press my legs together to suppress the embarrassing movement below my waist and suck in my lips for fear of any involuntary drooling or utterance of some nonsensical words that could reveal how tempting the idea of having a new girl sounded. Kunle does not believe any man can be satisfied with one woman, but I have stopped arguing with him. Does it ever occur to him that his wife could find out? What if Tara finds out? By the way, does she have a right to complain since she has failed woefully in that department consistently? Hmm, can I cross this line? Never! I quickly chide myself.

Mike gulps the last of his stout and heaves his tennis bag from the floor. "I have to go mates. I take it you'll all make the party next Saturday." He goggles at Kunle, waving his middle finger. "And you, no African time."

"On my honour sir."

"Running away?" Big Sam challenges Mike, but he does not respond. Flora, Mike's wife gave birth to their third child, a girl, a month ago and the christening was low-key at the hospital because of some complications before she was discharged. She later insisted on a thanksgiving party for close friends and family members. That woman appears to be the one in control of that family in a way we all refuse to acknowledge. Shortly after she got pregnant, she barged to the club to drag her husband home, accusing us of keeping him away from her at her most period of need. When she noticed Kunle had a girl with him, she asked him why the girl was sitting so close him, to which he kept mute.

She moved back to her husband and continued ranting about him going AWOL when he should be lending a hand with the twins. Afterwards and without any consideration for our feelings of uneasiness, she faced the girl and stared intently at her as if to make her disappear. "Can't you find someone your age to settle down with or you don't know he's married? How would you feel if you were his wife and he is cheating on you? I guess you think you're having fun and you can't be bothered about that now. Listen carefully, one day it's going to be your turn, in fact you will have it worse than this."

We all sat there speechless. The girl, who had gone quite pale, opened her mouth but quickly shut it when Kunle shook his head. I wished I could sneak under the table on her behalf. Mike tugged at Flora twice, but she jerked her heavy arm free. She had grown even bigger after the twins. "Leave me alone. Just thank your stars that she's not sitting beside you."

"That is enough!" Meek Mike urged.

"What is enough? Have I done anything?" Still seething, she went to the girl's side, shifted the table and stood akimbo opposite her. "And what are you still waiting for?"

"Flora stop!"

Too late! Kunle got up as the girl looked at him for support, he nudged his head towards the door and the poor girl grabbed her bag in a fury, while Kunle walked behind to lead her out. Flora hissed. Big Sam cleared his throat. "Flooooora!"

"Big Sam, there's no need to worry, I won't tell anyone." She glared at her husband and headed for the door.

"I'm sorry mates, I don't know what got into her." He grabbed his bag and followed, just as a chick hurries after its mother.

Of a truth, Flora's size is imposing – the female version of Big Sam. Possibly, I would be afraid of her if I was married to her too. Since then and to the unspoken acquiescence of us all, Mike would disappear from the club before or at the dot of eight thirty or as soon as any girl strayed to our table courtesy of Big Sam or Kunle. Maybe I should start heading home too, since my overwhelming urge to take on Kunle's offer has subsided a little. So what will happen to the extra girl? That should not be my business since he invited them without my consent. It will be a lame excuse to try and convince myself that Tara is the cause. God help me, it is so difficult seeing all those girls wearing miniskirts and transparent blouses jiggling all around town.

Do I want to become another Kunle or Big Sam? No! They never seem to have enough of sleeping around. Better not to start at all, that way I can go to church with a clear conscience. Maybe God will smile on me for being a good boy tonight and I can get a passionate session with Tara. Just maybe.

* * *

Tara

I rouse from my slumber when Tokunbo drives in, exchanging words with Yisa, the gateman.

"Nobody come *oga,* madam *dey* for house since morning." I let him in through the kitchen back door instead of waiting for him to use his key.

He startles. "Hey, what are you doing up?" As usual, the smell of alcohol oozes from his breath. He steps aside for Ola to bring in his jacket and his briefcase.

"Good evening madam." Ola greets with a slight bow. Until about six months ago when I persuaded Tokunbo to let Ola sleep in the spare room in the boy's quarters during the week, the poor boy had to travel to and from Mushin - a distance of about fifty kilometres - every day, not minding the fares he has to incur and the safety of the roads, especially since Tokunbo started coming home late.

"Good evening, you can drop the briefcase on the dining table." I am not usually downstairs when Tokunbo comes back but I do not particularly feel comfortable letting Ola into my house at almost ten; coming into my kitchen is bad enough.

"Okay madam." He takes the briefcase to the dining room and Tokunbo follows him, while I wait by the door. "Goodnight sir, good night madam."

"Good night." I lock the door after him and return to the living room to meet Tokunbo removing his socks. He usually dumps every piece of clothing downstairs for Maria or me to pick up after him. He grabs the remote as if he expects me to struggle for it and quickly tunes to Channels TV. "Do you want anything to eat?" He shakes his head. "How was your trip?"

"Hectic as usual, I finally got an appointment with the sanitary wares factory in Ghwanzhou, so I'm travelling next week." The reason he went to South Africa was to attend an exhibition where he was hoping to make the Chinese contact for the sanitary wares. He sprawls on the three-seater in front of the TV with a loud belch. Like a religion, he always tries to catch the ten o'clock news on Channels TV. "I heard the news. How are things at your office?" He adjusts his glasses, which I hate so much because they make him look years older. Tokunbo is not one of those men one would describe as handsome; just okay. His round chubby face, flat nose and slanted narrow eyes give him the look of a Chinese man, except that he is dark-skinned, keeps a shaped sideburn, curly short afro and tops it with round rimless glasses.

If I did not know him well enough, I would have said he is trying to taunt me with that question, but he is too candid for such nuances. I lean on the staircase, poised to go upstairs. "Why don't you come and watch the news upstairs? You won't disturb me."

"I don't want to miss anymore of the news." He grunts. I remain by the staircase, undecided about what to do. I am often asleep when he comes home and I have never been one for watching TV at night, especially news since anything newsworthy would have found its way to me during the day. I decide to stay eventually and lower myself unto one of the marble steps. The newscaster raves on, mostly about government activities and politics, randomly slotting in occurrences about real people while Tokunbo complains about the news items one after the other, until the channel breaks for commercial. "What are you waiting for, why aren't you asleep, by the way?"

"I came home early today. I was laid off too." There is no way of saying it to make it sound like a normal occurrence and better to say it before the newscaster mentions anything about the bank.

He turns to look at me then. "What do you mean you were laid off, what did you do?"

"It's another round of retrenchment and it's bank-wide, I don't know how many people yet."

"I know about the mass sack, but I didn't expect you to be one of them. Do you think any employer likes to lose a good staff?" He turns back to the TV. I actually feel like slapping that caustic mouth of his, though I am not disappointed much. Very few people will agree that the banks have no fair defined parameters for the retrenchment exercise. With Tokunbo, anything that happens has to be my fault. "Well, I've always told you it's not the right job for you, so it's not such a loss."

"Tokunbo, I've spent all my working life in that one bank and the only thing you can say is that it's not such a loss, simply because you don't like the job. Can't you show some empathy?"

"You know if I had my way, you would have left that job a long time ago." He is unrepentant. "There are easier ways of making money than labouring over ten hours daily in the name of working in a bank. It's modern day slavery, this so-called banking. Even the people who make the most money close by five. Don't you have friends at LNG or Chevron?"

No need to argue with him yet again, about how there exists an anomalistic culture for bank staff to close after six, even when the contract of employment specifies working hours as eight to five. It is common to walk into a bank at seven or eight in the night and see people bent over files or staring at computers as if they have just resumed for work and they have no other life than that. There is a hypocritical expectation that no one leaves the office when the boss is still around, even if there is nothing to do except play solitaire. I have always been lucky though. The two managers I have worked with appeared to cherish their families and neither of them stayed in the office beyond six, except on very rare occasions, when they have to attend evening scheduled meetings that dragged late into the night.

Tokunbo does not like my working in the bank, even though he was instrumental to getting me the first opportunity. His assumption was that I would only work for a few years and then start my own business or at best work as a teacher. He started complaining about the tediousness of waking up too early and sleeping too late about one year into our marriage.

I thought the concern was about my health, until he started making snide remarks about the possibility that most bankers would be having affairs since they spent so much time with one another and at such ungodly hours. He did not like many things about my job: the fact that I closed as late as seven, the fact that I worked with men at all, either as colleagues or as customers, and the fact that I spent a lot of time and effort looking good to go to work. He did not like my unmarried colleagues; either male, because he may possibly be attracted to me; or female, because she may possibly influence me to have an affair; neither did he like the fact that I have to travel to Abuja with my male boss sometimes.

After a while, he bluntly told me he wanted me to stop working altogether, so I can focus on building a family. It was perhaps, the strain of working long hours that was hindering me from getting pregnant. Then one month later, I coincidentally got pregnant and he became the doting husband again, until two months after, when I had a miscarriage. The complaints started almost immediately, even when the doctor said there was no plausible reason for the miscarriage. Tokunbo conveniently attributed it to work-related stress. And now that the job has taken care of itself, God help me if I fail to get pregnant with this IVF cycle.

What if I am unable to get another job and I have to become fully dependent on my husband? I moan sadly, with a sudden longing to be loved, touched, and assured that everything will be okay. I want to cry, but sometimes crying is not soothing if there is no one to console you.

I leave the staircase to sit beside him and take hold of his hand, but he gawks at me suspiciously. "Tokunbo, I'm your wife. Does it occur to you that I may be sad, even if just a bit?"

"Are you?" He flips my hand over and turns to face me. "Why should you be? You don't need the money, you can do without the stress and if you're bored, you can look for something less stressful to do. What's there to be sad about?"

I do not know what to say and my heart is seriously seeking an outlet to shed some of its heaviness. How do I explain to my husband that it is sad to have something dear to you snatched without an immediate hope of replacement? Why should I not be sad, when I just lost something that has given me some form of usefulness and an identity other than being a rich man's wife? How should I explain that losing my job makes me feel less worthy than those that did not and that I partially agree with him that employers never let good workers go? The tears gush out now and I begin to sniffle.

He raises his brows and opens his hands in exasperation before pulling me to himself, placing my body against his in an unusual show of affection. I cannot remember the last time we sat this close. Romance has gradually continued to disappear in-between the arguments, the fights and the accusations that are stylishly thrown at me because I cannot not give him a child several years into our marriage. I cannot exactly remember how it turned out like this, I just woke up one day and he was not there to tell me, `I love you'. Sometimes, I wonder if he deliberately stays downstairs so that I fall asleep before he creeps into bed. As for lovemaking, he does only what he needs to do to try for a baby. Once he is done, he would turn over and start snoring almost immediately. It could not be worse being a prostitute.

"It's okay, Tara, look on the bright side of things. Just take some time out and don't rush into something else." His voice is soothing, I have not heard it like this in a long time and it is comforting.

"I just didn't think it would get to me." The tears flow unhindered with emissions of my sobs.

"No need crying over what is done. It's okay, it's their loss, not yours. Once in a while, we all get what we don't deserve, but you take heart as long as you know you did your best." He wipes my face with his white cotton shirt. I smile inwardly at this rare gesture and it almost feels good to have lost my job. "Stop crying please, I can't stand it when you cry. It's okay."

I quieten. "And someone hit the back of my car when I was coming home." I do not bother to mention who that someone was, not willing to chance anything to tamper with our new found cosiness by bringing in Fola Gomez.

"Oh!" Tokunbo switches off the TV, since the news has ended. "Only you in one day? Sorry my dear, you must have had a bad day. Have you gotten a police report?"

"I didn't bother, the man said he'll pay for the repairs. I'll take it to the Nissan Garage tomorrow."

"What if he doesn't show up?"

"If he doesn't, maybe I'll call the insurance company then. But it's not really much." I get up to follow his lead and to avoid him probing further.

"Will you need Ola to help you with the car then?"

"No, I'll be fine, I'm not going to work. Thank you." We take the stairs up to the bedroom.

Tokunbo retreats to the bathroom to perform his nightly ritual while I start changing, wondering if he will try to hold out until I am asleep before coming to bed. He does not, but switches off the light, slides into the six-footer bed and faces his wall as I have faced mine. A few minutes later, he rolls towards me under the Indian cotton sheets and hesitantly turns me to himself. Within a few seconds, he touches my forehead, and starts tracing the plane of my face in a choreographed movement. I almost shrink back, but I decide against it.

I try to focus my eyes to search out his through the faint light flashing through the curtains, to figure out if this will be different or just like other times, devoid of passion. He pulls back, just enough for me to see a tinge of desire in his eyes, before pressing his face on mine. His breath is fresh against my mouth as he starts kissing me fervently, while his hand fumbles under my satin nightie. I feel like telling him I miss this part of our relationship, I want to tell him never to stop, but the moment passes as his tongue and hands continue to probe, while my body gradually relaxes to this strange, yet familiar sensation.

"I love you, sunshine." He buries his face in my bosom again. For weeks, I have listened attentively to hear those words, but they have been lost somewhere in space. Now, uttered in this delirious state, he sparks up every fibre of my being with a burst of energetic desire I am beginning to forget exists. I wrap myself around my husband possessively, kissing him hungrily, begging him to take me and giving myself to him with an all-consuming passion of fulfilment and selflessness, while he waits patiently for me to reach his pulsating peak. He does not turn over to start snoring, but stays inside me in the warmth of our body juices. The glow inside my body is electrifying.

Sated, I relive the memory that this is how it used to be as I revel in the euphoria. Until a figure that looks like FG's appears and hovers in the background to cast a smother; it is a mixed feeling of bliss marred with a tiny bit of discontent.

CHAPTER FOUR

Tara

"Do you have a driver or should I send one to pick your car?" FG is still apologetic about yesterday's incident.

"I'll drive down myself, don't worry. It will give me something to do today."

"Okay, I've booked your car in for twelve, please get there on time, so you don't lose that slot. I've heard they are usually fully booked for repairs."

"It's not a problem. I'll be there."

"I'll talk to you later. Let me know if you have any problem with them or the car."

"I will, thanks." The workshop is just about ten minutes from me, but one can never tell with traffic. I sit on the stool in front of the dressing table to start my make-up and the girl in the mirror stares back at me disappointed. The phone rings again. It is Daisy. "Hello."

"Hello Tara, how are you today?"

"I'm fine, hope you're okay. How about your Dad? Sorry, I should have called you earlier. What's up with you?"

"Nothing really. Thanks for yesterday. Daddy is okay, it seems nothing can shock him anymore. It still feels strange, you know. I don't know what I'm going to do today. You won't believe I woke up the same time I wake up every day. "

"I'm sure we'll find something soon, just relax and take this as your overdue vacation. Tokunbo suggested I shouldn't bother looking for work, but I don't want to be a housewife and become fully dependent on him."

"Hmm, I envy you. I wish someone would volunteer to pay my bills, so I can cross my legs on the table and sip tea all my life. I don't understand how depending on your husband poses a problem for you. Being a kept woman can't be as bad as being a slave, where people dangle your life in front of you anyhow they wish?"

"So you don't mind living off a man? I know that's not true, because you can't stay in one place with your restlessness."

"When will it dawn on you that my restlessness is borne out of looking for what to eat? Let me have the money and see whether I won't become more homely than you. If I don't have to care about money, what will I be looking for up and about Lagos?"

"True, but life is much more than someone meeting your needs. What if he walks out on you?"

"I keep telling you God is on my case now and by the way, why would he walk out on me? Will it be because I don't spend his money well enough? I've told you, once I hook a man, I've hooked him for life." Daisy giggles into the phone. Picturing her gap-tooth, I wonder why she finds it amusing that men are not reliable.

"Well, my father didn't stay around with my mum and see where it got her." I can never imagine going through what my mother went through after the man turned his back on her. Without any support from her parents as a lesson in responsibility, she had to get a part-time job to be able to complete her education and to stabilise after. It was a rough time for me growing up, because we simply never had enough to spend on anything. Although her parents eventually reconciled with her, she had already become independent and did not take any hand-out from them no matter how broke she was.

"Omotara Akande, how many times do we have to argue that not all men are the same? You need to get that into your head. Some men are honourable, some are not. That's the way it's always going to be." Hmm, it is easy to believe the best when you are not the one in a situation. No need telling her that. "As long as you behave yourself anyway, you've got yourself a good husband." She believes Tokunbo is one of the best things that happened to me. If only she knew what he thinks of her.

"So it will be my fault if he leaves me, *abi*? Anyway I'm sure you're joking. It will be a boring life, someone like you will soon tire of it."

"Try me. Is anyone of your husband's friends divorced yet and looking for a replacement?"

"Daisy, what will I do with you? Maybe we can plot to chase one wife out for you."

"Ah noooo, I'm not that desperate. How far with your car?"

"I'm supposed to get to the workshop in about two hours, so if you get off this call, I'll be sure to get there on time."

"Will your Mr. Gomez be there?"

"He is not my Mr. Gomez and I'm sure he won't be there, he doesn't have to be. It's just to fix the boot."

"I need to confess Tara, I haven't gotten over his hypnotizing looks, I almost dreamt about him."

"You almost dreamt about FG! Now I know you are truly mad, you silly girl."

"Don't blame me. When you don't have a man in your life at my age, the only thing you can do is to dream about them." She chuckles. "You seem to have all the rich men in your life now. Let me leave you, if you see him, do tell him I don't mind him and…"

"I'm cutting you off now." I threaten her as I unknot my hair bond. "Good to see that your mouth has not lost its vibes. I'll talk to you later and see what we can plan." I don't need her endless rants now. She had been morose and hardly in any mood for her natural jabbering yesterday after Shoprite and I could not blame her.

The last person that needed a sack is petite, good-natured Daisy. The first of a family of three, her mother eventually died after a protracted battle with cancer, which caused her father to resign his civil service job in order to look after his wife. When they had to sell the modest family bungalow in Yaba to settle the unending hospital bills, the lot fell on Daisy to rent a tenement-converted three bedroom flat in Ajegunle, and to take up paying her sisters' school fees, both of whom were in university. Ajegunle, the most popular slum in Lagos, is not the ideal place for anyone to live, but that was the only place she could afford to rent the much needed space of a three bedroom flat for all the family and within reasonable commute to Marina.

When her mother died last year, she was secretly relieved and confided in me that her grief was not so much about losing the poor woman, since she had lived the last one year of her life in terrible pain, but the fact that the family had lost almost everything in trying to keep her alive. All for nothing! It was in the height of her mother's illness, after visiting their new apartment in Ajegunle that her last boyfriend whom she had dated for almost three years tactfully exited her life. Daisy in good spirits commented that she was grateful her mother did not wait for her to get married before taking ill, otherwise she would have become a divorcee instead of a jilted girlfriend. Although, she had been a regular churchgoer like me, it was in the middle of the crisis that she became born-again, embracing God in a new intense way. "There's always something to be grateful for, you know." That was her forgiving outlook towards her boyfriend.

At the age of thirty six, the breadwinner of the family, single and now jobless, Daisy will need a miracle as soon as possible to help her stay afloat. This is the time her God and carefreeness will matter the most. For how long? I wonder. We need to get back into work fast.

Maria, the resident help, brings in the clothes I gave her to iron. The possibility of running into FG had crossed my mind and having tried unsuccessfully to quieten the subconscious suggestion that I was trying to dress up for him without making it obvious that I put in some effort, I spent almost thirty minutes leafing through my wardrobe to pick a basic multi-coloured striped cotton shirt and black trousers. Being most bankers' trademark, the H & C shirt seemed to be my safest bet, to avoid appearing too casually dressed, in case I have the misfortune of running into anyone who may wonder why I am not at work on a Tuesday.

"*Make I serve your food?*" She lays the clothes on the bed, taking a comfortable position by the door.

"No, just check if Yisa has washed the car. I hope he has, otherwise get a cloth and wipe it quickly before going to your shop. I'm almost ready to go out."

"*Make I pack am for you?*"

"No, I'm not going to the office today." I pick up the trouser as a signal to her that I am ready to start dressing up.

"Yes ma."

Soon afterwards, my mirror tells me I look good enough to head for a panel-beating job. Instinctively, I send a text to FG. *'I'm on my way to the workshop.'*

* * *

I drive into the workshop five minutes past twelve. There was an *okada* accident on the highway, causing the road, which has been reduced to two narrow lanes, because of the on-going road construction to be further reduced to one. As is common with the stretch of the Lekki Peninsula, there is no alternative route. Sometimes, it does feel good to know that both the rich and the poor have common denominators, like when we all have to sit through traffic and struggle to squeeze one another's cars into the one tiny lane available. I was stuck for a while and almost sweating as the air-conditioner seemed to become less effective occasioned by the frustration with reckless *danfo* drivers and the tension of trying to beat time.

There are a few other Nissan cars parked there and a conspicuous Range Rover. A man comes to meet me before I finish parking with a small notebook in hand and politely asks if I am there for repairs or enquiries. He flips through his notebook after taking my name and then asks me to allow him drive the car in. After I hand him the keys, he asks if I will wait, pointing to the reception or if I will rather go somewhere and come back for the car. He does not know how long it will take to fix the trunk, but he can confirm for me if I wait at the reception. Feeling too tired to wait for a cab under the thirty-something degree temperature, I decide to wait at the reception.

"Madam, where are you going?" FG's girly voice flows from

the Range Rover before I get to the reception. I have always wondered how such a tiny voice could belong to someone with as big a frame as FG. If he spoke in a crowd, people would be looking for a doll-hugging girl.

"Hey, I didn't know you were here." My voice falters in surprise, although I must admit I am pleased to see him.

"The least a gentleman should do for a lady, especially for one he hasn't seen in a long time." His white teeth glitter through his subtle smile. He is dressed in a giraffe-print shirt and blue jeans. "Can we go for a quick brunch? I had to rush here so I wouldn't be late, but I'm seriously starving now. Have you had breakfast already?"

I shake my head and pretend to be picking a loose thread on my shirt button, avoiding his discomforting gaze. He retains his stare on me, until it becomes unbearable, so I respond. "No, I haven't had breakfast."

He does not seem to notice my uneasiness. "Good, why don't you pop into the car, I'll go over to the reception and confirm when your car will be ready." He leaps off without waiting for me to accept or protest his invitation. I drag my feet to the passenger's side and help myself into the Range Rover. It is an injustice to call this piece of evolution a car or an SUV for that matter; it is simply in a class of its own. There is nothing as refreshing as the good smell of leather with a mild scent of lavender and I close my eyes now to savour the aroma while it is still fresh.

* * *

The air is warm, but the closeness of the restaurant to the sea ensures the atmosphere remains fresh and cool. I particularly like to be close to nature whenever I have the opportunity, so I steer FG towards the gallery where fewer people are seated. It also has a more lively scenery. After placing our order, FG fills me up on the history of the restaurant and how they have expanded over the years. The original owner, a Lebanese who naturalised as a Nigerian, picking many chieftaincy titles along the way, has since retired to allow his son run the business. The old man had been a friend to FG's father.

The waiter brings our order and asks if we want anything else. I shake my head, but FG responds with a mischievous smile. "Yes, you can serve us anything that won't go on the bill." The waiter returns his smile and leaves. He picks his cutlery immediately to start devouring his portion of Smoked Salmon Omelette. I pick my cutlery, but the sea breeze keeps fanning strands of my long lace wig into my mouth. I drop the cutlery, sweep my hair to the back and self-consciously gather it into one piece. FG looks on in-between mouthfuls. "Why did you do that?"

"Because I don't want you to finish your food before I start mine." I am now free to start eating.

"You look very beautiful letting your hair loose." He sounds disappointed.

When was the last time Tokunbo told me I looked beautiful? That word alone makes me feel years younger. "Thank you, but sometimes beauty can become a burden." Considering the amount of time and effort invested in getting the hair to this state and I still need to fix it in public.

"Has it ever been a real burden to you?" He sets his cutlery down and focuses on me.

"What?"

"Do you think your beauty has ever been a real burden to you? How do you handle passes from men?"

"Oh! I didn't succeed with you, did I?" I shift my eyes to the man revving his sea bike to launch out. "Really, I'm not sure I qualify for that kind of beauty. The nature of my work shields me from all those stories you hear about some ladies. I don't go out much except for family and church functions, so Mr. Gomez I don't think I meet enough men to warrant being burdened. And I always wear my wedding ring." I raise my left hand to reassure him.

"Hmm, you underrate yourself." He keeps quiet after that, smiling with a kind of knowing privy only to him. The silence lingers as we both concentrate on our food while I try to blot out the thoughts of what our lives could have been if we had indeed married each other. I am surprised the pain still sears through me as if it happened yesterday. He has maintained his teddy look and he still looks attractively babyish even with the grace of maturity around him. If he was a lady, it would be easy to guess whether he has a family with children or not, but men have the luxury of keeping their body parts intact, except when they start building pot bellies with indulgent alcohol like Tokunbo is trying to do now. FG looks as trim as he looked in school, with just a little bit of added maturity, flesh and muscles. Why did he come to meet me at the workshop? Surely he did not need to be there.

"How many children do you have now?" I recline on the chair after laying down the cutlery, done with the food. He dusts his hands and wipes his mouth with the napkin, shaking his head. "None?" He nods. "Wife?" He shakes his head again. "You're not married? Why?" My voice rises a little bit.

He looks amused and shrugs. "What makes you think anyone would marry me when you didn't?"

"That was some millennia ago, surely you have a lot of admirers who would be too willing. For how long do you want to be the most eligible bachelor in town?"

"You read gossip magazines too? That is the problem, sugar. No lady has given me the benefit of a very good chase after you." His smile is vacillating now. He called me sugar, like he used to and the sound of it tickles my insides. Tokunbo calls me sunshine, but that has become infrequent lately, well until yesterday. "Believe it or not, it took me quite a while to get over you and the most frustrating part of it is that neither you nor mum told me what transpired between the two of you. That was a wicked thing to do, Tara. I still don't know why you hated me so much afterwards." He swallows and looks pleadingly into my eyes, waiting for an answer. "What happened that day?"

I shut my eyes briefly, deliberately inhaling the sea-fresh air, before I start recounting what happened that one time I visited his family home, after his mother came in. I had greeted her courteously, going down on my knees instinctively, even though he had told me it was not necessary. "Good afternoon ma."

"Hello, Fola, I've forgotten we were having a guest today. You can get up." She signalled to me. The woman was tall, beautiful and with an aura of unobtrusive but apparent elegance and authority. She was casually dressed in patterned white short sleeves top and bottoms, yet the expensiveness of her presence was not lost on me as I involuntarily inhaled the vanilla fragrance of her perfume. I had seen and admired her a lot from a distance as much as her pictures in soft-sell and fashion magazines would allow; never for once had it occurred to me that she could look this beautiful in real life, without being all-dressed up in outing clothes. Suddenly, my flowery blouse and jeans trousers felt fit only for a house cleaner.

"Mum, this is the girl I've been talking about, Tara."

She nodded at me and I could feel the weight of her eyes as they went up and down my figure like that of a commodity on display, forcing me to lower my eyes. "I see, take your seat and make yourself comfortable." She pulled FG aside and whispered to him.

He smiled and came back to squeeze my hand. "Give me some minutes, I'll be right back." He disappeared through the exit to the staircase.

His mother took a seat opposite me on the other sofa and removed the sunglasses she had on. My nerves were tearing apart under her persistent dissecting stare.

"Who are your parents?" She asked unemotionally.

"Me?" Of course, there was no one else in the room, but that question just flew at me. She nodded. "My father is a medical doctor, but I live with my mother. She is a nurse." I did not have the time to think before the words poured out.

"If your father is still alive, why are you not living with both of them?"

"They were never married, ma." Talking truthfully about my father and family circumstances was not my favourite subject for discussion, but sometimes there was simply no way to avoid it, like now. To claim my father was dead would simply be easier, but my mother insisted that would be a big lie. I hoped the bitterness I felt towards him did not reflect in my voice.

"Hmm." She clenched her fingers, rocking them back and forth. "Your mother is a nurse. And where does she live?"

"We live in Ketu ma."

"You live in Ketu?" It was a query with an incredulous inflection in her voice that surprised me. Even without my eyes raised to meet hers, I could feel her eyes summing me up again as my insides began to heat up. "You live in Ketu." She repeated. "And you come to my house as Fola's girlfriend. Does this place look anything like where you come from?" Her voice was so flat I almost missed the contempt in it. "Let me give you a piece of advice, if you like yourself, you will stop following my son and find someone on your level. I hope you don't think he's serious about you because he brought you home. Don't be fooled." She chuckled in between. "And don't let it cross your mind that he could even consider marrying you. What do you think you have to offer him?"

Conscious there was no way to escape the venom being spat at me, I continued to look down at the black shoes Fola had given me for Christmas.

She came to my side. "I don't want you to ever step foot into this house again. Is that understood?"

The wooziness besetting me knotted my tongue and my mouth would not open to utter any sensible thing, so I nodded. I would have left immediately; there was nothing else for me to do there, but the possibility that the dogs might have been let loose kept me on the spot. My head was drooped and my eyes blurred with tears that threatened to burst forth at any time soon. There was something about being poor; it gave you a ray of hope, otherwise any fool would have known our relationship would not last.

FG came in afterwards with all smiles and enthusiasm. "Mum." But she had left, mission accomplished. He had me in his arms. "Omotara, what's wrong, why are you crying, is it mumsie?" I nodded. "What happened, what did she do?" I continued sobbing, unable to speak. "Mum!" He left me and rushed out to look for her. She was long gone. I carried my bag and followed him. Never to return!

Fourteen years is a long time. That was when I walked out of his family home, and never spoke with him after that. What would it have achieved? Could I have asked him to choose between his mother and me? That would have been too much to ask of anyone, especially an only child. I definitely would not have been able to withstand the arrogant Mrs. Gomez; she would have crushed me to bits. With Tokunbo's mother's interference in our lives now, I am convinced as ever that I made the right choice, leaving FG to find himself a deserving girl from a rich family that would meet his mother's specification.

I turn my head to the sound of clattering plates and cutlery as the waiter clears the table, leaving the bill. Beneath his carefree gorgeous façade, I sense that vulnerability FG never revealed to anyone in those days. It is ironic, how many guys I knew back then who envied him for his good looks and wealthy background, and how many ladies that longed for him just to wink at them. Yet here he sits, hiding forlornly behind his persuasive baby smile.

"I'm surprised your mother hasn't gotten you a wife by now since she said I was too poor for your family and that she never wanted me near you." Now I can say it without feeling inadequate about my background or family fortune. Tokunbo is by no means a poor man. I wish I could tell FG much more, but I put a rein on my mouth, knowing it would not avail to any good. How would he feel if I told him what happened after we parted ways? Guilty, heartbroken, regret? I will never know, because I will never tell.

His touch is tender as he reaches for my left hand which is resting on the edge of the table. A familiar sensation shoots through my body. He shakes his head sadly. "I guessed it was something like that, but I didn't know what to do since you shut me out completely."

I subtly withdraw my hand to stem the threatening release of oxytocin in my body, even though it feels good. "I hope it's not too late to say I'm sorry, I couldn't be the one to cause a feud between you and your mum. But seriously, why haven't you gotten married."

"You could have given me the benefit of making that decision. Do you know how boring it can be to always have what you want, when you want it? No push, no incentive, no thrill because you know you'll always get it. I'm looking for that girl that will challenge me as much as you did, and hopefully she won't bail out on me because of my mum's indiscretion. Enough about me, what have you been doing with your life beyond getting married and getting sacked. Do you still bake?"

Bake? Oh yes. FG would remember that. That is one of the reasons I was sugar to him. Apart from being his girlfriend at school, the other thing that made me popular was my baking business. I used to bake in school and sell to supplement my pocket money. I was the one everyone came to for Valentine and Christmas cakes and I was the mysterious girl who delivered the little surprise gifts as peace offerings when things went a little bit awry between lovers. He helped me build that business by making his oven available, continually buying me the needed equipment and baking books at every opportunity.

When I started dating Tokunbo, he practically took charge of my finances and had gradually weaned me off making cakes for money. Although I have stopped selling cakes, baking has become more than a way of making money; I find it a means of expressing myself without having to apologise to anyone and whenever I get down to it, I come out creating unrestrained designs. Working at the bank made it impractical for me to make cakes with the creativity I love to bring to them but I still find time to bake for friends or family whenever there is cause for celebration. That in itself saves me the hassles of thinking about appropriate gifts to buy for celebrants, and everyone knows what to expect from me.

Some years back, Tokunbo started on my case to resign and suggested that I should open a confectionary shop, but he made it seem like he would go to any length to lord his agenda over me, so I stopped baking unless it was absolutely necessary.

I shake my head. "I hardly have time to bake. You know how bank work keeps us unnecessarily busy." I must admit I miss that hobby; talking about it now makes me feel like a whole page of my life has been erased, while I stand looking on, unwilling to do anything about it.

FG's eyes widen. "You don't make cakes anymore? That's some talent you're throwing away." It feels like someone just dropped a truckload in my heart as I remember how FG and I used to play around to produce each piece of art. "Maybe that's what I miss most about you." His mischievous voice sounds as if he read my mind.

"I haven't stopped altogether, but not as a business. Well, one person can only do so much after work and family."

"That's true. Now that you've stopped working, maybe you'll have time to rediscover yourself." So nicely put, that he did not remind me I was sacked again. "And I can give you a contract to make a Christmas cake for my office party."

"Christmas cake?"

He winks. "Yes, that's the only thing I can think of as an excuse."

A flash of the last Christmas party I had with him and a few friends in his flat brings a hot flush inside me as I remember the rubbing of his smooth skin against mine; it feels almost real right now with his eyes piercing into mine. I shake myself out of the reverie. "But I can't charge you for baking you a cake." Back to the present, my mind races to my house and I see Tokunbo's scowling face over me in the living room. Should I not tell FG I cannot make a cake for him outright? What will I tell Tokunbo? Not that he will ask me anyway, but it will seem like FG is intruding in my house and it already feels like I should be guilty of some wrongdoing. Getting him off my mind since yesterday has already been a tough task.

He smiles wilfully. "I never refuse a gift, and not especially from you, so if you want to make one for me for free, I don't mind. Just make a nice one. Now that we're on it, I can't wait to have the cake. It's been a long time." He reaches for my hand again and his fingers trace my palm as if he is trying to read my future. It feels familiar good, so I let him continue.

"I will have to see about that if I'm not too busy." It does not really sound right, this Christmas cake business. But the thought of him desiring my cake and the way he is touching me send disturbing signals to my brain, I cannot just refuse him absolutely. I know I should remove my hand, but my brain tells me I have been longing to be touched like this, like a fragile piece of chinaware. I want it to last forever.

"Busy?" He grins. "Well, what can I say, children? How many of them have you got now?"

"None yet." I look away from him and set my gaze on the sea, gripping the glass of orange juice.

"Oh, really?" He stops his probing fingers. "What are you waiting for? I hope he doesn't mind?" I cannot exactly describe what he is thinking. Is it shock or curiosity or even pity? But it does sound like what I am used to; that I am the one who has problems with having children. "So what will you be busy doing then?" He corks his head when I say nothing. "Are you happy with him?"

Am I happy with Tokunbo? I withdraw my hand. The reference to him gives me a jolt. "I married him, what do you think?" He raises his brows and flips his hand without responding. "I'm as happy as I want to be. Happiness is a choice, you know and my husband is a good man." I wish I could have said loving.

"You're a good woman too. The best so far."

"Thank you." I flush under his intense gaze, but I slowly pick up my glass and guzzle the remaining juice in one swoop. Maybe I am a good woman in his mind because we did not end up getting married to each other. Sometimes, the fact of never knowing what could have been on the other side gives us an illusion that it would have been better. "We should start going."

"So do we have a deal on the cake?" Tara, get a grip of yourself and let him know there is no deal. "Take it as a business request."

I shake my head with a smile. "It's not like I need the money, but I'll let you know if I can come up with something. I have to get back into the job market quickly before I get too comfortable being a housewife. Or maybe I should take a holiday and give myself a break from everything."

"A holiday won't be a bad idea. Where are you thinking of?"

I raise my brows to look at him. "I'm not thinking of anywhere yet, it just crossed my mind now."

"Well, whatever you come up with, let me know. You never can tell ..." He shrugs and leaves it in the air.

I look at my watch on impulse after the long pause. "They should have finished with the car."

"Yes, sugar. Whatever you say." He looks at his watch too. "They did say it would take about three hours, but we can get going. He lifts himself up slowly; his biceps shoot out, accentuating his masculinity. It looks so deliberately sensual that it almost seems rehearsed. He lands immediately behind my chair as I push back to let myself up. His fresh breath is close and overpowering, and I shut my eyes for an instant. My eyes refuse to lock with his by the time I open them again. With weakening slow steps, I let him walk me to his car.

CHAPTER FIVE

Tokunbo

Tara stirs to the sound of my movement in the bedroom from her sleep, her face exuding a peaceful smile like a new born baby yet to discover the world. With eyes still shut, she turns and pulls at the coverlet to cover more of her body. But not before revealing some fleshy part of her laps. The sight of her curvaceous body has never ceased to arouse me since I first set eyes on her. And sixteen years on, she still has that innocent charm of someone unaware of how beautiful she is and how much impact she has on men. I stand beside the bathroom door, looking at her, reluctant to wake her up, yet longing to have her in my arms. But she is already on her side of the bed and that is a sign for me to keep off, unless something changed since yesterday.

Ironically, the effect of her dismissal at work last Monday made her let her guard down, although she immediately recoiled back to herself the following day. Why can our relationship not revert to how it used to be, when she was not all closed up and consumed with getting pregnant? It seems so long ago that she looked to me for affection and made any attempt to innocently lure me to bed with those short revealing negligees; bending over to pick imaginary items she dropped at odd places, and later, when I caught up with her, curling up to me and shyly ask me to make love to her.

It seems so long ago that I first set eyes on the angel-like image at the boutique below my office. A fire alarm had started shrieking and people were rushing out from the high-rise office block opposite. I had thought it was a fire drill until the persistent noise became an unbearable distraction; only for me to look out from my second floor window to see the smoke increasing in height and thickness from what appeared to be the fourth or fifth floor of the building across the road. Street hawkers, pedestrians and the notorious o*kada* riders were converging in front of the office block and drivers were slowing down to steal glances at the building, causing traffic build-up. Some police officers were strolled down while some people stood far off, recording the scene with their phones; some other people were on the phone talking frantically, hugging files and folders. A few looked on in shock, and stood almost transfixed like zombies. Two women were crying with contorted body movements as though they were mourning and their colleagues hovered around them.

Suddenly, a mild explosion ruptured and fire spluttered through some windows. The people on the streets ran in different directions, only to congregate again. I buzzed my secretary then to ask her to call the fire service. She said she had called and they had confirmed receiving several calls about the fire, but they were short of trucks as there had been another fire incident in another location on the Island. I shook my head at the futility of relying on government agencies when they were needed them the most.

Distracted and unsure if I would be able to offer any help, I left my office for the ground floor. By the time I got downstairs, two fire trucks had arrived and the policemen were trying to disperse the onlookers, while the fire fighters set up their equipment. Rather than join the other people from my office block and scorch myself in the heat of the furnace-infiltrated sun, I turned to enter the boutique. There she was, akimbo, behind the sliding glass door, and immersed in the events across the road. At first, I thought she was a mannequin, clad in a black long skirt with a glow transferred from the blaze behind me. When I looked up, I saw a smiley face matched with a pair of lively eyes and perfectly attached to a long neck, with a body toned between caramel and honey. My eyes locked with hers for a few seconds and her curved lightly-glossed lips parted slowly as she uttered something and moved aside before Abba, the owner of the boutique reared her face.

"Good morning Mr. Akande, you saw the fire?" Abba slid the glass to let me in, but I almost missed my footing. "Oh, sorry."

"It's unfortunate, isn't it?" I stepped into the shop, grateful for the air conditioning. "Hello." I beamed at the graceful young lady, who effortlessly made me lose my bearings. Her face had that guileless beam, like the image of a sunflower as if she was born with it. She was tall, definitely taller than me; her hair was tied back, revealing her rounded spotless face, high cheek bones and unusual flawless nose. Her well-endowed chest stood distinctly upright and accentuated her small waist line.

Even with little or no makeup, everything about her body seemed deliberately and perfectly moulded. She had a grace of nonchalance and naturalness of beauty that made her more intoxicating.

"Good morning sir." She greeted me without meeting my eyes, rather glancing at the watch on her smooth textured wrist. Her nails were short, well-manicured and lightly coated. I did not think I looked that old; why would she address me as sir? I should have stopped Abba from addressing me as Mr. Akande a long time ago, but I had not wanted to encourage any familiarity. "Auntie Abba, I'll come around when I close if you're still here." She moved towards the door, expecting me to step aside.

Should I let her leave without even knowing her name? "Do you know what caused the fire?" I stood my ground by the door.

"Me?" She looked at me, then at Abba as if she would be scolded if she responded to my question. "I don't know anyone there. I was on my way up to the office when I heard the explosion."

"Oh, I see. Do you work here too?" She nodded and moved from one leg to the other. As I swapped my own legs too, I inhaled the scent of her closeness, despite the smell of her cheap body spray. "My name is Tokunbo, my office is on the second floor, Toxy Development Company." She did not look like the type that would be impressed but I stretched my hand to her and she glanced at Abba again before shaking it.

"Okay sir, I have to go now. Thank you." I stepped aside then and she exited immediately.

"She's on a vacation job at Providence Chambers, I thought you'd have met her." Abba did not wait for me to ask before volunteering the information. I wondered why she was smiling, but I simply nodded to stop her inquisitive stare. Providence Chambers was owned by my friend, Big Sam on the first floor. "I introduced her to Big Sam and he confirmed that she's been doing well. Her name is Tara."

That information was consoling. Despite being married, Big Sam was notorious with girls, but since he had a fling going with Abba, it was unlikely he would be digging it in with her friend.

"Good for her." Fully armed with the information I needed to find my way to the smiley face, I tried to feign dis-interest, turning to face the sad spectacle across the road. "I came down to see if there was anything we could do to help out, but since the fire-fighters are there now, there's nothing more to do." I trailed off and with that, I left Abba's boutique to fathom what to do about that smiley face.

She was in year four and had come to work for Big Sam so she could get some work experience and make some money to help ease the burden of school fees on her mother. Almost twenty two, she said she found addressing a man who was eleven years older than her by his first name totally disrespectful. She already had a boyfriend she was in love with and would never think of cheating on him. I met the charming chap twice and I envied his youthfulness, his looks and his ownership of Tara's heart. But he could not stop me from leaving my door open for her, and gradually, I began to win her trust and reverent friendship. Apart from her boyfriend, she did not seem to trust any other person, neither did she have any close friend, which made it easy for her to come and talk to me about her studies and relationship, and most of all about her father.

She missed not having a father figure, especially since she knew her father was still alive. She longed to have a bit of him in her life, but she knew her mother would still disapprove of her trying to reach him. About a year after mentioning her father, I located the man, lecturing at a University in the UK. He was married with three children. Tara had not wanted to contact him; she only wanted to know if he was alive and doing well. It left her distraught that the man was indeed alive and would not extend a hand to her. She expressed hope that one day, he would come looking for her.

That singular act made her trust me and depend on me more and by her last day at work with Providence Chambers, she reluctantly called me Tokunbo at my insistence, still keeping her eyes away from meeting mine. As much as I wanted her, she would not even spare me a hug because of her deep immersion with that Fola boy. I had to respect her loyalty and commitment to her boyfriend. Yet I could not stop myself from continuing to fall in love with her. Somewhere deep in my heart, I knew I had touched her life and I was not ready to let go. I remained her brother, friend, mentor and confidant and we stayed in touch.

Once in a while, when she visited Providence Chambers, she would call at my office and we would have lunch together. She was not like any other girl I had dated; no pretensions, no arrogance and no demand on time or resources; just the simplicity and candour of someone who was comfortable enough with herself not to hide her vulnerability and humble enough to depend on me without taking advantage. My girlfriend at the time, if I could call her that, had made it clear that getting married was not on top of her list. And I wanted a wife desperately. Tara was all I wanted in a wife and more.

When she went to Law School, she kept working part-time with Big Sam and we continued our cat and mouse game. Until the day she walked into my office, and I was finally able to hold her in my arms. I knew something was wrong immediately I saw her. She had lost some of her exuberance and confidence; her frame was gaunt and her shoulders stooped; her ever-beaming eyes looked listless, almost hollow; even her otherwise glossy skin looked pale. Everything about her was screaming for attention. She agreed to have dinner with me after work, where she poured out the misery of losing her precious FG the week before. In good conscience, I should have advised her to have a sincere talk with her boyfriend, but I had wanted her for so long, her loss in love was a prayer answered. I did my best to weave myself into her life slowly, but steadily. She did not have to say yes, because I did not ask her formally. I knew she was ready for me on her twenty-fifth birthday, when I leaned to kiss her and she turned her face to offer her lips instead of flinching or giving me her cheek as she used to. It was three long years later that she became my wife; because she insisted on starting her career on the right track to justify her mother's struggles in sending her to school. How time flies!

It seems so long ago that we had any spark in this marriage, except for last week when she curled into me after the emotional strain of losing her job. It seems so long ago since I made real love to my sunshine and for that, I was almost glad she lost that job, self-serving as it may sound. Anyway, I have never quite shared her obsession with wanting to work for a livelihood. I make enough for her not to worry about anything money can buy now or in the future.

Although she would not talk about it explicitly, I feel it has something to do with her desire to be independent, to avoid being abandoned the same way her father abandoned her mother. It is an indication that she does not trust me enough and I often wonder why I have to suffer for her old man's misdeeds. What would make me leave Tara? I cannot fathom, and right now, that is not what I want to think about.

Once more, the image of the ample breasts of Kunle's girl at the club earlier today creep into my head. I should not bother going to that club tomorrow, Fridays are usually flooded with girls.

She stirs again in her sleep, gradually opening her eyes to

adjust to the light before glancing at the wall clock. "You're back early." She stifles in between a yawn.

"I'm sorry I woke you up." I switch off the light immediately and slip back into the bathroom to splash some water on my face to douse the rising cadence of the flames trying to burst through my loins. But the imperious images of that girl's voluptuousness and Tara's glowing thighs flowing in my head both conspire to maintain my erection. It is a futile exercise. I sneak back to the bedroom, into the double bed.

Her back is already turned before my hands reached her shoulder and she stiffens lightly without turning to face me. My nose trails the flowery scent of her flesh to her nape and I inch closer, rubbing my body against hers in the smoothness of her silky nightgown. I grabble for her breast under the red illumination of the fabric, hoping that will rouse her to life. She mumbles as if she is still groggy, but I cannot make out what she says, neither do I care. Is she not the same person that talked to me a minute ago? I continually brush my turgidity against her back, so she can feel how far gone I am.

She lets out a moan and I persist by stroking her nipple until she turns towards me. "Tokunbo." Her murmur only stirs me on. I cannot allow her talk, otherwise that will be the end of it, so I reach out to bury my face into hers, making out her lips. She turns her head aside, but I follow still, until I intertwine our lips, arresting her in a deep kiss, gently using my body to turn her over on her back and slightly pinning her arms to the bed as I begin to tease her body with my lips.

She emits a quiet noise of complaint, but I press on, until it turns into intermittent purrs of pleasure. She gradually surrenders to my sensual exploration of her body, encapsulating me in the magical warmth of her womanhood. It is a conquest I would rather not have, but this is the way it has been for a long time.

CHAPTER SIX

Tara

I pick my phone from the console to check whose call I missed. It was FG's. My stomach churns. Why did he call me this morning? In fact why did he call me at all, I muse uneasily. *'I set up an interview for u on Thursday. I hope u can make it. Pls call to confirm & send me your CV asap folag@gholdings.ng FG'*, his text reads. An interview in one week? That is good news. Can he make things happen this fast? It was only last week Monday I ran into him. Or is this how fast the labour market is? Sheer energy seeps into my veins. Should I tell Tokunbo? No, better not, not now anyway. I need to update my CV and put myself in the right frame of mind for the next forty eight hours.

'Ok, I will call u later. Tx'. I go back to the dining table with my cup of tea, suddenly not in the mood to join Tokunbo on the sofa with his newspapers. We have been having breakfast together since last Tuesday, now that there is no longer an office to run off to before the break of dawn, and he can

afford to leave for his office as late as he wants. How thoughtful of FG. I did not tell him I was sure about looking for a job, yet he has gone ahead to make contacts for me. Getting an interview at such a short notice must be a miracle at a time like this, especially when he does not have my CV. Wonderful.

"Mama is coming in on Saturday." Tokunbo's voice comes at me as my phone starts ringing again.

"What? Which Mama? Why, when?" I almost splutter with my mouth full of tea. I thought I did something right last night, but all Tokunbo has done this morning is to make my blood boil.

"Which one do you want me to answer first? Bimbo called to inform me she's booked her on a morning flight on Saturday, so I'll have to pick her up. I don't know how I can manage that with going for the church programme and Flora's party. Or, what do you suggest?" I stare at him blankly. Mama has spent almost one year with Bimbo, Tokunbo's younger sister, since she gave birth to her fourth child. After Tokunbo's father died shortly before we got married, she abandoned the family house and now lives in three cities – Lagos, New Jersey and London; between Tokunbo and his two sisters. It must be a wonderful thing to be able to interfere with other people's lives without any repercussions. "If you won't come to the airport with me, then you'll have to drive to church." He pauses for an answer, but I am speechless. Then he raises his shoulders. "Well, just sort it out and let me know what you want to do."

I push the plate of potatoes away and get up to walk towards him, but stop and walk back to the table, facing him. My body temperature has gone up suddenly and my body feels so bloated it needs an outlet. Tears trickle down my eyes. "You're travelling next Friday, what's the point in having her here when you won't be around?" Sobbing through my words, I struggle to make sense of the impending visit.

"Why are you crying?" Tokunbo stands and gapes at me. Why am I crying? Even I cannot say why I am crying. "Is it about Mama coming here or something else?" He comes to hold me by the shoulder while I wipe my eyes with my hands without saying a word. He sits me down and sits opposite me. "This is my mother we're talking about. Is she such a terror to you?"

"Honestly, I didn't mean to, but I can't explain it, I'm sorry." I groan inwardly, still swallowing. Tokunbo's mother is not such a terror, she is just a cunning woman that manages to get on everybody's nerves, including her son's. The last time she was here, the only news she had to share was of every family member giving birth, including the dogs and cats. Then she would tactfully look at me and ask if we were still checking that nothing was wrong with either of us. What will I be doing with her from Monday through the week, since there was no office to use as alibi?

"I think it's your hormones acting out all over again." Tokunbo shakes his head. "I don't care what the outcome of this one is, but let me tell you straight up, this is the last IVF we're going through."

"Tokunbo…"

"Don't start." He cuts me short. "Anyway, I've postponed my trip, so you won't be alone with her. I hope that's enough consolation."

I sniff the residue of my sobs. "I've said I'm sorry, you don't need to cancel your trip." My phone rings, but I ignore it to continue talking. "I'll be fine, I'm sure."

He holds his hand up again. "Pick your call." He gets up and goes back to the TV.

"Hello Daisy?" I force a smile into my voice.

"Why can't you answer your call, woman? I've called you before."

"Sorry, I was in the middle of something. What's up with you?"

"Are you okay? You sound distant. Anyway, you're always okay, miss smiley face." Daisy is chatty as usual. "I've missed you seriously and right now I need someone to talk to."

"Go on, I'm listening."

"Can't you feign some excitement? My car arrived."

"Oh, finally. That's good. After the long wait." She paid someone about four months ago to import the fairly-used car from United States and we were beginning to think the car would never arrive as the man had different stories of mishap to tell her each time she called him. "That calls for a celebration. When are you coming to take me out?"

"Take you out?" She chuckles. "That's the problem with this car arriving now. I hope it doesn't become a burden because if I don't get a job soon, I may have to put it up for sale. What I need is a job, not this car." Her voice flattens out. Maria comes in to pack the plates.

"At least we can rock it for a few weeks first and who knows, you may get a job next week. You have to switch on some positivity to see the bright side."

"I hope so. I just wanted to see how you're getting on. I miss you and I haven't eaten cake since the last time I was in the office. Can you imagine that?"

I pause for a moment. "Don't worry, I'll see you after my interview on Thursday." The words are already out before I remember Tokunbo is still within earshot. I sneak a peep at him and I am not surprised to see him staring at me, cross-legged, with eyes threatening to tear the phone from my hand.

"You have an interview? Where? You didn't tell me you've started looking. Please are you sending my CV out too?"

Tokunbo tunes on the TV loud enough for me to know he is still there. "I'll have to get back to you about that." It is difficult to follow through on this discussion while I am struggling to make up what to tell Tokunbo after getting off the phone, stiffening my insides. "I'll try to see you then, or maybe Friday. Can you hold on till then?"

"Do I have a choice? It seems you can't wait to get off the phone or off me for that matter."

"You're actually right about that. Enjoy your weekend." I exhale, relieved to be getting out of the conversation, but she quickly chirps in.

"No, no, please hold on. Don't drop yet. There's something else I need to tell you."

"Daisy, please." I try to keep the irritation from my voice.

"Sorry, sorry. Although I don't know what's eating you this morning." She complains before switching to an almost whisper. "The other thing is, I think I'm pregnant."

"You're what?!" I almost drop the phone. Tokunbo stares at me and adjusts himself up from his comfortable position. I shake my head, wave him back, and cover the mouthpiece. "Sorry, it's nothing serious." He sits back. "Daisy, are you pulling my legs, that's not possible. How can you say you think? How did that happen? For whom?"

"Not a joke at all, my sister. We need to catch up and talk and it has to be fast. Will you come or should I come?"

"Then I should definitely try to see you, maybe tomorrow." I wish I could share in her excitement. "No, let's do Thursday, I'll come to the house once I'm done."

"You promise? Not later than Thursday, okay I'll survive till then." She hangs up.

"That was Daisy."

"Don't you think I should be able to figure that out?" His response is snobbish. Count one to ten under your breath; that is what the doctor advised me when I complained about my bouts of crankiness. I count, but before any word leaves my lips, he barges in. "What was it she said that made you shout?"

"Oh that." I pause, unsure whether I should tell him or not. "She said she might be pregnant."

"Is she married now?" I shake my head. "I thought you said she has become born-again. Or has she stopped being a deacon in church?" I shake my head again. "And she's been sleeping around, what kind of double life is that?"

"That's not fair. I'm not even sure she wasn't joking. Daisy doesn't sleep around."

He nods derisively with a crooked smile on his face. "The same way you said she didn't have a boyfriend. So it's either she's been sneaking around with a guy you know nothing about or you're in on this with her. I've told you there's something wrong with a lady who can't find a husband at thirty five and that's the person you call your friend."

"Can we please not talk about this? Why are you being judgemental? You haven't heard the full story."

"What story is there to tell?" He refuses to back off. "I hope she knows the father of the poor child."

Why could Daisy not have called at a better time? More like why did I use her story to cover up for my interview gaff? "That's uncharitable of you. Anyway it's none of your business and I probably shouldn't have told you. So if we don't have any other thing to talk about, you can leave now."

"You are joking, right?" I cork my head in defiance. He smiles and folds his newspapers. "Will you come with me?" His subtle smile is patronising. "I don't have much to do today and we can go out later, anywhere you want to go."

My fighting stance falls apart, but I shake my head all the same. "I'm not coming with you. You know I don't like visiting to your office." I walk towards the door and call out to

Ola, who comes in and picks up his briefcase. He continues to smile mischievously as he walks towards me, and the door. "Enjoy your day, don't worry about me, I'll find something to do with myself." I pat him on the back like a boy going to school. He turns and gives me a peck on the lips. As soon as I hear the car drive out of the compound, I exhale and a torrent of tears come pouring down. What is wrong with me?

* * *

Tokunbo

The meeting with the CEO of Petra Services was successful and he has promised to send the contract papers before Friday. It is our first business with the company and even though we quoted the lowest and will make no more than fifteen to twenty percent profit, I am convinced the contract will yield more deals for my company, TDC. All we have to do is to position ourselves as the most competitive with the best promise of value in terms of delivery and timeline. Over time, we will have them in our kitty. That is one lesson I learnt from my father. He had reminisced about the English proverb that in business, he who laughs last laughs best; and explained that one should not be afraid to lose at the beginning of a new relationship, as long as there is a likelihood of repeat business.

The good thing about this deal is that they will pay in dollars and TDC will not suffer from the negative foreign exchange fluctuations. The contract is to build six model homes of four bedroom duplexes for their expatriate executives. We started from one million and five hundred thousand dollars. Although we continued arguing back and forth as I did imaginary calculations on sheets of paper, I strongly sensed the CEO had another candidate favourite; and the only way to beat him was to go below the one million and two hundred thousand dollars threshold, which no other company would have accepted. After about one hour of explaining how we handle quality control by sourcing building materials ourselves, I eventually agreed to fifty thousand dollars less. The treacly expressions on the other executives' faces betrayed their relief and sense of victory. Only the CEO was somewhat subdued. My adrenalin shot up then, so much that I almost exploded. But now, I feel rather empty thinking about Tara.

I walk to the window, trying to make sense of our marriage. Out and down below is the familiar scene of people traipsing the street to fit into the daily routine. There are men and women who, despite the hot weather are clad in dark-coloured suits, chasing deals or meeting up for lunch. The hawkers ply their wares to traffic victims for whom the display of items is irresistible, and *okada* riders try to beat the traffic odds by squeezing in and out of tight spots, not minding whose car is dented or whose leg is bruised. It is always a chaotic scene, sometimes injected with fresh but predictable bits of drama; yet it has become part of everyday life, that anything short of this would be rather abnormal. It is a symbolic scene of the rat race to which almost everyone in Lagos has submitted themselves.

I believe things can be better, or can they not? When hustling is all you have known about making money, every other thing would seem like an aberration. Or how else can one define Tara's obstinacy at working in the banking sector? If I take a poll of those sweating suit-clad figures on the streets, most of them would be bankers, when ironically the people making the most money are behind their comfy expensive desks in places like Shell and LNG. Almost all my friends' wives run their own businesses and they seem fulfilled and have more time running their homes. Why not my own wife? The way she is going on about getting a job makes me wonder if she feels trapped in our marriage and merely using work as a means of liberation. Could she really be unhappy? But why, how? I know many women who would be happy to be in her shoes right now. What exactly is her problem? Does she think she is the only one that wants a child? Is she unaware that I also feel self-conscious when people talk about children?

Three gentle taps on the door take me back to the L-shaped polished brown table adorned with various office paraphernal objects as Ebi pushes her head in. She follows with the rest of her small-sized frame, carrying her bulky file of to-do documents. In the little time she has spent with TDC, she has demonstrated high levels of resourcefulness, professionalism and forthrightness. She was introduced by the coordinator of the Women's Ministry in church and was actually interviewed informally by Tara, which makes me treat her like family sometimes. She has proven to be a great asset to the company unlike my previous personal assistant who lacked the initiative to do anything on her own. Ebi is the one who has the most audacity in the office to challenge me and my decisions occasionally. And when I refuse to shift position, she humbly lets me know she is not convinced, but compelled to carry out my directives. Of course, I hardly acknowledge it to her, but that quality does keep me in check every now and then.

What I really feel like doing right now is to tell her to go away, but I nod her to sit all the same, swivelling to the left to pick a pen from the crystal pen-holder. Turning back, my eyes land on her cleavage, staying there for some seconds. What is it about a woman's chest that pulls a man's eyes like magnet? Her dark green jacket is cut a little too low this time and very much in my line of vision, it is difficult not to see. I wonder what her personal life is like. She said she is engaged, but in over two years of working here, I have never felt the trace of a boyfriend. She maintains a high level of professionalism and reasonable aloofness to let me know she is here to work and I like it like that, although, I have seen her chatting familiarly with Kunle twice. That Kunle, I cannot trust him with anything in skirt and it is not impossible that he would have tried to work his way through to Ebi. I even caught him staring at Tara lustfully once. Reasonably, there was no way I could have protested without making it an unpleasant issue. But I believe he still has some degree of honour. No matter how much he looks, he will never cross the line with my wife or anybody's wife for that matter. Tara thinks otherwise, advising me to surround myself with more friends from church. The few ones I have tried to get close to hardly have social lives, and most of our discussions revolve around church and charitable activities. When I want to talk about real life issues, I have a feeling I would be judged because they all make it seem like their lives are perfect. I am not sure I can ever be comfortable enough with any one of them to share my silly fantasies with.

Ebi opens her file. "Sir, the accountant brought the budget for next year. He said it's the first draft and he'll be at the warehouse if you need any clarification." She pauses and raises her head, waiting for me to stretch out my hand. She flips the document over when my hands remain behind the table, tapping almost inaudibly with the pen. "Guess what, they've acknowledged delivery of the two containers at the warehouse. The sales manager said they'll start shipping them out to the sites and customers by Monday. Someone brought this card from the chairman's office, it's about their daughter's wedding. It falls on the day of our planned Christmas party, so we need to discuss the possibility of shifting our date sir." She pauses again, probably disappointed that I am not as excited as I should be. She opens the beautifully crested envelope, yet I have no response for her. Her perfume seems to be overpowering today and it is almost chocking me. "Providence Chambers sent back the contract agreement. Big Sam said you should look at the circled areas and he'll come back and discuss them with you. I've called the IT technician and he apologised and promised to get it fixed, I told him…"

"When are you getting married?" I interrupt her.

"Me?" Her widening eyes contort her brows as she hastily withdraws her hands from the file to lean back a bit.

I nod hesitantly. I am not sure where that came from, but now that it is out, I would really like to satisfy my curiosity. Her facial muscles loosen up a little and I am glad that she is not taking it too seriously, rather she maintains her demure posture, meeting my eyes with a glint.

"Next year sir. We are proposing mid-year, July." Although, I cannot see her hands, her motion tells me she is twisting that small ring she has on her finger. I recline in my seat, smiling and nodding, hoping that will urge her on. "We would have gotten married around Christmas, but my parents want us to wait another year because my elder sister got married earlier this year. You remember the wedding Sister Tara attended." I nod and she goes on as if she has also been waiting for this opportunity. "We are currently having our pre-marital counselling classes. He attends our church, but we've not been able to see you in church. He works with First Bank, Alaba branch. He's been eager to come and meet you sir, but you know Alaba is just out of this world. I planned to ask Sister Tara if we could visit you at home."

Hmm, really? "Oh, that's good. It will be a pleasure to host you two. That means you're sure he won't back down." She lowers her eyes and I hope this conversation is not sensitive or embarrassing to her, but that is the first step towards answering some of my own nagging questions.

"Definitely not sir, he's a good Christian and he's serious-minded."

"Does he make enough to take care of you?" She raises her brows and looks at me quizzically. "I mean, like the wedding. He can afford the wedding, right?" She nods. "What about after the wedding, can he still take care of you, like if you have to suddenly stop working?"

She jumps from her seat, her floundering right hand almost knocking down the crystal clock on the table. She handsprings her palm to me inquisitively. "Sir, have I done something wrong? I do my job with all commitment and you've never complained about anything. Why do you want to sack me?" Her voice quivers from her petite structure.

I must have said a wrong word and I wish I could placate her by petting her on the shoulder, but I remain on my seat, just shifting out a little. The last thing I want her to think is that I am trying to patronise her and since I have started I need to finish well before she starts having wrong ideas about me. "Sit down. It's nothing like that." She sits cautiously, ready to bolt again if need be. "Of course, you're doing a great job." She relaxes a little and releases some tenseness from her face. "What I meant to ask is, if he has the capacity to really take care of you. I mean, what if he asks you to stop working after you get married?" I hope she will not explicitly tell me off and warn me to steer clear of her personal affairs.

She sighs warily. "Seriously sir?" I nod. "He's mentioned that he thinks it will be tiresome for me to continue working on the Island, with the traffic and stress, and he would prefer that I spend more time at home when we start having children. He doesn't seem to like the idea of the two of us working eight to five."

"What do you make of that?" I am eager to hear more.

She shrugs. "Well, I like my job and it's been a tough discussion, but I've agreed that I can start a gym and health club once we settle down and we can afford it. I believe I can find fulfilment in helping people make healthier life choices." Indeed, she has stylishly recommended an exercise routine for my midsection. Even this small girl knows what she needs to do to make her boyfriend happy. Is it that Tara just does not care anymore? "Sir, I hope it's alright, what I've said. Definitely, you know I'll give good notice if I'm leaving, and the wedding is still next year. I hope it's okay sir." Her voice is weaker than when she first started talking.

"Oh sure, It's okay. I was just thinking that I've never met that boyfriend of yours and I was wondering. These days, you never can tell with those young men."

"Thank you so much sir, I appreciate your concern. But really he's quite a reliable person and I've never had any doubts about his commitment."

"Good to know, I'm happy for you." I reach out for the file. "I'll look at the documents later. Let me know what you agree with the other staff members about the Christmas party. Any date is fine with me as long as I'm in town. You need to change my tickets for next week, but I'm not sure of the day yet?" She nods. "Let Tara know your plans for the Christmas cake once you've decided. Maybe she would have some ideas for the party too."

CHAPTER SEVEN

Tokunbo

"Where are you going?" I roll over to see Tara dressed up in a black skirt suit and applying her makeup at the dressing table.

"I have an interview for twelve and I think it's best to set out early and stay around VI, to avoid any unforeseen incidence."

I yawn, rub my eyes and help myself to a sitting position. "And you don't think you should tell me?"

"Oh, I didn't tell you? I thought I did." She glances at me through the mirror, while brushing her cheek.

"Maybe you told me in your mind. Unless you term overhearing you the same as telling me. I thought we agreed you wouldn't bother about work for now. Another bank job?"

She nods. "We didn't agree, you merely suggested it."

"And my suggestion carries no weight?"

"Please I don't think this is the right time to talk about this. I count myself lucky that I got this opportunity within this short time. I'll get rusty in no time if I continue to stay at home. I don't want to spend the rest of my life unproductive, parading about like someone without a sense of purpose. I need to work."

"You don't need to work, because you don't need the money. That makes me feel like I'm inadequate and can't provide for you."

"Even you know that is not true." She comes to sit at the side of the bed and pats me as if I need pacifying before she puts on her shoes. "Seriously, I can't complain about your generosity, but you should know by now that it's not about money."

"But it doesn't have to be a bank job. I've told you I don't like the idea of having a wife I don't wake up to find beside me. I don't like the idea of being left alone with Maria in the house every morning. If I didn't have the distraction of going to the club, I would be home almost every time before you."

"What has Maria got to do with this?" She empties the contents of one bag to another. My tirade has done nothing to interrupt her proceedings and I cannot help wondering if it is possible that she actually does not understand the importance of what I am saying or she does not care.

"Is Maria the only thing you heard in what I said?" I stretch and swing my head back and forth to exercise my neck, making a mental note to change the pillow. "And what if you're confirmed pregnant and you get this job? Have you forgotten the stupid policy that you can't get pregnant until after one year?" I am not even sure what to say anymore, but I need to get her to see how disruptive her work life is to our relationship.

Without looking at me, she responds as she continues to arrange her bag. "There's no policy that says I can't get pregnant. Maybe I won't be entitled to maternity leave, but that's the worst case scenario." Now she raises her head. "Please I need to be in the right frame of mind for this interview. Even if you don't feel like wishing me luck, you shouldn't try to make me feel guilty. You knew I wasn't a lazy person when you met me and I'm sure you know my mother didn't send me to school for me to hang my certificate on the wall for display. Please I beg you, let's stop this discussion about me not working." She sounds like she has rehearsed the line over and again. She glimpses at her watch and reflexively I glance at the wall clock too; it is a few minutes to nine. "I'll have some breakfast before I leave and I'll set your meal on the dining. Or will you join me?" I am too stunned to talk. "No?" She is already by the door. "I'll talk to you later then." She closes the door behind her as she goes downstairs.

Why do I feel like I am losing it?

* * *

Tara

I turn off the radio to try to run through questions the interviewers could likely ask me, but my mind is so clogged it is difficult to think through appropriate answers. Although I spoke with the HR Manager yesterday to confirm the appointment, much of what she said was unclear to me because of her American accent. I cannot help feeling apprehensive. I have not been in an interview for over six years because my former bank had been one of the three highest payers in the industry. If not for the CBN intrusion, the staff turnover was relatively low; except for those in Business Development who always jettison from one bank to the other in search of non-existing lower performance targets.

FG sent me a text reminding me of the appointment and wishing me luck. I am grateful for that, otherwise Tokunbo would have succeeded in depressing me as he had planned to. Why is he not reasonable about his expectations of me? Why does he always have to be right and everything has to be about him? If he wanted to, he could have been the one to introduce me to a job, instead of FG. I am sure he did not even tell his friends that I needed a job. God bless FG.

Traffic is light this morning and getting to 1004 had been easy, but just at the roundabout, drama starts playing out. A *LASTMA* official hails an old model Mercedes 190 to stop, but the car keeps moving, almost brushing the official aside. Reflexively, the official starts banging on the car, trailing it as it tries to turn into Ademola Adetokunbo Street.

Then the car stops, right in the middle of the road, and a hefty man dressed in army uniform with beret jumps down, throws his beret back into his car and lashes out at the *LASTMA* official, kicking and boxing him at the same time, even though the official cowered to the floor, covering his face with his arms. Hawkers scamper off to a safe distance and other *LASTMA* officials run to the aid of their colleague just as people parking on both sides of the road rush to restrain the soldier, but he seems resolute about killing someone today. It is beyond rational thinking when someone paid to protect you with money taken from your tax becomes the same person who mistreats you, yet no one can curb their excesses.

How can one explain the conduct of this gentleman in uniform this early morning, not minding the consequences of his actions? Cars start honking from all around me. I pray it ends soon and not become chaotic as the traffic light is not functioning and people have started parking to intervene in the fracas.

An *okada man* jolts my mind back as he suddenly hits my

right side mirror while struggling to manoeuver past me. His passenger, holding a crash helmet in one hand peeks at me and waves apologetically with the other hand; the scowl on his face confirms his aggravation as he yells at the rider. The *okada man* turns back to glare at me as if I am a nuisance and says something I cannot hear while revealing his darkened teeth and bloodshot eyes. He pauses a little, reverses enough for the passenger to re-adjust my mirror back to its position and off he goes to the next car. I can only shake my head as I remind myself that I need to listen to Tokunbo sometimes. If I had used the back road, I would not have witnessed this, but who knows what is on the other side too? I still have about one and a half hours to get to the bank, and I hope I will not end up on an o*kada* myself.

The honking around me tempers down, even though the crowd has not dispersed yet as people are still trying to appease soldier-man. Something must be amiss for people to stop honking. I peep into the mirror to check what is happening behind me. A smooth looking, diminutive man dressed in grey kaftan, flanked by two soldiers is making his way towards the front, almost casually, yet briskly. *Haba*, could soldier-man have called for reinforcement just to deal with a traffic warden who was merely doing his job?

What a country! I hope they will not kill the poor guy. Who can stop them? The crowd that gathered around soldier-man has been able to pacify him a little, but he is still fuming and raving at all the *LASTMA* guys now, throwing intermittent kicks at the one on the floor. Now it is apparent he was waiting for his comrades to come and finish what he started. It looks like a big clash is about to play out here.

However, the unexpected happens. As the diminutive man and the two soldiers approach the scene, soldier-man straightens up immediately and does a salute, freezing to attention mode. The other two soldiers salute too, but not the diminutive man, who instead faces soldier-man for a few seconds before pulling up the *LASTMA* official and hands him to his colleagues. They thank the man with a unified salute. The two soldiers exchange words with soldier-man, now looking morose. They escort him to his car. The crowd start booing and clapping; two *LASTMA* officials get back into post and start directing traffic while the diminutive man stays with the others by the *LASTMA* truck. Thirty- five minutes of my time gone.

Prime Bank is in sight and I drive past to the next roundabout to turn around to reach my destination. Of course, parking is another matter and I join the queue of cars waiting for spaces to be freed up to get a slot. Twenty-two more minutes. I will not take the risk, so I call the security man and ask him if there is any other place to park. He directs me to another car park a bit further down the road. I quickly drive down to the parking lot, staying a while to calm myself down and refresh my makeup. FG has sent a text to check if I have gotten to the bank. I reply him immediately. *'I'm there now. Tx, I will let u know once I'm done.'* No call or text from Tokunbo, not that I am expecting one. None from Maria, which means everything is okay at home. Thank God. I mutter a short prayer and walk into the hot atmosphere.

As directed from the reception downstairs, I make my way to the front lobby of the Human Resources department, where a bespectacled male secretary takes my name, nods me to a seat and informs me his manager will see me soon. The lobby is informally but tastefully decorated with a mixture of white and red, and a little infusion of grey one could almost miss. A large silver-rimmed picture of not less than thirty people on whose heads is inscribed 'The Winning Team' hangs on the white wooden wall beside the secretary. About fifteen minutes of my flipping through the bank's annual report placed on the centre table, a young man comes into the lobby, loaded with files. He opens the inner office after a nod from the secretary. Before the door shuts, the HR manager's voice squeezes out. "This shouldn't take long, I've got to be somewhere."

I hope she attends to me before going off to wherever she has to be. I shift my attention to the flat screen TV, just in case CNN will be more interesting than the annual report, only to realise the audio has been tuned off.

"Do you have a copy of your CV?" The secretary turns to me as I dip my hand in my bag to check on my phone, which I set on silent before entering the building. I bring out my CV envelope instead.

"Sure, this is it." I go to his table and hand him the CV. He gets up for the first time since I entered the office and goes to the photocopier to makes some copies. The minutes tick on. The secretary divides his time between answering the phone in low tones, staring at the computer screen and typing furiously on the keyboard; the young man does not come out of the office; my mind wanders back and forth; and getting restless, I bring out my phone.

There are three missed calls: from my mum; Daisy; and FG, and a text message from FG, '*How far*'.

'*Not so far, still waiting 2 see HR*'.

'*Does she know you're there?*'

'*I believe so*'. Or does she not? I turn to the secretary and fake a cough. "Please does she know I'm waiting?"

He nods, using his finger to section the paper on his table before lifting his face. "She knows, but there's a board meeting on Friday, so everyone is busy. I'm sure she'll attend to you soon."

"Thank you." I quietly inhale some air through my mouth to curb the dryness. Board meeting, I know about all that.

About two minutes later, the young man comes out without his files, one hand in pocket. "She says you should come in." He looks at me shiftily and stays with the secretary.

"Oh, thank you." I get up, adjust my suit and take a deep breath before walking into the office. The HR manager, a towering dark-skinned lady, professionally tucked in a striped cotton shirt with black trousers gets up from behind her desk to shake my hand meeting my eyes with a smile. She would have been intimidating if not for her friendly demeanour. Her slim broad structure, her skin tone, her pointed nose, oblong face, natural dreadlocks and the nametag on her table explain the semi-nasal accent I thought was fake. She is probably American or Jamaican? I can't tell. Her tone is apologetic and her smile seems warm and sincere. "Good afternoon." I also manage to project a smile.

"I'm so sorry, dear. FG gave me a call. I didn't mean to keep you waiting." Amy Lawrence points me to a chair as she takes her seat, shakes her head and starts scanning through documents. I make myself comfortable as much as I can. "It's always a mad house here. Not sure how long I'm *gonna* be able to cope. You won't believe I've only been here for five months and I'm strung up already." She raises her head and waves her hand. "Excuse my manners. Tea, coffee?"

"Thank you. I'm okay." I shake my head, even though she has turned back to the desk. Does it mean I would still have been waiting if FG had not called her?

She extracts some sheets from the documents. "I've got a meeting to attend, so this won't take time. Yeah, I got your resume here." She is tapping a pen on the CV, sounding like she is unsure of what to do with it. "This is just formality really, FG spoke highly of you. Sorry to hear you lost your job, those things happen you know, even Tiger Woods loses sometimes." I am unsure how I am supposed to respond to that. I hope she is not about to give me a lesson in moral instructions. I did not expect her to be on such familiar terms with FG. Is she his girlfriend? No, she looks much older than he does and she is wearing a wedding ring too. Why is she doing him a favour then? "You'll be talking to the guys in Legal. If they're okay, then the Company Secretary will see you, although I can sway that. He's told me there is no space, but I'm *gonna* give it a try, so you may end up in Business Development, wherever, as long as you come in. We can move you around later. Is that okay?"

I nod. "I'll take my chance." Do I have a choice in this? I pray it is not Business Development. I cannot imagine being grilled for funds mobilisation targets.

She lets out a deep breath. "Let me see, what else do I need to know that's not on this resume?" She looks at me pointedly.

Her change of tone jolts me. "Professionally?" She nods. None of the answers I prepared in my head will be appropriate for this, but it is the only reasonable question she has asked me since I stepped into her office. "I'm resourceful and hardworking, I'm equally versatile and intuitive and I can easily manipulate words to suit the audience. I'm very good at producing and reviewing documents for loopholes and I ..."

She raises her hand to stop me. "Okay, okay, good enough for me. I just needed to hear you speak. You haven't talked much since you came in. My secretary will show you to Legal." She gets up, indicating the end of our discussion. I follow suit, thank her and shake hands with her before opening the door. The file man straightens up quickly and bolts into the office, probably afraid Amy might find a way of escape.

"Please give me a moment. I'll take you to Legal." The secretary stands, but continues to type.

"Thank you."

It takes another two hours, forty-three minutes to see the

so-called interviewers in Legal. Almost three solid hours of idleness, restlessness and exasperation; of watching CNN newsflashes severally until the sequence became predictable; of staff going and coming until some faces became familiar; of not knowing whether the interview would still hold or not; of not being able to decide whether I should wait or leave; of ignoring Tokunbo's calls because I could just be called in at any time; of FG texting to pacify me and explaining that he would have intervened, but he did not know them; and of me trying to figure out if I really wanted this job. Two hours, forty three minutes before a lady comes to lead me to a conference room, and another six minutes of staring at white walls before two men hurriedly come in one after the other.

"Hello, I'm so sorry you had to wait this long." The first one apologises. "I am Jude, and this is Malik." We try to smile, exchanging pleasantries as we shake hands. Both men have notepads and pens in hand. Jude is a short, slim and distinguished looking man, wearing a black suit and black-framed glasses that give him an air of standoffishness; he looks like he would rather be somewhere else. Malik looks more relaxed in a starched white shirt and tie, tall, muscular and front-balding.

"I'm Tara. Thank you for seeing me."

We sit down at the six-man round table, while the butterflies in my stomach try to perch peacefully. Malik starts by making small talk, asking random questions while Jude interjects infrequently, but keeps taking notes and sometimes looking at me. For a brief moment, I could have sworn he was staring at my chest, but maybe his height naturally defaults to that level. We go on talking about mundane issues for a few more minutes until Malik introduces the professional questions and starts referring to my CV. People barge in from time to time, to talk to either of the two and some come in with documents requiring their signature. They ask about my education, my work experience, briefs I have handled and documents I have contributed to or introduced to the organisation. By now, it has become certain that Jude is struggling to keep his eyes to meet mine, even when he is talking to me. Malik does not seem to notice and he talks on, exuding smiles now and again, and gesticulating appropriately. I try to focus on Malik and brush off the self-consciousness of the ogling eyes. Malik asks me about conflict resolution and how I draw a balance between legality and morality. I share an experience I had with a customer who had been involved in a serious car accident, and the bank was threatening to sell off their family home when the monthly repayments stalled. After several discussions with the client, I did a paper to give him a six- months respite and continuously worked with the man to ensure he fulfilled his obligation.

"How do you handle personal conflicts with colleagues?" Jude asks tersely. I try to recall if I have had any serious conflict with anyone in my former office, except with customers and I hope I won't start with Jude if I do get this job.

"I manage conflicts effectively by being objective and professional at all times, I try to be positively assertive and I stay within mutually defined boundaries. But at the heart of it all is being able to listen and communicate with clarity and the willingness to accept that I am not always right."

They both smile. Malik asks me if I have any question to ask them. My impulse says no, the only thing I want to do is get out of Victoria Island as early as possible. But I succumb to my gumption and ask questions about the structure of the department, how performance is evaluated, the work and relationship culture, and a few other things. In the course of these, Jude's eyes continue straying, responding only to one question. I take a cue that the interview is over when Malik gets up, nods and stretches his hand towards me. Jude is the last to get up and waits for me to walk ahead of him. Malik walks beside me to show me out and finally I am able to breathe when alone as I wait for the elevator. I rummage through my bag for my phone. Over four hours have gone since I stepped into the building. There are several texts and missed calls including one from Tokunbo, three from FG, two from Flora and several from Daisy. I will call Tokunbo once I get into the car. I read the text from Kola David, my former colleague, whom I sent my CV to last week. He says he has gotten Daisy and I an interview with Diamond Bank. I send one terse text to both Daisy and FG that I have just finished. Flora's text says she was just checking up on me. All too well, I know that means she has something to gist about, so I will find time for her later.

"I'm going to break somebody's arms if you don't get this job." The tiny voice booms behind my ears on my way to the car park. No mistaking that voice, it is FG's.

"What are you doing here?" I turn to face him. He is so close I almost collide with his sturdy frame. I can smell warmth, freshness and his scent of masculinity. My stomach butterflies disperse in different directions now.

"I had a meeting at Eko Hotel and I wanted to find out how the interview went. I'm sorry, I didn't know it could take a whole day to interview just one person." He walks on beside me towards the car park. "It shows how important you are."

"You shouldn't be sorry, you're only trying to help. I should be grateful. And thank you for putting in a word with Amy." I expect him to explain to me how Amy has a right to call him FG.

He offers no such explanation. "It's a small thing. You know I'll do anything for you. If it was up to Amy, you'll start work tomorrow, but let's keep our fingers crossed. How did it go anyway?"

Interesting! He has that much confidence in her. "It was okay, I guess. I haven't been to an interview in a very long time, so I can't really tell. Ah, but I hated being kept waiting, I never knew being on the other side was that bad." I lament, recalling how it was customary to keep our customers waiting, sometimes we even avoid seeing them at all. We are by the Murano now. "Where did you park?" I lean on the driver's door, facing him, my heart pumping faster. I feel so complexly close to him, even though he is standing a safe distance away.

"Eko Hotel. I thought it would be faster to walk than sit through the traffic and good exercise for me too."

"You walked?" He walked to see me. Tokunbo will not raise a pin to find out how my interview went, except to confirm my movement. "You didn't have to. You've done enough already. Thanks a lot." My heart thaws into my body the way ice-cream melts from the top. I turn to the door to resist the magnet trying to pull me to embrace and kiss him and he reaches out to open the door for me, his hand brushing mine. My hand shudders at his touch. "Should I take you back to the hotel then?" I ask without facing him. That seems to be the only reasonable thing to do after what he has done today.

"Don't worry, I'll walk back. It won't take me twenty minutes, and I can bet driving won't take less than thirty minutes." He makes to leave, but opens his arms. It looks like the normal thing to do, but my heartbeat and my parched breath say otherwise. I lean into his arms with my side and he plants a kiss on my cheeks. I breathed in his scent and I almost turn my lips to him. "I'll give you a call to find out when you get home." He disengages, his tiny voice almost inaudible. He leaves immediately, and by the time I enter the car, my nipples are as taut as rock.

CHAPTER EIGHT

Tokunbo

"Welcome Mama." Tara greets, smiling as Mama drags her chubby frame out of the car, while Maria goes for the two suitcases in the boot. "Hope you enjoyed your trip."

"I thank God for his mercy. I was expecting you at the airport." She accuses Tara before putting herself forward for a motherly hug. In between a series of dozing off and waking up from the airport, until I drove through the gates of the house, she has complained about everyone and everything except the weather and me.

"I already told you she had to go to Flora's party to represent the family." I remind her as we make our way into the house. It is too early for any antagonism between these two women. "How was the party?" I turn to Tara.

"The party was okay, they all asked of you and Flora said I should say hello ma."

"Peace be unto this house." Mama makes the sign of a cross

over her face before taking a seat. We all chorus amen. Maria waits with the suitcases by the staircase.

"Should we take your bags upstairs ma?" Tara is wise enough to ask her. The last time Mama was here, she complained about how difficult it was to climb the stairs even though she refused to move downstairs. Tara has taken precautions by preparing both the rooms, upstairs and downstairs.

"Do you need to ask me, at my age do you think it is easy to climb these stairs daily like you people?"

"Sorry ma." Tara signals Maria to take the bags to the guest room downstairs. "What should I get you to eat ma?"

"I'm not hungry, I'm just tired. I need to rest my back after sitting down for so long in one day. I don't know how you manage to live in this Lagos. Imagine driving three hours from the airport." She pauses. "Maybe I should take small pap."

Tara looks at me and shakes her head. "There's no pap ma and we can't get pap in this area at this time. Will you manage custard or tea?" I respond.

"*Ngbo* Tara, there's no pap, were you not expecting me?"

"I didn't tell Tara on time that you were coming. You know we usually don't take pap." I reply before Tara utters any word.

"Ah, okay o." Mama sounds resigned to her fate, patting her hands. "I didn't know I should give long notice to be able to get food to eat in your house. I should go and sleep then."

She makes to get up and Tara rushes to her aid. "I'm sorry ma, we'll get it tomorrow. What of some beverage?" Tara collects her handbag.

"Don't worry, I've bothered you enough." She yawns and we both follow her to the bedroom. "Goodnight."

"Goodnight ma." We both greet back and I shut the door. Tara goes to the kitchen, leaving me to settle down to Silverbird TV to catch up on the analysis of the day's football match. Thank God I was not home to watch the thrashing of Arsenal yet again. Since the sale of Nasri earlier this year, I have finally become disenchanted with Wenger. Now losing 8-2 to Man U is just about much anyone should be made to suffer. If I venture near the club tomorrow, the taunting will be too much, especially by Kunle who has been teasing me about following Nasri to Man City. People cannot seem to understand why we keep supporting Arsenal when it seems the team has forgotten that it needs to keep scoring goals to keep us happy. Still, staying loyal to Arsenal is like the prescribed drug for my ailing soul; I need to keep to the prescription whether it is sweet or bitter. After all, if there had been no Arsenal, there would not have been a Samir Nasri for me. He would not be the first to be sold, neither will he be the last, if Wenger's quest to make money for the team persists. That is one consolation at least. Profitability!

"I'm going upstairs." Tara heads for the stairs, while I continue staring at the TV, even though my mind is torn in-between staying put and following her immediately. If I miss the replay match between New Castle and Fulham, it will be a double loss for me if Tara decides not to play ball. And going by precedence, Mama's arrival alone is a show-stopper. I wish I could get a time machine to transport us back to when we first married.

The early days of our marriage were passionately wonderful. As the first and only son in a family of three children, my mother had continually harassed me to get married immediately I turned thirty and stabilised in business. She did not like my last girlfriend, because of her sanguinity and expectedly, her tribe. When she met Tara, she had been full of praise and prayers for her for rescuing me from bachelorhood. She soon became agitated and aggressive when the grandchildren did not start coming immediately as expected and she began picking on Tara at every given opportunity. We were all overjoyed when she finally got pregnant the second year of our marriage, but she had a miscarriage in the second month. It was a traumatic time for everyone. Tara had started decorating the room in preparation. For me, the part where I had to politely sit through people offering her empathic advice was especially tiresome and depressing. All attention was on my wife and no one asked me how I felt. Yet, I mourned inside and looked for some form of consolation from friends or family, but the guys only patted me on the back and it was like just get on with it. I so much wanted to share my burdens with someone, but no one listened, especially not Tara. I also had to deal with Mama's disappointment and lack of empathy; she even hinted that Tara may have deceived me into believing she was pregnant. That was when I started drinking again.

It may not have been so bad if my wife did not push me away. Yes, she was a reserved person, but she internalised her grief so much, she simply retreated into herself as if she was the only one that suffered the loss of the child. Somehow, she convinced herself that I blamed her for not being able to see the child to full term, simply because I suggested that she should slow down at work. Apart from church, her job and the African Magic channel, every other thing in her life, including me started fading into irrelevance. Three months after the miscarriage, she was still not ready for sex. After rebuffing my advances several times, I let her be.

It was another two months, when I was too tipsy to be proud that I pleaded with her and she allowed me pour myself into her. When she got pregnant once more, she handled it with so much fragility that I would have been the devil's incarnate if I had made any allusion to sex. I probably would have been consoled if she had brought the child forth, but alas! I prayed fervently, pleading with God to let the next child stay, so I could have my pretty sunshine back. Then we started IVF treatment and she got pregnant after the second cycle, and she must have been pleased when the doctor advised her against any physical activity including sex until they could put a stitch around her cervix. The cycle of no sex continued, but that did not stop the miscarriage once again. By that time I had almost totally lost interest, as we both picked either side of the bed, rarely meeting in the middle save for the few times I got lucky, which I suspect could be attributed to her ovulation period.

The match starts in two minutes and I know that even if Tara is ovulating, Mama's presence is enough reason to make her forget.

* * *

Tara

The TV is on in the living room, with Mama lying down on the three-seater and backing the staircase. I avoid the temptation to switch off the TV and instead, remove my shoes and tiptoe towards the stairs. Maria said Mama came out to the living room at about noon and has been at that spot sleeping. Although she complained she was tired yesterday and did not follow us to church, I did not think she would sleep through today again. It is almost seven and I will rather she wakes up when Tokunbo is back home.

"Why are you sneaking into your own house like a thief?" she sits upright, yawning.

I drop my shoes and let my guard down. "I'm sorry ma, I thought you were sleeping and I didn't want to wake you up. How are you ma?"

"Which work did you give me to do since morning that I

will be so tired and be sleeping now? You are asking how I am at this time of the day. Did you see me in the morning to confirm how I was, or didn't we both sleep in this house? How are you ma?" She sniffs and mimics. "Hmmm, as you can see, the grace of God has kept me. How did you expect to find me?"

I mumble inwardly. I should not have to face this woman after all I have been through today. What am I supposed to say to her? "I didn't know I'd be this long, I had a lot of things to do on the Island and I got delayed. There was heavy traffic on my way back too. I told Maria not to go to her shop today so she can make you comfortable. It's because of you she stayed at home ma."

"Did I complain that I wasn't comfortable? Maria did her best. She switched on the TV, the AC in my room has been working since and she's been asking me if I want anything. What else is she supposed to do or has she not tried?" She unties her scarf and ties it again.

"I'm sorry. Is there something I can get for you before I go upstairs to change? I've had a hectic day."

She pats her hands. "Anything you like, do, *sebi* I've been at home since morning, did I die?" She rolls her eyes at me.
I close my eyes for a second and ask God for wisdom. "Mama ...."

She interrupts me, although I have not fully decided what to say to her. "You and your husband abandoned me here, all by myself since morning. You say Maria was at home. Did I come to see Maria? I've spent only three days in this house and you can't be bothered to spend time with me. If there were children, I would have them to play with when they come back from school. Don't you think it's right for us to say hello to each other before you leave the house? But you left as if I don't mean anything."

It always has to go back to the non-existent children. I think about the day I will let myself loose on her but for now I hold my peace. "Ma ..."

She interrupts again, this time with a raised hand. "Hold on, I've not finished." She pauses and I remain quiet. "Come and sit down." She pats the sofa right beside her. I drop my bag beside the shoes on the staircase and take the patted seat. Silence is likely to be the best line of defence in this monologue about to play out. "I'm sure you are thinking to yourself that I talk too much. I have to let you know when you offend me, because it's wrong to hold grudges against anyone. Otherwise I don't have to say a thing and before you come back I would have left, and probably not come to your house again." She looks at me, I nod. "You too, think about it, how will you feel if you travel all the way down to see me and I don't' spare time to spend with you. When that girl came to tell me breakfast was ready, I thought we were all eating together. I didn't eat the food, because I didn't come here for lack of food to eat. *Abi*, if it's you, will you eat?"

"It's not like that ma. I had a job interview and I left early, I thought you'd still be resting and I didn't want to disturb you. I already told you why I came back late, you..."

"Wait, you went for interview? But Tokunbo told me you will be starting a business."

How dare Tokunbo? "We haven't agreed ma, he only suggested it."

"Hehe, I don't understand you. Is it not because of money you want to work? Your husband said you should start a business, you said he only suggested it, what's the difference?" Jesus Christ, how will I cope with this woman in this house? Any answer I give will only evoke more condemnation. Can I ever do anything right? God where are you when I need you the most? "And you will say you want to have children, how can anyone have children with all the up and down stress in this city? By the way, when you have the children *sef*, how do you want to take care of them? Will they ever know their mother when they don't see you during the day? Or is it Maria that will bring them up?"

When I was growing up, my mother used to complain that I hear with my right ear, but I let out the words through the left. That is the mode I need to switch to right now, otherwise I'm going to curse this woman. But instead, I burst out crying.

* * *

Tokunbo

Carzola just got a yellow card. "You know what?" Mike interjects forlornly. "If we don't win tonight, I'm going to say my final goodbye and cross over to Man U for real." He pauses and I eye him surreptitiously. "I'm serious about it this time. We can't afford to keep losing money as if …" He trails off, hisses and folds his arms across his chest, while beating his slippers-cladded feet against the tiled floor.

We both know he is not crossing anywhere, but my pounding heart makes it easy for me to ignore his tirade and I inch more out of my chair, just enough to be seated as Estrada positions the ball for a free kick. What if they score? This might be the game changer with the first half only a few minutes to the end. No, they cannot score now! Shutting my eyes will not do the trick this time since my eyes have remained glued to the large screen ahead of us. My eyes pick the ball delicately, trying to fish out someone to pass on to. Yes! My hand bangs the table as Giroud comes along to collect the ball with a header. There are some loud cheers from other tables as

I release my breath, giving Mike a thumbs-up, not fully at ease to celebrate yet. We both stare on.

The first half of the match between Arsenal and Montpellier is almost over with neither team scoring any goal. Not that Montpellier should score, but it is almost becoming hopeless having so many chances and not being able to make a clean goal for over forty minutes. If we lose, Mike and I will be losing fifty grand to Kunle and Big Sam. It is not so much about the money, but the taunting and bragging by our opponents who do not understand what loyalty means. As far as we are all concerned, Montpellier is fatherless, and no one cares if they lose. But if Arsenal loses… I dare not think about it. We are lucky that Mike and I got to the club before Kunle and Big Sam, and Mike had the foresight to drag us to sit unobtrusively at this corner to wait for the match to start, way out of everyone's poking and *yabis*.

The whistle goes off after forty-six minutes of a goalless precarious game. Now I can have a go at my Carlo Rossi Sangria, but the alcohol hits hard against my tongue. I hail a waiter. "Get me some ice please, Mike, another bottle?" Mike adjusts his glasses to look at his watch. "Don't tell me you're not going to finish this game with me." The game started at seven forty five and Mike is already past his curfew at eight thirty.

"One small stout." He tells the waiter. "I already told Flora I'd be late, but I'm not sure I can sit through it here till ten, so maybe I'll call her to record the second half."

"You must be joking, you want me to face these sharks all by myself?" Across the bar, two unfamiliar faces have joined our usual table with Kunle and Big Sam, one of them a lady caressing the back of Kunle's neck. Except for that and Big Sam's head moving as he talks, there is little activity around that table. Definitely, the other fellow with them cannot be a

Gunner, otherwise, Kunle would have been dancing around him in victory by now. How he must wish we were sitting beside him.

"Then I should drag you with me when I'm leaving."

"Come on Mike, it's not going to be the same." A tall man wearing Arsenal jersey passes by our table, swinging to the background music. "Gunners for life." He turns back and gives me a stretched-arm salute.

"Up Gunners! I'm sure we're going to beat them silly. Just wait and watch." The man boasts with the confidence that I lack about this match. He continues to sway his waist like a slow Indian dancer. If the match was not being broadcast live, I would swear he knows the outcome of the match.

"Sure, no other way to go, but up." Mike chips in. The man sways on and joins a group of four. "These boys really need to get their acts together. Can you imagine Kunle insisting that if Adebayor hadn't been sent out last week, we couldn't have won, even with a clear three goals ahead?"

"You know Kunle will say anything to win an argument. Although if we had been in top form, Bale shouldn't have scored that second goal with one man down." The waiter brings my ice, allowing me to savour the smooth taste of the victory we had last week again. I pick up my phone that had been flashing red for some time.

'Where are u, when are u coming home?' Tara's text reads. Definitely, she knows where I am, why is she asking? Another text from an unknown number. *'Call me, we need to talk.'* Who is this? I go over the number again looking for any familiar pattern, but none comes to mind. This must be a terrible joker.

Mike's voice bounces off my head as the referee blows his whistle for the second half to start. "It's their tough luck. Getting a red card is part of the game. If they were good players, they should not have earned the red card in the first place."

"Brace up buddy, this is play time." I refill and take a gulp of wine before responding to Tara's text. *'At the club, I hope u're okay. We're playing 2nite and d 2nd half is starting now.'*

"I miss Walcott, men. That boy does some wonders in my team." Mike laments after setting down his glass of Stout. "By the way, how is Mama settling in? Flora suggested we should stop by and say hello over the weekend."

"You know my mum, she's her nagging, trouble-brewing self. Thank God I don't have to spend all day with her. It's Tara I pity, this morning... goal! It's a goal."

"Gooooal! Half of the bar including Mike and I are on our feet, banging tables and clicking glasses. I manage to hold the table from tripping over. It is hardly five minutes and Wilshere has put a ball into the goal post.

The man in the Arsenal jersey pirouettes to our table and extends high fives to us, as if he just won the lottery. "I told you." He yells, patting me on the back, while pointing a finger to his Tee shirt. "I told you my boys will deliver. It's Arsenal we're talking about, who is Montpellier?"

"We've only just begun." Mike grins at him before he glides back to his seat. "I want these boys to give them another two goals at least, that way no one can say it was a chance goal."
I pour the last of my wine into the glass and pick it up. "Let's join the others, we need to jeer Kunle before this moment is lost. *Chopping* fifty grand has never felt so good." Mike does not bother to argue.

Big Sam points and hails when he sees us moving towards their table. My phone vibrates again. *'Mama hasn't gone to bed, I think she's waiting for u, and I can't leave her all by herself. Are u coming any time soon? What should I do?'* I feel like asking her what she will do if Mama is her mother, but I am not in the mood for any back and forth texting. It is better I enjoy this moment and attend to her later.

Mike grabs two chairs and pushes them to the table before shooting his middle finger at Kunle. "We are going to do you in this night. Do you want to top up your bet?" He poses in front of Kunle with arms folded like a mafia boss, deliberately waiting to catch someone in his trap.

Kunle bolts up, chuckling and unceremoniously dropping his lady's hand on the table. "Er, I pity you. The masquerade that dances early in the show ends up watching others eventually. You should be ashamed of yourselves, only one goal since morning, and you open your mouth to talk."

"I need to call Flora, Toks, finish this boy." Mike nods me to Kunle as he moves away and I step up to the enemy.

"*Even if person take one day old pass you, senior na senior. Abeg siddon make we watch game.* When champions *dey* talk, make you no *dey* open mouth. If you still doubt who the champion is in this game, just stake another fifty." I challenge Kunle. It is easy to get money out of him when he is with his girls. He says when they think he is a spendthrift, it gives them hope that one day he will lose his senses and make them rich.

"Okay, if that's what you want." He sits down and cuddles the girl who readily snuggles up to him. She must be a new one. Surprisingly, she is dark-skinned, but typically heavy-bosomed. "Big Sam, another fifty on this game."

Big Sam growls and shrugs, typically with his arms resting on his belly. "Toks if you haven't scored another goal by now, Montpellier may still catch up with you and seriously, it's going to be a shame. Anyway, let's watch. How many more minutes? Twenty."

"We'll see how it goes. It's not over until it's over." I try to figure out what to text Tara. Maybe I should have stayed at home with them, but I know neither of them could have made the night as interesting as this. I can handle Mama by simply ignoring or indulging her, but Tara... what is the point in staying at home when I cannot have a simple discussion without fear of her taking offence for some flimsy reasons? I still cannot figure out where we started drifting apart. Is it possible that she does not find me attractive anymore? Not much has changed about me. Hmm, could she possibly be interested in someone else? No! Perish the thought Tokunbo, you know Tara is ... "It's a goooal, Podolski!" I spring to my feet, shaking Big Sam's shoulders profusely as Mike runs towards me. "Did you see that?"

Mike hands me a reverberating high five and wiggles back to Kunle. "Who is the boss now?" The whole club is gyrating with screeches and movements, and our tall friend has resumed his slow dance steps.

Kunle nods. "I must acknowledge that was a good one. It caught me unawares. Well done guys."

I pick up my glass of wine to raise a toast. "To Arsenal."

"To Arsenal." Mike, Big Sam and Kunle's girlfriend raise their glasses.

Kunle grabs his girlfriend's hand before it makes the toast. "Are you serious at all? That's my hundred grand you're toasting against. What's your problem, can't you see?"

"Er, aarh, sorry, I didn't know." She emits in a shy tiny voice, looking across the table in a bid to avoid my eyes. They also have to be dumb to be with Kunle.

"I'm sure we'll be able to finish them off with one more goal." I boast.

"Today is definitely your lucky day." Big Sam cheers. "But if I were you, I wouldn't rejoice too soon." He pats my hand on the table. "A lot can still happen in twenty minutes."

"Hmm, unless the dog in a book can bite." I snigger and pick my phone to reply Tara. *I'll be home soon, we are winning.*' Not that it makes any difference to her, but that is the best I can do for now.

CHAPTER NINE

Tara

The shrieking sound of my phone interrupts the answers I am subconsciously considering for Tokunbo's imaginary whisper and my mother's nagging voice. I dart my eyes to the phone briefly from the road to see who is calling. It is Daisy. With another furtive glance at the phone, I press the speaker icon while slowing down the car speed. "Babe, what's up? I hope you're not calling to cancel because I don't have any other thing planned for today." I have not gone to see her since the first interview as I promised and we spoke two days ago to agree to meet at Yellow Chilli after my appointment at the clinic.

It is a good excuse for me to stay out of the house and have some nice lunch rather than hanging around Mama all day. Who knows, we will probably be celebrating once I confirm that I am pregnant. God, let this be positive, I beg you. I try to ignore the sensation piercing through to my lower abdomen, but it is proving difficult as the possibility of a negative result hovers. My hand unconsciously goes to rub my belly. Please make sure you survive this time, I am going to take care of you and even God will be proud of me. I appeal to the life forming inside me.

Daisy's voice is filled with irritation as she tries to contend with some noise in the background. "Ah, cancelling is out of it." She hisses. "But, this traffic *no get* rival, *I never see this kain before*. We've been stuck on Carter Bridge for over thirty minutes and it doesn't seem like we're moving anywhere. I'm definitely going to be late. I just hope it clears on time."

"Aren't you driving, where is that noise coming from?"

"Drive ke? Don't worry, I'm as comfortable as I can be." She muffles into the phone, still unable to douse the other voices around her. A sudden loud revving sound and another exciting shout of *'Oya,* let's go'. "Oh, it's started moving." However, hisses and exclamations soon follow.

Being stuck in traffic in one of those dingy, un-ventilated buses with this temperature is unimaginable to me. "Daisy." I drawl her name. "Why didn't you get a cab? You could have insisted I come over. Why do you like stressing yourself?"

"Who is stressing now? I just called to tell you I'll be late, okay. I'll see you soon." She hangs up on me.

What will I do if I have to wait for Daisy? I wonder. It will take me less than ten minutes to get to the restaurant from the clinic. If Daisy's bus is still on Carter Bridge, then I will have over thirty minutes to wait, even if the other roads are clear. Can I just pop in to the salon for a pedicure? No! The last time I tried that without an appointment, I almost quarrelled with them for making me wait for over an hour.

At the approach to the Lekki roundabout, I beckon to a newspaper vendor standing by the roadside with his stock on his head and some newspapers at hand. I veer off the road to wait behind other cars and avoid causing traffic. I ask him which newspaper has been in high demand today and he shows me a magazine – Dazzlers. He runs through the pages, explaining that it is new in the market and on promotional sale for one thousand naira instead of two thousand. Flipping through the magazine, I fail to see any other thing dazzling about it except the print paper; until I reach a page that catches my attention with the caption 'Lady G Launches Silk Range'. It has the pictures of FG and his mother splashed all over.

"I'll take it." He offers me the magazine's glossy envelope. I must say the publishers have done a good job with the packaging. "Let me have Guardian too." Maybe I will find an interesting article or probably a job advert. It is ironic that the last thing one looks out for when looking for a job is job adverts. The way it works is keeping one's ears to the ground, because by the time the jobs make it public, the positions would have been filled. I should have enough to keep me busy before Daisy arrives.

* * *

Trepidation hits me as I manoeuver to park my car at the clinic. My breathing speeds up and I start muttering to myself to cool down. God help me. Please, you are the only one that can do this for me. This is the fifth time, please let this one come through. You should not allow me to continue suffering. Please, I know I am not perfect, just look beyond my sins and grant this one desire. I step out of the car and greet the security man, who asks for my car keys in case they need to re-park the car. My short heels squeak against the paved floor. Of all the days to wear attention-seeking slippers. What if it is negative? Now I wish I heeded Tokunbo's advice to wait for him to return from his trip and for us to come together. No, the last thing I want are his patronising words, even though he will claim to be trying to comfort me. The last time he followed me for the test result in the other IVF clinic, he held me and said soothing words as I cried in the car on the way back home, assuring me that everything will be okay and God will somehow answer our prayers.

Shortly after that, we went back to our non-eventful relationship and he showed no interest in trying again. Until one of the managers at work, who was in her late forties got pregnant and successfully delivered a set of twins, after which she became an advocate for Grace Life Centre. The centre is acclaimed to have the highest success rate of IVF for older women in Nigeria. When I told Tokunbo, I was shocked by his lack of interest, and I did not speak to him for three days. It was as if he came from the enemy's camp to frustrate our chance of success. I even accused him of infidelity, insinuating that he was not interested because he probably had a child by another woman. So the arguments started again.

After two other ladies, one in her late thirties and the other in her forties became noticeably pregnant in the office, I persuaded myself to try the Grace Life Centre and Tokunbo reluctantly agreed for us to pay for two cycles. He was on a business trip when I learnt the first cycle failed. Although he was gracious and understanding on the phone, I still cried my eyes out and locked myself in for two days, before Daisy came and dragged me to the office, believing that I was sick. How many people can I tell that I am going through IVF treatments when I am not sure it will work? Most people will only share their success stories.

There are two middle-aged couples and a younger woman waiting at the reception. It never looks busy, this clinic, same as the other IVF clinics I have visited. They all have the feel of affluence different from the regular clinics. Well, what with the exorbitant fees one has to pay? How many people can afford it, no matter how desperately they want a child? Thank God for choices. I greet the people seated, trying to cover my embarrassment with my heels squeaking as if they are on a mission to dent the granite floor.

"Good morning, Mrs. Akande." The pretty receptionist beams a smile before I reach her desk. I wonder how she manages to remember everybody's name. No matter how much training I am given, I am not sure I can ever be good with names.

"How are you this morning?"

"Very well, thank you." She quickly presses some keys on her keyboard. "Please sit down, I'll let the nurse know you are here."

"Thanks." I take the chair closest to me and to the door, to avoid the intrusion my slippers will make. Not much else to do except to watch SKY news on TV or flip through one of the magazines on the side stool. I bring out my phone and start fiddling with it like the others in the room. There are five messages on BBM, one from my mother, one from Flora and some other motivational messages. One of the couples starts chatting in low tones, but the woman's 'no' comes out a bit loud, and she raises her head to look around. We all pretend to be busy with our phones. The man puts his phone to his ear, says 'hello' and hurries out of the room. From the corner of my eye, I can see him pacing back and forth, gesticulating frantically. I quickly switch off my phone. This is neither the time nor place to allow phone calls to distract me.

"Mrs. Akande." The receptionist's gentle but distinct voice calls out. "Please go to room five."

"Thanks." I squeeze out a smile, almost reluctant to get up as the reality becomes imminent. God I beg you. My stiff breathing resumes. Brace yourself Tara, what is the worst thing that can happen? A gentle knock and I enter the room infused with the all too familiar vanilla fragrance. I wonder how she and others like her manage to remain impassive at such times when they discover their patients' expectations have not be realised. Really, is there any good way of breaking bad news?

"Hello Mrs. Akande, how have you been? Please take a seat." The nurse points to the only other chair in the room and turns to her side to take her syringe pan to draw blood.

I shut my eyes in anticipation of the sharp pain as the syringe pierces through my skin. In less than a minute, we are done and I head back to wait at the reception. The only thing I can do is pray as I wait endlessly for the call. The receptionist calls the woman whose husband went to answer a phone call outside and she goes outside to get her husband. The man raises his hand to signal he still needs some time on the phone just as another couple enters the reception.

"Mrs. Akande, the doctor will see you now."

I keep praying under my breath on my short walk to the office. Half-bald Dr. Sandip turns his chair round to face the table as I open the door. "Mrs. Akande, how are you feeling today?" His voice sounds the same as always, with a heavy accent. Despite his seemingly professional aloofness, his elderly mien and the fact that he is Indian give some sort of assurance that all will be well, even when he promises nothing.

"I'm okay and optimistic."

He pushes the file on his table out a little bit and I can read my name upside down. "And your husband? He didn't come with you." He looks straight at me. I shake my head, quietly urging him to go straight to the point, while trying to subdue my twitching body. Does he act like this too when the result is positive? I wonder. "Have you had your period or any spotting?"

My muscles flatten out and all I can do is to close my eyes and puff out some air. Here we go again. If I am pregnant, why should he be asking about spotting? Am I expected to spot? By this time, I already know the pattern.   "No, not at all."

"I'm sorry to let you know, the test came out negative." My head contracts and relaxes, pulsating with a fast rhythm. Dr. Sandip tries to fill the silence. "I'm as shocked as you. I thought we had a good chance but these things happen and sometimes you just can't explain what the end result would be. I'm sorry. I know you are disappointed, but we did all we could have done."

I swallow hard and pull in my lower lip. "I really thought it would work this time." Thinking about some of the conversations I have had with Tokunbo, I know a sixth IVF will take a miracle.

"Well, maybe we shouldn't conclude too soon. Some women may have a negative test result and then go home to realise that they're actually pregnant. Let's wait a few days and if your period hasn't come, we can have another test."

"And if I am not?" All the doubts I pushed to the back of my mind come stumbling down. With the faith I continually shored my entire being with throughout the process, I have even fooled myself that I could get away with twins, when I witnessed one of the eggs splitting into two after the fertilisation took place.

Dr. Sandip raises his brows from under his glasses and purses his lips into a half-smile. "I'll say let's wait and see. You won't be taking any medication, but take things easy and go about your normal routine. No stress and no weights." I shrug and he goes on. "You don't look enthusiastic."

I raise my shoulders again. Does he expect me to start dancing? "Not really, I just want to know what my options are, worst case situation."

"If you want to try another cycle, we'll give you a discount, but you should take some time to think over it."

With nothing more to achieve here today, I push my heavy body up and force a smile. The doctor gets up as well and extends his hand, which I grab with disappointing reluctance. "Thank you so much, I'll let you know my decision next week." I say in a bid to keep up the appearance of hope."

* * *

"Hey Tara."

I almost jump at the sound of the unexpected but familiar voice over my head, but a firm clasp on my shoulder follows immediately. I lift my head from the Dazzlers magazine and turn around to see FG wearing a warm smile looking down at me. "What are you doing here?" I barely manage to keep my voice down after closing the magazine I have been engrossed in for some ten minutes. I wonder how he recognised me from the back. I arrived at the restaurant, which was one of our favourites about thirty minutes ago to wait for Daisy.

I am seated at the back of the restaurant obscuring myself from the comings and goings with my back turned to the entrance. Is this simply a coincidence? Definitely! There is no way he or anybody for that matter except Daisy could have known I would be here.

"So sorry for startling you." He comes to face me and looks at me intently as he always does. "What are you doing here too?" Impulsively, I look around the restaurant and look back to lock eyes with him. He pulls out the chair opposite me. "Can I join you?"

"I'm waiting for a friend. Oh, I think you know her. Daisy, the lady you saw with me at Shoprite"

He nods. "Do you think I forget anything about you, sugar?" A tiny flicker tugs at my heart as his eyes hold mine, causing a shy smile to form on my face. I am not quite at ease with him calling me sugar, but it sounds nice all the same. He picks the magazine and flips through the edges without fully opening any page. "You bought this too?" He stops at the centrespread splash of his mother's event where he stands out like an icon.

I smile, lifting my shoulders. "What better pictures to look at apart from those of the indomitable Lady Gomez?"

"She thrives on parties and publicity. That woman." He shakes his head.

"She makes it look like she's promoting her business rather than cheap publicity and you didn't look like you were not enjoying the party either." I tease him. In one of the pictures, he is holding his mother's hand to cut the tape at the event. They are surrounded by a bevy of young beautiful models all adorning different colours of the silk clothing. Before he came to me, I had stared very long at that picture, wondering which one of them was his girlfriend, or which one of the skimpy-clad girls would have propositioned him. Then I thought FG is not exactly into girls, only to remind myself that was a long time ago. So many things would have changed about him especially with his eligible single status in this town where competition for eligible men is rife. "So what brings you here, truly?" I clasp my hands and stare at him, waiting for an answer, while hoping he will have a plausible one.

"I came for lunch with a friend." He looks out to the overflow and waves at a chubby clean-shaven man, smartly dressed in a suit sat at a corner, with just a glass of water. The man waves back with a perfunctory smile and I wave at him too. Instinctively I know the man is a banker, probably pitching FG for his accounts. "Have you ordered lunch?" A waiter brings a glass of juice that looks exactly like mine. Did he order before coming to my table?

I shake my head. "I have to wait for Daisy." I was already on my second glass of orange juice when FG came to me and I have forgotten how hungry I was after burying myself in the Dazzlers. Mentioning food now makes my tummy whisper, but I have to contain myself until Daisy comes so I can unleash all my sorrows on her first. Recalling that I switched off my phone at the clinic, I fish it out from my bag. It has been almost one hour I spoke with her when she was on Carter Bridge. She should have been here by now. She has called three times and then sent me a text that she would be going back because she was not sure if she would ever get to Victoria Island today. Everyone on the bus with her got off as well. "She's not coming anymore." Without any thought or effort, my heart and body droop in disappointment and a well of emotions spring up to my eyes to create a mass of water, which starts flowing down.

"Tara." FG's voice is alarmed as he flails his hands with his widened eyes. Immediately, he is up and beside me, stooping to my level to squeeze my shoulder. "What's wrong? Is it me, what did I do?" I cannot trust myself to make any body movement or open my mouth to utter any word without turning this into a full wailing scene. I have been looking forward to talking to Daisy and holding back my tears for her. Reading her text just now releases the grieving emotions I tucked away when I was leaving the clinic. Another dashed hope, probably my last since Tokunbo has said he is no longer interested in the process. I am not even sure how to tell him.

"Excuse me." FG mutters to the people sitting behind me and squeezes himself into the chair beside me, turning to face my side as my face remains focused on the window ahead. He takes my hand and starts patting it gently. "Did something bad happen to your friend?" I shake my head, sniffling and a tear drops unto the sleeve of his white shirt, staining it with a faint dot of black eye liner. I sniffle again. "I'm sorry, but it's okay to let go of whatever is bothering you." A waiter approaches our table, but FG waves him away. Still sniffling, I rub my tears with my free hand and in that instant, my head fuddles up with different scenarios of what could have been if I had waited around to marry him. I am at the door, watching him with two chubby five year olds– a boy and a girl – in a luscious garden, playing hide and seek. A red scarf, one of mine is covering his face and he walks cautiously in the garden, stretching out his hands to find his way as both children call out to him from different directions to confuse him. The girl suddenly pounces on his back and gleefully shouts, 'Got you daddy,' as they fall, rolling on the carpet grass. Then his mother's voice calls out, 'Omotara!'

I come back to reality, to the touch of FG's soothing continuous hand strokes as he sits there quietly and patiently. Another spring of tears bursts forth. How I hate that wretched woman! If not for her, we could have been one happy family with our children. How can someone so unkind be FG's mother? I close my wet eyes to try to shut her out before I start cursing her, but it is difficult to bear this loss alone and I cannot tell FG. A few more sniffles and the emission of a big wheeze help to pull me together. I retrieve my hand from underneath his and both our hands intertwine briefly. Finally, I turn to face him. "Thanks, thanks a lot." I nod. "I'm okay now." I use both hands to pat my eyes, hoping to save any form of make-up that survives.

"You're sure you're okay?"

"I'm okay." I nod again, grabbing the cup on the table and guzzle the little juice remaining to smoothen out my voice. I force a smile. "I'm sorry. That was embarrassing."

"Embarrassing? I just sent someone to get me a bowl in case there's more where that came from." He smirks at me.

"Nice try." I eye him with a genuine smile now. "I better start going, before your shirt becomes my hankie." I reach for my bag and start foraging for my purse.

"What do you want to do? Of course I'll pay. Don't insult me."

I bring out my sunglasses instead. "Seriously, thanks for being here and all that."

He pushes his chair back, I do the same, suddenly self-conscious and hoping the people behind me would not have heard my mourning. "Have you heard from Prime Bank? How is that going? Or have you gotten another job?"

A load of guilt suddenly falls on me. "I'm sorry. I should have called you but I don't want you to go barging on Amy again. One of the people at the interview called and said they'll get in touch with me, but they haven't and I've been pretty busy. I attended one other interview last week too, but I don't feel positive about that. I think they already know the people they want to employ. "

"I should be having a meeting with Amy next week and I'll ask her. Don't worry I won't harass her. At least not on your behalf." He pats my hand, smiling. For the first time since he joined me, he drinks his orange juice. "Hmm, this tastes good."

My skin tingles with the weight of his eyes on me as he frolics with his lips to savour the drink. "You don't need to bother her. Really, I'm sure they'll call me when they're ready." I have not had to look for a job in a long time and I don't know the protocols anymore.

"If you say so." Again, he brings his hand on mine in a gentle consoling caress. My head is still a bit fuzzy. "If you don't want me to talk to her, I'll leave it. Just promise me you'll be fine." His tiny voice rings of sincerity and tenderness.

Truly, does he not know the effect he has on me? He gets up after me. "I'll walk you out." I nod.

He goes ahead to open the door to let me out of the restaurant without referring to the fact that the man who waved when he joined my table is no longer there. "Thanks." I stop myself from asking about his friend.

"Sorry Miss." A man mutters, catching himself from stepping on me as we almost jam by the door.

"It's okay sir." I whisper and raise my head to meet the man's face. The face of Kunle, Tokunbo's friend confronts me with twinkling eyes; then shock, followed by a mischievous smile as he steps back to smoothen his crinkled linen shirt while thrusting himself in front of a lady, who seems to be his companion.

"Ha, Tara, it's you. What are you doing here?" He looks at FG, who is almost pushing behind me.

"I had a meeting with a friend, but she didn't turn up. I'm just leaving." I supposes I should ask him the same question, but I let it go as I take some steps from the door to let FG pass and indicate to Kunle that I am not about to wait for a chat.

FG walks on without a word and Kunle's eyes follow him, nodding. "Your friend?"

"Yes, from University." Kunle is about the only one amongst Tokunbo's friends who makes me uncomfortable around him. His flirtatious smile and roving eyes always make me awkward and I can swear I have caught him staring at my breasts more than once, but I have never mentioned it to Tokunbo to avoid blowing it out of proportion. Only God knows what would be going on in his mind about FG and me.

"Oh, you should have…" He starts taking a step forward but stops as I cut in.

"Don't let me disturb you, and you shouldn't keep your friend waiting." The lady smiles in response to my acknowledgement and tucks her hand into Kunle's elbow. I start walking towards the gate. "Enjoy your lunch. Please greet my friend and tell her I miss her." I walk straight out of the gate, leaving him with his girlfriend and his thoughts.

* * *

Tokunbo

After thrashing Mike Mba at three games of table tennis, we both manoeuvre to the bar to join the others, greeting and backslapping randomly along the way. The inside bar is already filled up. The loud volume and the mixed voices of mild to extreme tipsiness filter through to produce the regular ricochets of cacophony over the assorted plates of food and bottles of liquors. Kunle and Big Sam are at our favourite table talking in raised voices and flailing their arms. Kunle moves his chair to make room for us as we drop our bags and drag two empty chairs to join them.

"Who won?" Big Sam's alcohol-laced belligerent voice roars, followed by the arm that was comfortably resting on his paunch, pointing from Mike to me. Even when he has not had any drink, his whisper is loud enough for anyone to hear from a forty-foot distance.

"I'm ten thousand naira poorer." Mike drops on the seat and drags the waiter passing by to place an order.

"So tonight is on you." Kunle stretches out to me for a handshake with a bow and pats me on the back. "Good work, Tokunbo. Now this boy will stop blabbing his mouth against me." I shake hands with Big Sam after Kunle. It is customary on Tuesdays to have a wager between the incumbent winner and a contender, and the loser gives the winner cash and settles the bill for the night. Last week I beat Kunle, and Mike teased him unrepentantly. Mike adjusts his rimless glasses and fakes a punch at him.

I check my phone to see if Tara has called or sent a text. No! I have called her severally since landing at the airport before stopping by at the club, but she did not pick up. I have been checking my phone since, hoping she would at least tell me the result from her visit to the clinic. I would have gone home straight from the airport, but I received a text from my contact at Petra Services telling me his CEO would be at the club this evening, and I thought it would be a good idea to get in his good books after winning the contract to make my life easier. He was shocked to see me, but started loosening up when one of my Arsenal buddies stopped by to chitchat about Arsene Wenger and we both discovered we were mutual Arsenal fans. He left with a promise to introduce me to a friend of his.

After he left and Tara was yet to call, I became apprehensive that the test was negative, but I was not ready to accept that reality. I decided to join my friends and challenged Mike to a game of table tennis to get my mind off thinking. She still has not called nor sent a text. Does she not think I have a right to know as well? I called her yesterday and pleaded with her, for us to go together tomorrow. But no, it has to be her way. Wait a minute, is it possible that she has not gone to see the doctor and probably waiting for me? I suddenly become restless and cannot wait to be home with my wife.

The intense feeling of possibility secretes some adrenalin into my brain and I jump up. "Hey guys, I have to go." I pack my bag as the three of them react at the same time, muttering words that are lost on me.

* * *

Luckily, Tara is awake watching a *Yoruba* movie on African Magic with the lights out.

"Sunshine, how are you?" I whisper with enough excitement to cover my feeling of guilt.

"Welcome." Her voice is low and flat.

"Sorry, I had to stop by at the club to meet someone. Remember Petra Services? The CEO. Thank God I went. How was your day?" She reduces the volume of the TV and raises her brows. "Has she been up to any mischief?" I point to Mama's room and Tara shakes her head as I lower myself beside her on the sofa. "Tell me, how has your day been?" Her silence worries me and coupled with my apprehension, I am not sure if I should ask her directly about visiting the clinic. "Did you…"

"I did." She blurts out with a gale of tears. She does not need to say anymore. I hold her in my arms to comfort her and to stop her from seeing the tiny lump of water in my eyes.

CHAPTER TEN

Tokunbo

"What do you have to lose?" Tara's mother edges towards her.

"It's not about what we have to lose, mummy. I've told you severally and I will repeat it, I don't believe that deliverance is the panacea to everybody's problems. If I can't solve my problem, I don't want to add to it by thinking that one witch or stupid spirit is responsible." Tara faces her mother squarely. This is not their first time having such a discussion and I am indifferent. "I am not going, simple." She crosses her legs and turns slightly right, using the sofa to support her elbow below her chin.

We are both sitting on the two seater sofa in Tara's mother's sparsely decorated living room, having responded to her tacit summon at her insistence that there was an important issue to discuss with us. It is difficult to imagine now that Tara used to live in a smaller flat about three streets away, when I consider that even this flat is rather small. Irrespective of the minimalism of the flat, it never ceases to feel like home.

Tara's mother had been living in the other one bedroom flat for God knows how long. After we got married, Tara offered to move her to Ajah or Ebute Metta, but the woman refused, claiming that she wanted to remain in a central location to be close to her friends, her workplace at the teaching Hospital and most importantly her church at Ketu. We could only persuade her to move to a bigger place. Her life seems like a revolving door of – work, church, home and sporadic visits to family members. Save for a few, she had become ostracised by her family when she got pregnant with Tara. Tara is probably the only worthy person in her life and her uncle that walked Tara to the aisle.

The flat is on the middle floor of an old building of six flats close to a terminal bus stop. The street outside is lined with old houses; some cracked, some completely un-plastered and a whole lot that have not experienced the slightest touch of paint for years or decades, except for a few squeezed into pieces of land that have been scavenged from existing buildings. Those few represent new money, a connotation of the polarised one-eyed in the land of the blind.

Almost every house has a sort of shop or kiosk overflowing into the road to reduce the breadth available for the thronging pedestrians and vehicles. From within the flat, one can easily pick up bits of different activities going on all around; people talking at the top of one another's voices; bus conductors hollering for passengers; *area boys* harassing bus drivers for levies; horns blaring; screeching tyres; and an infusion of different musical concoctions. The script remains the same day in, day out, except for Sunday perhaps. It is easy to empathise with those errant kids who run away from home in such a place. The environment simply holds no incitement for anyone to aspire for more, save for those to whom education or sheer providence offers a way up the ladder. Yet some have lived here for two generations or more. The flat itself bears no resemblance to the chaotic realities outside.

When her mother went on a one-week retreat in church, Tara secretly arranged for a complete makeover of the entire flat. Now the living room is covered with satin-sheen cream wallpaper, tiled with brown granite and fitted with a split unit air-conditioner that works only half of the time because of the electricity current in the area. There are two sets of two-seater fabric sofas, two side stools, one dining table, a small wooden table sitting on a centre rug and a thirty two-inch TV hanging on the wall above a brown mahogany chest of drawers. The big standing fan drowns some of the atmospheric noise with its own humming sound.

"Tokunbo, won't you say something?" Tara's mother turns to me looking for an ally, her eyes beaming with the plea of motherly love, yet with a tinge of sadness. She folds her arms back to her midriff, looking at me with puzzled resignation. "If you say my idea is bad, then what is your alternative? It's not like I'm asking you to follow me to a herbalist."

I groan silently, placing my glasses on the stool in front of me and turn Tara's crossed knees back to me. I would rather not be part of this conversation, but she and I have agreed that we should always present a united front to both our parents, so we have made it clear that all issues pertaining to us should be discussed freely and openly, otherwise this should have been exclusive to the two women. I know her mother means well as she tries to convince us yet again to attend an all-night prayer and deliverance session at her church. She has been inviting Tara on the phone about the special service tagged 'Barrenness No More', and it is no surprise that she is still pushing to get us to attend. Understandably, Tara tries her best to stall seeing or talking to her mother since they could not communicate without an allusion to our childless state. After the very first miscarriage and continuous barrage of invitations for deliverance sessions, Tara avoids the topic with her mother as much as possible.

"Ma, there's nothing new I'll say that hasn't been said. If God is the one we're praying to, then it shouldn't matter where we pray. Do you remember the time you warned me about not playing religious adultery. That is exactly what you want us to do now." I pick up the glass of the fresh mixed-*zobo* juice Tara made from a mixture of fruits we brought for her mother. I only take a sip as it feels like lead against my tongue right now.

Tara's mother has not touched her juice at all, choosing rather to focus on her mission. She is the personified image of a beautiful woman dragged through the dregs of a tiresome life and left behind in a hollow to look at the world from the inside. I cannot help but wonder at the difference between Tara's mother and mine. Her demeanour always reminds me of the nun that taught me in primary school as a young boy. Even inside her own house, her scarf covers all except her face, no make-up, no jewellery; just a tiny watch adorning her small wrist. Her dark complexion is a sad reminder that Tara got more from her father's genes than from her.

The one thing that casts a ray of light on her personae is that same natural smile that Tara wears on her face. According to Tara, her mother has not always been this religious or conservative if the pictures of her young adult life were anything to go by. Tara believes she gradually embraced the charismatic prayer-warring church due to her state as a single parent, without a hope or probably, desire of a husband. Despite the fact that she always looked resigned, her smiley face conveyed contentment and a lack of aspiration for anything more than what she already has.

"Mummy *ewo*, leave that matter. God will do what he will

do. Have you had lunch?" Tara parks her leather slippers with her feet and looks at her mother for a response. The woman shakes her head. "You won't eat?" Tara makes a face at her. "I want to make rice because we didn't eat from home. I thought you'd offer us lunch, at least let's help you use your dining table." Tara goes to shake her mother teasingly. "Cheer up, God has heard your petition, it's just the manifestation we're waiting for."

I wonder if she has any belief in what she just said or she is merely trying to lift up her mother's spirit. When we talk about kids, I always end up trying to pacify her.

Her mother extricates herself from her and nods her back to the sofa. "Leave me alone and sit down, there's another issue I want to talk about."

Tara comes back to sit beside me, her lips frizzed in a half smile. "*Today na today*, what is it again? Can you call Mary to come home on time and make some food? Seriously, I'm hungry." She gives me a side-glance to which I merely shrug. Mary is the house help Tara got for her mother against all resistance. Her mother maintained she was quite capable of taking care of herself, but Tara brought the girl anyway, insisting that beyond helping in the house, her mother needed a real human stimulus outside work and church. Tara enrolled the girl as a tailor's apprentice within walking distance to the house. After adjusting herself to a comfortable pose, she juts out to face her mother squarely.

The woman shifts in her seat uncomfortably and exhales. "Your father contacted me last week."

"*Hen!* Who, whose father?" A wave of heat transfers from Tara's body to mine. Her outburst obscures my mouthed question of 'who', and I shut my mouth almost immediately. Tara's eyes widen and a crease of wrinkles appears on her forehead. Her mother remains calm, but exhales heavily. She breaks into a derisive laugh. "You're joking, *abi?*"

Her mother shakes her head. "No, I'm not joking. He came to the hospital last week." I take Tara's hand and start rubbing it gently; her stiffened body begins to relax. "He asked after you, and I told him off, but he's been coming every day since and still asking to see you."

"Well, I don't want to see him." Tara bolts up, retrieving her sweating palm from my hand. Her flesh goes pale as she starts pacing the living room behind her mother. "Why are you even telling me? We agreed long ago, he wasn't going to come into our lives."

Her mother turns in her seat to face her. "You are much older now and I believe some things will make more sense to you than they did when you were younger. Relationships can sometimes get complicated without logic and with no clear indication of whether you are wrong or right. It's going to be your decision whether to see him or not, I can't force you, but ask yourself this question, 'What would Jesus do?'" She reclines in her seat and a trace of sniffle escapes from her. I wonder what the woman has had to deal with since the only man she has probably ever loved and not seen for almost forty years strolled back into her life. How does life get this complicated?

Guessing Tara may brusquely retort that she is not Jesus, I respond quickly. "Ma, this is a tough one." Is there a better way she could have broken this news to us? Tara leans against the dining table, staring into the emptiness in front of her. I feel a deep tenderness towards her and glide to her to take her in my arms. She does not resist, gradually unleashing the weight of her body and heart on me. Then the random snivels of holding back a full outburst, followed by teardrops. I wipe her eyes and lead her back to the sofa. "It's okay." I whisper.

"Didn't you tell him we've managed fine without him? What does he want from us? Did his family abandon him the same way he abandoned us? Why is he coming now? Mummy, what did you tell him, how did he find you or did you go looking for him and you don't want to tell me?"

"Tara." I am torn between letting her rant on her mother and calming her down. Finding her mother should be one of the easiest tasks in this world. Since I have known her, almost everything about her has remained constant. I recall I saw the man once, when Tara mentioned the possibility of reconnecting with him. It was easy to understand why he had been able to sway Tara's mother, married man or not. The man was both a looker and a charmer, at least from what I saw then.

"So what do you want us to do now?" Tara expects a response from her mother, who merely flips open her hand.

"I think you should relax first and take some time to think about it. Or what do you suggest ma?" I add my voice.

She sighs again as if that act in itself lightens the yoke of an uneasy task before starting out. She drops her face in her hand, shuts her eyes and says nothing, rocking her hand over her brow from side to side. It is a deep silence, and a very long one.

"I think we should leave not." Tara says finally. As much as I want to tug myself from all the unpalatable emotions in this room, I am not sure we should leave without deciding any course of action. Yet, I cannot find the words to say as the two of them have bottled themselves up in their cocoons. I look at her and shake my head, but she ignores me and starts packing the unfinished drinks from the tables.

"Don't worry, Mary will tidy up when she comes." Her mother suggests unconvincingly, knowing fully well that Tara will clear up. "Please, can we pray before you leave?" She demands when Tara returns from the kitchen. Tara shrugs, but sits and adjusts herself to clasp her palms in prayer mode. "In

Jesus name..."

"Amen." We both chorus, heralding the rain of gratitude and supplication her mother starts to churn out. Tara's eyes are dripping wet as we get up to leave.

* * *

With the intensity of emotions that transpired in the house, the happenings on the streets went on without any attention. We come out of the flat to be confronted with residue of debris left on the pavements. Scores of people are engaged in clearing the gutters on both sides of the road to release little pools of flood from different low-level buildings remind us of the heavy rain fell for a short period. The woman in the kiosk downstairs packs some of the wet debris into a big rusty drum that serves as bin, while her teenage daughter sweeps whatever is remaining in front of the kiosk back into the gutter.

I have never understood how people cannot appreciate the futility in clearing debris from gutters onto the roadside, since the rubbles will always find their way back into the gutters and then another rainfall will bring people back together again to clear the gutters.

I drive on listlessly, with the heaviness hanging between us in the car, thumping the steering and looking straight ahead as I try to piece together what is going on in Tara's head. I draw a blank, but my mind strays back to her mother. The poor woman is alone to deal with shock and mixed feelings of relating with the man. No matter how short-lived or inappropriate, she must have felt some affection to have an affair with him in the first place. Unless she was just in for a fling at the time, which I doubt very much. But again, one never knows these things. Deciding to keep the pregnancy must have been one big choice for her to make in her life; waking up every day with the growing life inside her, and facing rejection by both lover and family could not have been any easy for a girl of nineteen in those days.

Could she have deliberately gotten pregnant because she wanted the man to marry her and then her ploy backfired? That does not add up, otherwise she would have tried to force the man to accept paternity, no matter the impact on his marriage. Maybe she just did not have the resources to fight back then. Why do I want to make her look like the victim when she could not have been entirely innocent in that tryst? Because as a lady, she is the one that has had to carry the plaque of indiscretion all these years. For all it is worth, it is possible that not a single person from the man's family was aware he had a girlfriend, talk less of a beautiful thirty something year old daughter.

A strident buzz from Tara's phone announcing a text message intrudes my rumination and splinters the awkward silence. She hisses quietly as if forced to break from an important task, but reaches inside her bag to search for the phone. She hisses again after looking at the phone and drops it carelessly back inside the bag; so that next time, she would have to search for it again. Women! With all the pockets in their handbags, one would think they would have a specific place to keep a phone.

"Do you know what it feels like growing up, not having a father, knowing that he's well alive, yet you have to tell everyone he's dead? Not having someone unpack your school bag or having a present to talk about on children's day with my friends? Do you know what it feels like not to be able to ask any question about your father from your mother simply because he is a bitter memory? Do you know how it feels walking on the streets and thinking that every pointed finger is at you? She purrs like someone reciting her questions from a script. "Do you know how I felt as a child, not being able to attend family parties or play with my cousins because they'd make me the laughing stock? Can you imagine what it was like when it was just me and my mother every Christmas, because she didn't want people asking about me? Me, the mistake child, the one that wasn't meant to be. Hmm." She laments and shakes her head. "And she wants me to meet the man responsible for all that."

"She said she'd leave you to decide on that. You don't have to meet him if you don't want to. But I think you need to take some time to sleep on it."

"And what do you think will change when I wake up?"

"Probably nothing. I'm just saying give it time. You don't have to see him if you don't want to. You can call your mum back tomorrow and find out what she wants to do. I don't think it's something you want to decide in a hurry?"

"You know what, I don't want to think or talk about him. I need only positivity in my life right now." She waves me off to end the discussion. After a few minutes, she blurts suddenly. "What if the man is dying?"

"Tara." I drawl, expressing shock at her trail of thoughts and almost missing the traffic light turning red at the 1004 junction. A white ambulance suddenly turns on its siren and pulls out from behind me, trying to manoeuvre its way between the rows of halted cars. I steer a little bit to my right to grant it passage. The ambulance is not that lucky with the other two cars ahead of me as they keep their spots, ignoring the fact that the ambulance may indeed be on a mission. Not that I blame them. Ambulances have a reputation for blaring sirens even when they are transporting a dead body to the mortuary. Siren blowing is one of the many oppressive and atmospheric-polluting actions we face daily on Lagos roads, from military personnel, police, politicians and even church leaders. Thank God, the government has been able to stop the hooliganisms manifested by the banks' bullion vans.

"What?" She remains adamant. "Does it not add up? What kind of man seeks his abandoned child after almost four decades, if not for something dire? I need to be convinced otherwise. He probably wants to make peace before he dies."

"Your mind is amazing." Although, it makes sense. "You and your mum need to discuss this further. For now ….."

"Don't you know she'll still have a soft spot for him?" She cuts in, looking at me with eyes that ask if I am stupid. "I'm sure all these years, it was her prayer point that he should show up at her doorstep, and that prayer has now been answered. I can't trust her to make any sound decision about this issue. If she wants to romance him, she should go ahead and not bring me into it."

"Romance?" I chuckle despite the seriousness Tara attaches to this. I cannot imagine her pious mum romping with anything that has a semblance of masculinity. "Your mind has really travelled far." The light turns green. Now, the two cars ahead wait for the noisy ambulance to speed off. It is almost certain there is no one seeking urgent medical attention in the trunk of that car.

She grieves on. "I don't know what to think. It's … it's just …" She stutters, failing to find the words to complete her statement. I reach out to her knees and pat her hand.

"It's going to be okay sunshine. Just trust your heart." It is easy to love my wife when she lets her vulnerability free. I squeeze her hand tightly to assure her of my support.

CHAPTER ELEVEN

Tara

With all the aggressive road rehabilitation works the government has embarked on in recent times, the road to Daisy's house remains untouched; untarred and uneven with various depths of potholes and blocked gutters. Because of the hot temperature, dried grass lines the dry road and debris, particularly pure water sachets litter the surface, flying whichever way the wind blows. Most of the cars parked on both sides of the road are covered in different degrees of dusts. Many of the houses are built very close to the open gutters so there is no provision for off-the-road parking.

Almost every house has a mobile kiosk or shop at its front, vending everyday consumables and operated by wrapper-tying women or children whose hollow faces reveal their disenchantment with their current tasks. There has to be a way to ensure these children go through primary school at the least. Two girls, one of whom is wearing a faded worn-out uniform are seated on a bench, struggling viciously over a wooden toy, while the two women beside the kiosk keep talking without as much as a glance in the children's direction.

Further into the street, a group of dishevelled teenage boys are playing football, barefooted; most of them without tops. It is as if there has been an agreement to make the place a football pitch, as there are no cars parked anywhere close by. Even with my AC on, I feel the need for a bucket of cold water to be splashed on my face. The one acting as a referee blows his whistle and raises up a hand, so I bring the car to a slow stop for the players split onto the two sides of the road. The referee uses his other hand to pass me on like a traffic warden. I resist the urge to shake my head at the sheer waste of talent and youthfulness in such a place as this, rather keeping a straight face as I drive through the parade of footballers. They rush back into the street as soon as I pass. These are the things I sometimes miss when the lifeless silence of my street gets so intense that it winds me up. The familiar sight of the woman fanning the embers underneath her *boli* stock leaves me salivating. It has been a while since I had a good snack of *boli*, especially after the task force demolished the makeshift stalls opposite the office.

Daisy's house, a tenement bungalow, converted into a three bedroom flat looks no different from the others on the street, except for the un-rendered low fence wall and black gate. How she manages to live here and get along with all these people without any expression of discontent makes me respect her. Especially with her daily exposure to people of affluence at the bank. I honk sharply and she peeps through the curtains. I turn off the ignition and exchange the flip-flops I use for driving with my three-inch black wedge slippers. She opens the door and pushes out the upper half of her body.

"Omotara baby." Daisy hails as I step onto the plank sitting on the gutter as pathway into the house. The plank has been replaced with a wider and firmer one since the last time I was here. With my second step on the plank, I remember the *boli* vendor down the road. "You look splendid as you always do *mon ami.*" She gives me a side hug and collects the un-iced carrot cake I shove at her. "You and cakes, you shouldn't have bothered."

I retrace my steps hurriedly. "Please let me quickly buy *boli* from that woman. Do you want one?"

She shakes her head. "*I don chop tire*, but you can buy two *sha.*"

I head for the woman's counter, two houses back. She is a dark beautiful woman, with her beauty tucked behind the weight of toiling under the sun and many other hardships that must be going on in her life. She has a baby cradled on her back, peacefully sleeping. She starts peeling another plantain to put on the coal mesh to make up her stock. I greet her and point to two *bolis*, asking for the price. Before she replies, she takes a second look at me with some scrutiny from head to toe and tries to hide the fact that she is glancing at my car.

"Pay three hundred naira for the two." She pats her hands cheerfully, without taking her eyes off my face, making me uncomfortable. I gasp. "You know things are expensive madam, and with all the up and down to get all these things together. You know it's not easy. Should I pack them for you, do you want groundnut?"

I know three hundred naira is way out of it, but I do feel sorry for her like I always do when I go to the open market to buy foodstuffs; one of the reasons I stopped going. Really, sometimes I wonder how much turnover these people need daily to make a proper living. People keep saying there is dignity in labour, but I wonder why that dignity cannot be liberating. I hesitate on whether to give in to her entreaty or go for the bargain and I reach into my red Prada bag. Even if she sells all her wares every day of the month for one year, she still would not have sold up to the value of this bag, yet I am thinking of haggling with her. "But you know it shouldn't be that expensive." I just have to say something, so she does not think she is the wiser. I bring out five hundred naira and she stoops to collect it from me.

She starts wrapping the *bolis* and adds two sachets of groundnuts without waiting for me to ask. "God bless you ma, thank you ma, God will keep you and your children, you will never lack, God will send help to you too, thank you ma." She puts everything in a black nylon bag and hands it over to me, untying the edge of her wrapper to give me the change. I collect the change and thank her, but on the count of three steps, the compulsion to give her the money is strong, I turn back and hand it over to her.

"Use it to buy something for your child." I quickly turn away before she says anything, but I hear her voice trailing behind me."

"*Hee*, thank you ma o, God will do wonders in your life, ah, God will surprise you, thank you…."

Daisy has left the door open and I burst in with relief ready, to devour my precious *boli* that cost me five hundred naira.

* * *

Daisy

Tara dumps herself into a seat in our compact living room and pushes away the centre table with the cake on it, to create legroom. She looks fatigued and relieved at the same time. Anytime she comes here, I am amazed at how much she feels at home despite coming from her posh palace. She says our house gives her a liberating experience because we seem to have purposed to drop our baggage by the door outside. What else can one do, having gone through that dark season of life? One reason I love her is because of her unpretentiousness. I have always known her to be rich by virtue of being married to Tokunbo, believing she came to work for the sake of avoiding boredom. When she said she came from a humble background in the office, we all sniffed at her, until I followed her to her Mum's home.

"You don't look bad at all, I shouldn't say joblessness does you good, but then I'd be lying. I think I've missed you." We both laugh at her compliment. I am wearing a cream T-shirt on a pair of brown combat shorts while Tara is wearing sequined *ankara* top on red linen trousers.

"Don't be so modest, I didn't think you could survive one week without seeing me, talk less of a month. And please don't protest, I am making *moinmoin elemimeje* for lunch. You can't come to my house and not eat." I take the seat opposite her.

"After this expensive *boli* I can't eat anything, but you can pack the *moinmoin* for me to take home. I've missed your cooking as well. How is your dad?" She unwraps the paper of *bolis* and groundnut on the table and starts attacking it. Despite all my resistance, I dive in after her.

"Hmm, that one." I smile mischievously about my dad. "He went out with his new found love. I think it's going to work this time. I feel so relieved to see him trying to move on with life and get some fulfilment. He is very busy these days. He has been helping her out with her business and they've decided to run it together. You can't imagine how having something to do has changed that man. If you meet him on the road, you'd hardly recognise him. He looks much younger, he is easily excitable and always in the mood to chat. It's been a long time

I saw him this happy. These days, it's difficult to get him to come home once they're together."

"That's good to hear. Maybe we need to find my mother in-law a man too, so she can stop harassing everybody. That woman ..." Tara trails off, without finishing. "Anyway, I hope you are getting along with your future stepmother." She eyes me mockingly.

"Yes o." I am actually excited. "But, what's my own, don't I have my own issues? And daddy is old enough to take care of himself." I ask her if she wants a drink and without waiting for an answer, I get up to go outside. I yell out to one of the boys at the house opposite to get me a big bottle of coke. We usually rarely stock up on foodstuffs because of the state of electricity. Also, most items are readily available from neighbours and I can get what I need by just peeping out through the windows. The boy soon brings in the bottle of coke after a gentle tap on the door

I excuse myself to check on the *moinmoin* and return with two glass cups in a tray, placing it beside the coke. The aroma of the *moinmoin* fills the house and Tara pleads for me to ensure she does not forget her takeaway portion. I tell her about the two interviews I have attended so far and how I was extremely disappointed at the last one. They kept me waiting for so long that by the time I saw the interviewers my body had started shaking with anger; which probably showed on my face and tone of voice, because the interviewers spent half the time apologising. I confess I am almost sure I will not scale through that interview. The first one was through the colleague in the office and that was okay. The good news is someone in my church has promised to get me into AMCON. It is ironic that AMCON, which bought over the bad debts of the failed banks, was employing staff from the same banks the CBN wrote off. If all that fails, I have already decided that I will simply join the state civil service; one of our former bosses, who got an executive portfolio has helped a few of our former colleagues into his ministry.

Tara mentions how her husband has been trying to manipulate her into starting her own business, which she is not particularly keen on doing. She also fills me in about her interviews including the one FG scheduled for her.

"How is that FG of yours?" I can see the uneasiness on her face at my question before she shifts her eyes from mine.

"He should be fine, at least he was the last time I saw him. And you should stop calling him my FG."

I switch on my moonbeam face, with some mischief stressing my every word. "Was he that good to you?"

"Who?" She rummages through her leather bag to divert my attention from her face, but she cannot fool me.

"Don't try to be silly. Who else are we talking about? You're such a lousy pretender?"

She takes a deep breath. "FG? I don't think there's any need talking about him, he belongs to my past."

"And I don't intend to bring him to your present. I just want you to talk about him and acknowledge your feelings. You have a way of bottling things up to yourself and sometimes I wonder about you when you say you're okay, if you're not just keeping up an appearance. You should try to let go a little bit. It's like there's something about you that cringes when someone tries to get close to you."

"Ah!" She finally musters enough boldness to look me in the face. "Is this about FG or something else?"

"You tell me." I cock my head. "You keep telling me I'm the closest friend you've got, and you sit around watching me wag my tongue about my entire life. But as for you ..." I pause and shake my head slowly. "It seems your life has to be perfect and sometimes I feel like a failure around you. I can't say I know what your weakness is if anyone asks me. What kind of friendship is that?"

"Daisy." She inflects my name. "If this is about FG, you know I'm married and no matter what I think of him, it's not going to change anything and take me out of Tokunbo's house."

"Oh, so you think about him in that way?" I chuckle. "Please don't leave your husband, I can never be party to that. He's a good man and he's my brother. I am only curious about that guy and you since we met him. That day, you looked so smitten and unnerved you can't even begin to imagine." I go to sit on the centre table to poke my face at her. "I want to gossip a little bit about my friend. What really happened between the two of you? I'm surprised you've never mentioned him all this time. I've always thought Tokunbo was your first love?"

"Tokunbo, first love?" She shakes her head. "By the way, I'm here to talk about you. Remember, you said we have an urgent matter to trash out."

"There you go again. Do we ever talk about you at any time? No! So I'm not telling if you're not." I get up from the table and go back to my seat folding my arms across my chest and eyeing her furtively.

"There's nothing to be said about him." She raises her brows and smiles satirically. "Okay, we met in school and he was my first love. I really loved him and we were into each other a lot. Until I met his mother." She goes on to tell me about the drama at FG's house with his mother and how he came begging, but she did not go back to him because there would have been no future for her there.

"Poor you. But you could have given him another chance. You know if it was me, I would have given that woman a piece of her own bitter cookies she would never forget, since I would have known I didn't stand a chance of becoming her daughter in-law."

"If she had let loose the dogs on me that day, who could I have reported her to? My dear, when you are from a poor and broken home, it's double *wahala* if you have to fight someone like FG's mum. Common sense should tell you to run for safety. Now that FG is still unmarried, I'm almost convinced I did the right thing. But I must confess I thought I had gotten over him until that day at Shoprite." She had that longing look on her face as if she wished she could go back in time.

"I know. I saw the effect he had on you, although the two of you were pretending. I've played this game too, you know." I gloat. "But what kind of guy won't stand up for his girlfriend if he was really serious about you?"

"We were young and thinking back now, I don't think I gave him enough room for that. Anyway, enough about me, what's this joke about you being pregnant? I thought you were abstaining for the right guy. And how did that happen without my knowledge? Which other secrets are you keeping from me?" Now Tara is the one who comes to sit on the centre table to face me.

I inhale and shift my eyes from meeting hers, choosing to focus on chipping nail polish off my fingers. "It's a long story and one that should never have happened. It was that weekend you travelled with your mum for your niece's wedding and I was so ashamed of myself I couldn't bear to tell you when you came back. Who would have thought it would lead to this?" I look at her and she stares back without saying a word, so I continue. "Remember we were supposed to attend the institute's dinner at Civic Centre. Paul was there."

"Which Paul, who is Paul? It can't be the same Paul I know."

I groan. "Yes Paul, the same Paul that left me." I continue, my voice going quieter. "He was at the dinner and we sat together throughout the night. After the dinner, he asked me to go with him to another party, and I guess that's when I should have declined and taken a cab *jeje*. I think I wanted to impress him so much I let him cajole me to drinking alcohol. Besides, talking to him throughout the night made me realise how lonely I was and how much I missed him. It felt really good having him lust after me that I got carried away and simply let go." I raise my eyes to Tara's with a plea for her to understand. "*Ore,* I'm tired of being single. Sometimes I get very lonely, I start thinking of a million and one things I can do with a man. I want to have a man in my life that I can call my own..." I lament resignedly as my eyes glistened and a tear slithered down to my cheek. "Although this is not the way I planned it, but to be honest with you I can't even convince myself that I regret it. I know it's all wrong, so right now I don't need anybody to preach to me. I've asked God for forgiveness that night, then this happened to remind me that I won't get off that easy." I wipe my eyes with my thumb. "But I just need to move on."

"Hmm. My only fear is that Paul may decide you're looking for who to pin this on and he won't want to be the victim. How can you convince him one time got you pregnant? The last time I heard, he didn't want to be with you." Tara scrutinises me.

"Trust me, it was just that one time. It couldn't even have lasted more than five minutes in that Xterra." I stifle a pleasurable giggle. "You know I think sometimes God wants to laugh at us. I've been asking him why he would allow a child from this when he knows you need one more than I do at this time of our lives."

Tara shuts her eyes and I wonder what is going through that head of hers. "Have you told Paul then? What did he say?"

I shake my head and look at her blankly. "No, Paul is

engaged. He told me so that night."

"He's engaged? Daisy…"

I raise my left hand to cut her short. "I know, I know, but it's too late to start telling me how stupid I am, I already told myself a few times. He didn't hide that fact from me, he even told me her name but I can't remember it now. I don't want to be the one to cause a break-up in anyone's relationship just because I don't have one. I am taking full responsibility for my stupidity. I can't be responsible for causing another woman grief. I don't intend to tell Paul." I shake my head. "And I don't intend to find out what his reaction will be. It's my cross and I have to stop making a fool of myself at some point."

Tara exhales, goes back to her seat and reaches for another glass of coke. "Why should you bear the brunt alone? You want to bring up the child alone? What will you tell her when she grows up and asks about her father? Haven't you learnt anything from my own story?"

The picture of a smiley, gap-toothed beautiful girl with dainty multi-coloured ponytails emerges in front of me, but I shut it out. "I don't want Paul to abandon his fiancée and marry me out of pity. I'm going to get rid of it." I say curtly.

"What!" Tara springs up, spilling some coke on her trousers. "*Lailai,* you won't do that! Are you out of your mind?"

"I'm not asking for your permission." I turn my face away but behind that defiance is a struggle to listen to the voice of God and of reason. My affliction of guiltiness makes me feel very reluctant these days.

"Daisy, you can't do that. We're talking about a life here. Even if Paul doesn't want her, that girl has a right to live. Do you know how many women out there looking for what you have? If you don't know of any, at least you have an idea of how much I want a child of my own. I wish I could trade places with you, but that can't happen. Please don't do something you'll live to regret. You're the one always preaching to us, what do you think God feels about that? Or have you shown him the way out? You can't do that. I feel inadequate preaching to you, but you know what I'm saying is the truth."

"It looks like you have a name for her already. God should have given her to you then." I snicker. "Anyway as far as God is concerned, I don't think having an abortion makes any difference to him than committing fornication, so let me add to the list of sins I'm going to be asking forgiveness for. That will be better than living with the shame of everyone fluttering their tongues at me. Then the pastor will use me as a topic for his sermon and announce that Deacon Daisy has been suspended for having sex outside marriage." My tears stream down now and I hiccup. "You know how all those married women look at you in church, as if the only reason you can't get a husband is because you have been more wayward than them. Some of them behave as if you want to snatch their husbands anytime you open your mouth to talk to them. Meanwhile, only God knows what every one of them did while they were single. No Tara, it's too much for me to face." I shake my head. "And what will I tell the man that finally decides he won't mind marrying me? It's tough enough without a child. How many men do you think will want me with one born outside marriage?"

"Hmm." Tara exhales from the depth of her belly and reclines in her seat. I am sure the first thing that comes to her mind is to tell me I should have thought of all these before frolicking with Paul. "I know what you mean. My mother and I had our fair share of backbiting and side talks from family and friends who only fell short of calling her a slut." She pushes herself forward to look squarely into my teary eyes once again. "I want you to listen to me carefully. No matter what decision you take, it's not going to be easy either way. But I will urge you to do the right thing that the God you preach expects of you and not because you're afraid of what people will think of you. You know part of my story and some of the challenges I've had to contend with. What I've never shared with anyone, except my husband is that I had one abortion, and probably that abortion was one too many." I raise my head and purr quietly as I entwine my hands over my stomach. Tara nods and continues. "Yes, that is one regret I'm living with as long as I've been trying to have a child of my own. For me, I don't understand how I could have deliberately done something wrong, then ask God to forgive me, and even if he does, I still have to live with myself. Can you live with yourself if this is the only daughter you can ever have? I don't know why I've been saying daughter except that I can already see her alive. But she needs you to help her live. That's what my mother would have said."

I have managed to stop the sobs and I let out a deep breath. "Hmm, just a few minutes of ecstasy and ..." I swallow. "It's tough."

"You don't have to do anything in a rush. Just remember that there are no guarantees in life. There are some consequences that are reversible and some that aren't. Whatever you choose will come with its own consequences, but knowing that you did the right thing can make the difference between sadness and joy. At times the one gift you have currently may be the only one you'll ever get and how you handle it will determine what else life throws at you." She clasps her hands in mine with a smile of relief. "And my dear sister, no matter what you decide, I'm here for you, without consent or condemnation."

CHAPTER TWELVE

Tara

Sometimes, the resonating silence of the house impresses a kind of bleakness in me that I wonder if it is worth it living in a big house simply because we can afford it. It is just Tokunbo and I in the main house since Maria also stays in the boys' quarter. There have been months on end that I would not enter any of the other three rooms upstairs or the guest room downstairs, save for the infrequent reference to the library books or the laptop in the room. Worse still is the fact that the streets are often quiet and empty, except the eccentric blaring of horns, which happens maybe twice or thrice a year. I grew up in a boisterous house on a rowdy street where mosques, churches, *okada* riders, *danfo* drivers and street DJs connived in competition with their loudspeakers to create a symphony of dissonance.

Tokunbo was living in a two-bedroom apartment at Ikoyi when I met him. As soon as we started making wedding plans, he began talking about moving into a more spacious place that would be convenient for a big family, understating the fact that his luxurious flat was a great advancement from living at my mother's almost century old flat.

When he took me to see our wedding present at Lekki Phase One, I felt angelic forces lifting me up to a spine-tingling mountain, where I floated like one of them looking at the whole world beneath, as if it belonged to me. I thought about Esther in the bible, who was segued from downtrodden Mordecai's household to the king's palace and I thought about Cinderella who was rescued from her oppressive stepfamily to become a fairy tale queen. Walking in and out of doors of the massive five-bedroom house that would be my home, I thought about how FG's arrogant mother could never have imagined me outgrowing my wretchedness to be fit enough for her son and it made me appreciate Tokunbo much more for turning my life around.

I started decorating the house shortly before we got married and the euphoria of moving into a big house in a posh area was so liberatingly consuming I did not notice that I hardly met anyone on the streets or that there were a lot of unoccupied plots. Maybe because environmental peace had been alien to me for a very long time, I initially embraced the tranquillity of the environs, the freshness in the atmosphere and the novelty of dwelling in a plush, newly built house close to the sea. Now, living all alone with Tokunbo often reminds me that it would not be so quiet if we had children capering about the house. Switching on the TV every morning even when no one is watching is one of the ways we have devised to have some semblance of life in the house.

When he came back yesterday evening, he was in high spirits despite being tired from his trip to Spain. He was ecstatic about the success of his business meeting because he finally got to visit the manufacturing site of the company he from which he was poaching the sole distributorship of washing machines in Nigeria. That is a giant leap and a new market for him. He had called me from the airport to meet him at Ikoyi Club for us to celebrate, but I tactfully declined. I knew his friends would likely be around and I really did not feel like facing Kunle with any guilty feeling. I suggested Jade Palace instead and unusually, he agreed. But by the time I got to 1004, I blamed myself after driving into gridlock traffic. We both agreed it was best I returned home.

My bare feet joyfully embrace the cold of the marble floor as I walk gently down the stairs to the living room; simple pleasures of life. The couple in the big frame on the console smile happily at me. We should have changed that picture a long time ago, but there has been nothing to replace it with. Tokunbo would not agree to another studio shoot without an addition to the family, and that does not seem to be happening soon based on the IVF result two months ago. His ringing phone shrieks into the silence as I make my way to the kitchen to ensure food is ready on time. Having an occasional breakfast together on Saturdays is one of the few rituals we still manage to observe and after last night, I should top it up with a satisfying breakfast.

Maria is at the marble worktop, peeling potatoes. "Good morning ma." She curtsies.

My phone rings and I wave to Maria in response, picking up my mum's call. "Hello mummy, good morning." I go back to the living room.

"How are you and your husband? You still haven't gotten back to me about meeting your father."

"My father? You're still on this issue. Let's be clear about two things here. First I don't have any intention of meeting him and second, please don't refer to him as my father because he is not."

"I'm sure you know you didn't drop from heaven. I don't want to force you and I'm hoping you'll to make the right decision. Just think about it. In fact, don't think about it, pray, just pray and seek God's face. If you think…"

"It's too early in the morning for this, please. Don't you want my peace of mind? I don't want to see him. Is that why you're calling?" I leave no space for her response. "Anyway, I hope you're okay."

"He's travelling next month and I wouldn't want you to miss him." Her tone is subdued.

"Good luck to him. I will try to see you next week." Without waiting for a response, I press the red button. What is wrong with this woman? I hiss and go back to the kitchen to check the cake in the oven; it still needs about ten minutes. I open the top cupboard looking to fish out a pack of green tea from the old browning packs. Life was much easier when I could simply trot down the road to an *aboki's* shop to buy a box of matches or a tin of milk at the very last minute. Now I have to buy provisions in packs and cartons; and every end of the year endure throwing away many of the processed foods that no one has touched for one straight year. I can imagine Maria takes most of them to her family members, but I never bother to ask her. "Make sure you split the eggs in two and fry one only half-done." Tokunbo is not keen on golden brown eggs like me.

"Yes ma."

With my tea in hand, I pick the neatly arranged newspapers Yisa left on the worktop and head for the living room to wait for Tokunbo to come downstairs. After placing my tea on the side stool by the three-seater, I pick the remote to switch on the TV, tuning it to CNN, which continues to run adverts. I start flipping through the newspaper pages with no expectation of anything interesting. What else can one do on a quiet Saturday morning with simply nothing to do? When I was working, the only thing I wanted to do over the weekend was sleep after going through a tedious week of work and traffic; but sleep is what I have been doing since I got booted out from my former office.

After the failed IVF and my father's sudden attempt at invading our lives, I lost the zeal to engage in any meaningful thought or action. If not for Daisy, who checks in to cheer me up with her regular banters, I would have slipped away from reality. Two days ago, when she called to tell me she has decided to have the baby and will need my support to go through with it, my body and soul gave me a reason to live and love again, eventually inducing me to bed with my husband yesterday.

Mama has gone to spend the weekend with Tokunbo's cousin, *Iya Ibeji*. Ebi called to remind me her birthday was on Monday, which gave me enough motivation to bake a red velvet cake; I am still trying to figure out how to decorate it. I should have thought about the design before baking with a twelve inch tin. I am not one to constrain myself to pre-defined patterns, preferring to follow my guts and stretch my creativity. I always come out with something extraordinary even if I say so myself. Except, I just do not feel creative now.

Tokunbo comes down as I return with one of my cake decoration books. "You could have stayed back in bed." I smile at his wink and his reference to last night. Even in my subconscious, it was a wonderful experience and I was grateful he had been receptive when I reached out to him. He looks good in the embroidered grey Kaftan and black leather slippers I got him for his last birthday, though I prefer to see him dress more casually in jeans that make him look younger.

Feeling flushed, I sip the last of my tea as I continue to flip through the book and adjust to make him comfortable beside me, handing him his newspapers. He smells fresh too.

He puts the newspapers back on the stool, collects the book from me and places it on the table. He cups my chin in his hand and looks me straight in the eyes. "Tara, I just want you to know that I appreciate you."

Is that it? My husband appreciates me. Why is it difficult for him to say he loves me like he used to do a very long time ago? I smile. "Thank you, I appreciate you too." How did life become this plain?

"Are you happy? Sometimes I don't know what to do with you. You've stopped talking to me."

Now, it is my fault that we hardly talk. "Don't you think I should be asking you that same question?"

"I don't know. I just want us to be happy, but you keep pushing me away. I don't like begging for sex, I want you back, the way you were, the way you were yesterday. You seem to be bottling up so many things and I don't know what to do if you keep pushing me away." I am always the one doing something to make us unhappy, never him. No matter how subtle he tries to make it sound, it usually comes back to the issue of sex or not having children. Maria is still in the kitchen and I go to shut the door, sensing that Tokunbo has more to say. He moves away from the three-seater and goes to sit on the loveseat, but he keeps quiet once I join him and I look intently at him raising my brows. He respires. "Can we adopt?"

My phone and my head start ringing at the same time; I ignore the phone. "What? God forbid!" I snap my fingers over my head. Adopt? Where did that come from?

"What do you mean by God forbid?" He seems to be genuinely surprised with his widening eyes almost popping out of his glasses. What does he expect, really?

"Adopt for what? Why should we adopt?"

"What do you mean? What's wrong with it?"

"How can you suggest that at this time? After all I've been through." He shakes his head. "Is that what you think of me, that I can't have my own children? We should go and pick up a child we don't know anything about? Tokunbo I'm not barren."

"I didn't say or imply you're barren. This is not about you or me. I just need us to move forward. I'd like to have children in this house, in our lives. Don't you feel the emptiness?" He stretches his right hand to gloss over the house, as if I am the one that asked him to build a big house. "I don't like how we are, and I'm tired of having sex only because you want to get pregnant."

Oh sure, I feel the emptiness and I hear that it is my fault all the time, but this dimension of going to adopt a child like it is another shopping expedition has never been in the picture. "Am I the only one trying to get pregnant? I thought we were in it together. I'm sorry, but I don't want to talk about this. I know I'll get pregnant again."

He exhales, shaking his head with eyes that are not looking anywhere. "Can you hear yourself? This is not the reaction I expected of you." He makes to get up, but changes his mind and lowers himself back on the seat. "How do you intend to get pregnant when we don't even have regular sex?"

I suppose yesterday does not count anymore now. "The last time I checked, it only takes one semen to get a woman pregnant." I say defiantly. If he wants to lay the blame on my doorstep again, he should have a rethink; he does not respond. The only audible sound is that of the humming generator. The silence seems to last forever as Tokunbo continues to stare ahead. After a couple of minutes, he gets up and heads for the cabinet by the dining table where he keeps his drinks. He rarely touches them, except when we are entertaining his drinking friends or when he is upset. He brings out a thick green bottle and calls out to Maria for a glass cup. After filling the glass, he sits at the dining table cupping his face in his hands. He downs two gulps and accompanies them with audible sighs. I go to lean on the dining table right in front of him and take his hand. "The doctor believes I can still have another IVF. Let's just wait it out."

He raises his eyes to look at mine. "Do you know what happens to you each time you've had that IVF? No, you don't." He tilts his head. "You become so focused on yourself, you don't even know what's going on around you. I don't want to tell you what you've done to me with those miscarriages, and just in case you didn't know, I don't find it amusing jerking off to extract sperm as if I'm some experimental tool? I don't want to turn to masturbation because I want to have children. You think it's just an ordinary exercise, but for me it's much more than that. And my dear, the way you're going, masturbating might be an attractive substitute to sex if we continue this once a month routine." Unlike me, Tokunbo has the irritating ability to keep his voice and face passive when he is most annoyed, so it takes a while for me to understand the import of what he is implying. He gets up and goes to pick the newspapers, suggesting the conversation is over.

"All of a sudden I'm to blame for all our woes." I yell out, with fury and tears welling up inside me. "Do you think it's easy for me either?"

"Well, it seems pretty easy for you to keep to your side of the bed every night. The only thing you haven't done is rebuild the Berlin Wall and I wouldn't put that beyond you." His eyes are still focused on the newspaper with indifference to me.

I ignore his sarcasm and retain all the calmness in me to put my thoughts together. "First, I think you should know that it takes two to tango, it would be nice if you could show some more interest and love towards me. Second, it's very insensitive of you to turn to that newspaper while we are talking." I pick up the cake book I was looking at and start flipping through. Two can play at the game. He drops the newspaper and comes to take the book from me. He gently draws me close to himself, places one hand on my shoulder and lifts up my chin to look into his eyes. The few times he has done this, I have felt like a foolish child being cajoled to do something right.

"My pretty sunshine, I love you so much it hurts me that we're going through all this. I don't know how to deal with it and I don't like not knowing what to do. I want us to be happy as a family, with or without children. But you've taken this too personal, it's breaking me to pieces. We need to do what's good for us, so that we'll still be together when the children come. Yes, I want children, but not at all costs." He sits me beside himself on the loveseat, clasping my hand in his. "Anytime I drive past that orphanage down the road, I wonder if we can't try to share that love with one deprived child and take our mind off things for a while. If we grow so far apart, I don't know how having a child will bring us back together, because then you'll start focusing on the child again."

The image of the orphanage's signpost flashes through my mind. I have actually thought about going in there to drop gifts, but never found the time to doing it. Now it is staring me in the face and Tokunbo is trying to make sure I never step foot in there. I let out all the breath I have been holding in. Even within his softness, I can sense the accusation in his voice, but I choose to focus on the real issue now. "I don't know what else to do beyond what I'm doing now." I eye him coldly. "But, if you're not that desperate for a child, why do you want one that you know is not ours?" What about those tales of people taking in *ogbanje* children into their homes and losing everything in the process? If I mention this, he will complain that it is because I have been watching too many home videos. "I'm sure I'll get pregnant if you let us try the IVF one last time. Talking about this right now is not helping me at all. I need your support." I take his hand. "Please." I stress.

He withdraws. Why is he acting stiff? "I'm sorry, I didn't know adoption would be a forbidden word with you. I thought if we had children in the house, you'd be more fulfilled and happier. We've been on this journey for a long time and there are many kids out there looking for someone to take care of them. I want children. Yes, and we've tried all that we can. Adopting has crossed my mind a few times and I thought I should mention it to you. Okay, maybe it's not the right time, but I didn't expect you to turn it into an argument." He is putting the blame on me again. "It doesn't mean I've given up on you. I never said you were barren, I just think..." He motions and trails off, but soon resumes. "I don't know what else to do Tara, I want to make love to my wife without feeling like a rapist or a greedy child begging for candies. I want a happy family."

"And you don't think I want us to be happy?"

"I didn't say that. Don't put words in my mouth. I've said what I want, why don't you say what you want?"

I groan. How else do I tell him I want him to court me, pet me, believe in me, encourage me and love me as he used to without sounding like I am whining like a little girl. "I just want you to love me again."

He turns to look at me like a bug he should mug. "Again? Have I ever stopped loving you? Even you must know how much I love you. What else do you want me to do? I do everything I can to make you comfortable."

"I need more than comfort, I need a friend."

He shakes his head. "I must be missing something here. You need a friend, and you keep turning your back on me." Before I can answer, Maria knocks softly on the door. Tokunbo gets up, too eagerly and opens the door for her to come in and set the table. "Do you want to eat now?" He looks at me after Maria leaves. That may just be the end of our discussion. How can he be settled to eat anything when we cannot even have a decent discussion and agree on issues? "Of course, you know I'm not using the dining." He returns to tune up the volume of the TV and sits on the sofa. This is just another one of his annoying habits, his subtle obstinacy at seemingly trivial things. Once again, I wonder why he bought the marble dining set when he would not be using it, except with visitors. I get his food and set it on a side stool. "Thanks."

* * *

Tokunbo

"Hey, where have you been?"

I turn around from the window to the sound of Big Sam's loud voice, abandoning my roaming thoughts about Tara's father's sudden incursion. I can't make sense of why the man should suddenly resurrect after all these years. To meet him or not to meet him is a question still hanging with my wife and despite her tough posture, I know there is something in her that craves a connection with her father; probably the reason she is refusing to talk about it.

"Big Sam, I have some architectural drawings on my desk to review, and I was going to come see you after. Where are you going with that?" I point to the big bottle in his left hand.

We shake hands and I take the chair beside him, facing him.

"I was hoping you'd pop in immediately you get my message. Anyhow, I'm happy to let you know we got the brief from Mesala Group." Big Sam's voice conveys victory and joy.

"Wow, you did? That's great news. Now I can uncross my stiff fingers." I gesticulate uncrossing my fingers.

"Yes, you can. Thanks for the intro, that company is a very big fish in our little pond now, and they'll force us to expand. Isn't that a good challenge? I really appreciate it man, you don't know what you've done for me." He clasps my hand and pats me on the shoulder.

"It's nothing really." To be sincere, it did not cost me anything. I was providing some updates to the group's chairman on their order, when he told me he desperately needed a reputable, small but aggressive law firm that would not be too busy to represent some of his companies. Mesala Group is indeed a big fish for Big Sam's firm. "So glad you got that."

He grins. "Sure, what are you waiting for? Get the cups, let's toast please. By the way, I've told Ebi, lunch is on us today, so we've ordered food and drinks for your staff as well."

I go to the door and ask Ebi for two wine glasses. "I hope I'm getting free lunch too." My phone starts ringing and I hurry back to the table to pick it up. Big Sam opens and pours the wine. It is the same unknown number that has called me severally in the past two hours without leaving any voice mail. I never pick up calls from random numbers, believing that if it is important enough they will leave a message for me to contact them; there are too many prowling timewasters and fraudulent people these days. This one seems persistent though, having called over ten times. I call out to Ebi and give her my phone to pick the call if the caller tries again. I raise my cup to Big Sam for a toast. "Here's to more big fishes and a bigger pond." The cold fruity taste of the wine against my throat is fulfilling.

"If you're up for it, we can go to the club later in the evening." Big Sam suggests. "It would be fun to celebrate with the boys."

I shake my head. "Maybe tomorrow. I want to surprise Tara by getting home early today, I'm hoping to take her out to dinner. It's been a while."

"Hmm, someone is feeling romantic now." Big Sam teases.

"Sir, it's a lady who says she's got a message from Zainab Mustafa, but she won't tell me her name." Ebi wields my phone in her hand and waits for an answer. "She will call again in five minutes."

"Zainab Mustafa?" Oh Zainab! My heart skips. Zainab is from a very distant past. What could be the problem? Why would she ask someone to call me? I collect the phone from Ebi and thank her, returning to my swivelling chair behind my desk. It takes great effort to follow Big Sam's feverish talk as I wait for the phone to ring.

"Hello." An animated voice booms back from the phone. She introduces herself as Ada and Zainab's best friend. Before I say another word, she goes on to say that Zainab was not aware of her plans to contact me, but I need to listen attentively. Listening to her, blobs of sweat gather on my brow and my finger instinctively goes in between my teeth. Big Sam gestures that he will come back, but I shake my head, asking him to stay as I slow down my pace around the room. Ada answers all the questions I throw at her to convince me her mission will work. I take a deep breath when I put down the phone and remove my glasses to wipe my face with a hankie.

"Everything alright?" Big Sam leans forward. "What's the problem boy?"

I fold my hands over my head, panting. "That girl just told me I have a fifteen year old son called Ameen."

"What do you mean by that? You believe her?"

"I don't know, but I don't think I doubt her. Or maybe I want it to be true. It kind of makes sense. I don't know if I believe her or not. Even if it's true, what can I do about it? Fifteen years? That's a long time. What do I tell Tara? Do you remember Zainab, my Hausa babe?" I rant on, leaving Big Sam to call to remembrance my long lost girlfriend. "This lady just told me Zainab was pregnant before we finally parted and she didn't tell me because she wasn't keen on returning to Nigeria or give up the boy. After having the baby, she came back but learnt I was getting married, so she left again and has never been back since. You know she was always playing cat and mouse with me. What am I going to do?"

"You don't need to work yourself up over what may be mere speculation. Where is she now?"

"She's in London, this friend of hers, Ada says she's in town for two weeks. She says Zainab is not aware she is contacting me, but she believes the boy deserves to know he has a living father and I deserve to know as well. Do you know what this means if it is true?" Big Sam shakes his head, frowning. I shake mine too, unsure whether the stirrings in my heart are of excitement or apprehension, or both "I also don't know. How do I tell Tara? She's my greatest concern. What should I do?"

"What you need to do is calm down and think this through. What if it's not true? Maybe they are desperately looking for a husband or just someone they can pin this on."

"How can you say that, don't you remember Zainab? She doesn't care about conforming to the societal expectations." I quieten a bit. "You know what I'm going to do? I'll go with this Ada to London and see if it's true."

"And if it is?" Big Sam's query is portentous.

"I don't know, but I'd rather find out the truth." I recall Tara's state of turmoil since she learnt her father came looking for her. "Every child deserves to know their father." I declare to Big Sam. I just hope I am not too late.

* * *

The traffic on the way home gives me time to reflect on the events of the past four hours. It is strange how something that was never part of your life can suddenly appear and become the most important item in your bucket as others pale to insignificance. Stranger is the fact that one can spend an entire lifetime chasing after what one already has. This is life! How could I have imagined when I woke up today that I would be someone's father without having to lift a finger? Without travelling to see Zainab, I already know that the boy is mine.

She was the only other girl I loved dearly, almost as much as Tara. However, there were some odds against us which neither of us was prepared to fight. She was a Muslim, I was a Christian; she wanted to live in the UK, I would not leave Nigeria; she loved to travel and see the world; I wanted a wife I could come back home to. One of the few educated and liberated Hausa girls I had ever met, she had a rich northern heritage and had her role cut out for her to join the family trading company after university. However, she defied her parents and went abroad to train as cabin crew after, which she joined British Airways. Now her friend tells me she has moved on to a property brokerage business.

Every time I asked her to marry me, she would tell me she had done enough to her parents already and did not want to be responsible for killing them by marrying a Yoruba Christian. We drifted in and out of our relationship several times and it was in the course of one of those drifts that I met Tara who also made it known she was not interested in me at the time.

"Sir, should I buy fuel now? The tank is almost on quarter."

Ola interjects my musing.

I lift my head. "No, just drive home."

When I gave Zainab an ultimatum on marriage, she simply disappeared. She arrived at my doorstep about six months later and I thought she had decided when she said she would spend the night but it became an emotional farewell tryst. I have not heard nor seen anything of her until today. God help me. True to her words, Ada sent me some pictures of Zainab and Ameen. Zainab looked exactly the same way she did when I last saw her: glamorous, bubbly and so beautiful. When I saw Ameen, I did not need to be told that he is indeed my son; he has my chubby cheeks, dark skin and robust body. He even has an afro cut. I hope the boy will learn to forgive me and accept me as his father. What has she told him about me all this while? Will he think I abandoned him? I have a lot to catch up with and I hope it is easy for us. Thankfully, Ebi was able to get a ticket for Monday. What will I tell Tara now? How will I tell her without breaking her heart? I have never been so confused in my life. All I know is that I am happy and afraid at the same time.

I hurry out of the car as soon as Ola finished parking, barely giving Yisa a wave as he tries to make incoherent conversation. Tara and Maria are in the kitchen. "Tara…."

"Hey, you're home early today." She mocks, unknowingly making me uneasy. "I haven't made dinner. I hope you can wait. I just finished making Mama's pap." We both go into the living room and she puts Mama's food tray on the dining table. "Are you still going out or you're staying?"

Mama comes out of her room as Tara finishes off her question. "Is that the question you should ask your husband? Are you not happy to see him? My dear, welcome."

I stoop to greet her. "*Ekule* ma." I go to my favourite sofa in front of the TV to start my daily motions of undressing.

Tara comes to join me, ignoring Mama. "That's your pap and *akara* on the table, don't let it get cold."

"Thank you, *Iyawo*. Actually, I have two more chapters to read from the Psalms. I came out because I heard you come in." She goes back into her room.

"Maria." Tara calls out. "Come and take these shoes upstairs." She puts the shoes by the staircase for Maria and comes back to sit beside me. "And bring the slippers. *Omo Mama*, what do you want for dinner?" She teases. I look at her blankly. The only thing I want for dinner is to tell her about Zainab and Ameen, but I cannot do that until I have seen the boy and know Zainab's plans. It is so complicated. "How was your day at work? Aren't you hungry?"

I am hungry, yet without any appetite for food right now. "I have to travel upper week. My contact said he was able to get an appointment with a new company. They've been looking for a reputable company to partner with in West Africa and he doesn't want me to miss the opportunity? So is it okay if I go on Monday, first flight, please?" I blurt out before my concocted story gets disjointed.

"You're asking me if it's okay for you to travel. Are you serious?" She gives me a strange look, opening her hands in confusion.

"It's okay, I just wanted you to know." My finger goes in between my teeth. I love my wife.

CHAPTER THIRTEEN

Tokunbo

"Today, we are dedicating ten babies and for the first time, we have two sets of triplets. Praise God." The congregation goes agog with different versions of halleluyah as the drummers beat out loud rhythm on their array of drums. The pastor shifts into a prayerful mode. "I just want to prophesy that if you've been looking up to God for the fruit of the womb, all you need to do is to hold on to his words. He never fails and he's never late. He knows what's best for you and he will come through for you."

An echo of amen oozes out from every angle. Tara clasps her hands with her eyes shut. I can almost bet that she is praying. How many times have we heard those words? Yet, year after year, we are here to watch other people dance to the altar with their children. And we are supposed to be happy for them. I don't know if it is natural to feel envious of those people, but that is what I feel. Envious and forgotten by God!

How are these people better than us? Yes, that sounds like self-righteousness, but I cannot lie to myself about how I feel. The choir leader hails people to dance as the instruments boom praise rhythms to set people in the mood.

The pastor raises his hand to signal the instruments to silence. "If you are trusting God for yours to happen, I encourage you to join them in celebrating. Others will celebrate with you in due course."

"Amen." The church booms. More people get up.

Tara looks at me. "Maybe I should go." I say nothing; we must have answered that call over a hundred times. She turns to ask her friend sitting on her other side for encouragement. Apparently, the answer is a no, because they remain seated.

Mama tugs at my hand. "Didn't you hear the pastor?" I ignore her.

The pastor starts calling out the names of the new parents. Then he calls a family that we know. "The family of Victor and Laraba Cole."

Tara and I look at each other with widened eyes and look back simultaneously to fish out Victor and Laraba at their usual seating spot. We are not the only ones turning back to look in their direction. Anyone who saw Laraba about three months ago like we did will also wonder how she hid her pregnancy. Indeed, she is gorgeously dressed, beaming in regal colours and carrying a baby with Victor smiling by her side. They dance towards the altar, followed by Victor's mother. People around them troop out to join as well. I nudge Tara now, and she and her friend join Laraba and the dancing congregation.

The last time we saw the Coles was at the car park, and Laraba did not look even one month pregnant talk less of delivering a baby just three months after. Two months, if I calculate that babies are usually brought to church for dedication about one month after delivery. Can I not tell a pregnant woman? "That lady wasn't pregnant a few months ago." I can't resist getting it off my chest to Mama.

"How can that be? She can't steal a child and bring the child to church. Well, who knows? Anything can happen these days. Were you looking at her stomach?"

"Do I need to stare at someone who is seven months pregnant? At that stage, will it not be obvious?"

She nods sarcastically and sniffs. "What do you know about pregnancy?" Why did I bother mentioning it to her? What did I expect from her? "You people should do what you have to do and let the children come. The pastor has prayed, go and do your own part."

No need trying to have this discussion with her, so I keep mute as people start coming back to their seats. Another pastor goes to the pulpit to preach after the children's dedication. Yet throughout the service, my mind keeps straying away to all the possibilities around the Cole's childbirth.

* * *

"Anytime I come here, I never stop wondering where all these people come from. And why they come." Mama starts as we make our way through the multitude trooping out of the church at the same time. Tara lags behind, staying back to chat with some of her friends. I stay close to Mama as much as possible to guide her and more importantly, to make sure nobody falls foul of her in any way. In a congregation of over one thousand, Mama expects that people should notice she is elderly and make room for her despite the throng of people moving in and out through the same gate. The last time a lady mistakenly stepped on her while trying to adjust her flowing *ankara* skirt, Mama almost caused a scene. She succeeded in creating minor human traffic as the lady apologised profusely in embarrassment after Mama advised her that the house of God was not for only fashion. "If half of these people are righteous, we won't have so many problems in Nigeria. But I think church has become a place of social gathering for your generation."

We step out into the road and start moving towards the car park. "You heard the pastor say church isn't for the righteous." I feel like telling her that anyone who knows about Nigeria's problems will trace it to her generation.

"Isn't that the problem, why should the pastor say something like that from the pulpit? Is that not encouraging people to continue in their evil ways?" She presses on. I would have been surprised if she did not come up with some negative comments about something, or nothing for that matter. I pause to greet a couple and Mama goes on ahead of me instead of waiting. I quickly excuse myself to catch up with her after pointing the couple to Tara, who I believe is enjoying her peace. "Those ones couldn't greet me, *abi*." She complains about the couple.

"They would have greeted you if they knew you."

"They didn't see the resemblance between us with you beside me?" Another couple I know stop to greet me before I am able to think of a response for her. She stops this time and looks back into the crowd coming behind us. "Are we leaving Tara behind or we have to wait for her? Because she's pretending that we didn't come together?" I follow her line of vision and catch Tara afar off, pointing in our direction while talking to one woman. Without Mama, we already have a trend of Tara trailing behind me when service ends because she always has more people to talk to, though she is always in time for me to pick her up from the gate.

"She will reach us before we leave the car park. Our drive

out will take some time." On the average, we spend between five to fifteen minutes tailing cars to be able to exit the car park. I definitely find the fortitude of the volunteer traffic wardens commendable as they deal with all kinds of temperaments every Sunday, rain or sunshine. Sometimes the intolerance exhibited at the car park makes me wonder what people would be like if it was not a church car park. Maybe Mama is right; if we cannot find good people in the church, what is the hope for the larger society?

Tara gets to the car just before the traffic warden asks me to move, after about ten minutes behind the queue of cars. She removes her high sandals as soon as she gets into the car and changes to flat slippers. "Mama, *epele* o." She turns to look back at Mama. "Are you okay? I hope the cake is not disturbing you or should I move it to the front?" She looks affectionately at the cake on the back seat as I drive the car along.

Mama adjusts her posture to face Tara. "There's nothing wrong with me. Why shouldn't I be okay?" Her tone is sarcastic. "Are you going back home with this cake or the person you brought it for didn't come to church?"

"Oh no." Tara turns to me. "I've sent Flora a text and she has confirmed they are home."

"That's the answer to my question?"

"No, yes, Mama, we're going to Flora's house with the cake." Tara insisted on baking a cake for Flora when I told her we might go after church. It has become her custom to take cakes or cookies anytime we are going to visit friends or for occasions. No matter how tired she claims to be, she always has that extra strength to put some dough together.

"Which Flora? Should you be encouraging her to eat cake? By the way, when did you decide that you're going to see her today?"

Tara keeps a straight face and looks ahead. "Didn't you

say you wanted to see their baby?" I pick up from Tara.

"Yes." Mama enunciates.

"And we decided to go today after church."

"Who do you mean by we? If I say I want to go and see the baby, don't you think you should ask me when I want to go?"

Tara rubs her right temple, remaining quiet. "But ma, do you have any other plan? I'm sorry I didn't tell you, I already told Mike we'll be coming when you said you wanted to go."

"So, because you think I don't have any plan, you can take me all over Lagos without my consent. Don't you think at my age I should know where I am going? When I talk, you will say I talk too much. If I had my own grandchildren from you to play with, won't I be busy? And will I even remember that Flora has a baby? Yet, you think it's your right to tell me that I don't have any other plan."

I swallow hard, trying to think of what could be appropriate to say at this time. From the corner of my eye, I see Tara turning her head totally towards the window and nodding her head slowly as if she is dancing and not part of the conversation in the car. I did not expect Mama to make an issue out of this at all. "Mama, do you think about these things before you say them or don't you think what you've just said is spiteful?" I ask in as unflappable a voice as I can muster.

"Which one is spiteful? That I don't have my own grandchildren or that you went above your right. Tara *ngbo*?"

"Okay, I'm sorry." I try to rescue the situation.

"*Eyin lemo*. You can take me home and go for your visit, I'll arrange my own visit another time. If I knew you planned to go and see the baby today, I would have prepared myself."

Tara turns her head slightly. "Ma, we're sorry, but you're okay to go like this. Visiting Mike and Flora is like visiting family." She did not have to say anything, but she knows fully well that if she keeps quiet for longer, my mother will find something to say about that.

"Thank you for reminding me. It's surprising that you want to go because of me, yet I'm the last person to know. And only because I reminded you about your cake. So if not for the cake you would have driven me there without my knowledge. Sorry I can't go and visit a baby with empty hands." She yawns as she turns her face back to the road. It never ceases to amaze me how my extremely reserved father was able to cope with this woman who manages to make a mountain out of every small stone. I manoeuvre the car onto the expressway. Either way, Mike's house is on the way home.

* * *

Tara's phone rings. She delves into her bag and starts fishing out some items before the phone eventually comes to the surface. She smiles into the phone. "Hello ... yes ... Oh, I remember ... I'm fine thank you." She glances at me, but I keep my face straight on the road. "No, I haven't heard anything... Oh, okay, thanks... Yes." Her voice takes on a sudden stiffness and impatience as if the caller changed personality. "No, don't worry, I'll give her a call myself ... No, no, that won't be necessary... Yes ... No ... Okay, thanks... Yes, you too." She looks at the phone, hisses and tosses it back into her bag.

We are on the way to Mike's house, after dropping Mama off at home since she stuck to her decision not to come with us. When I parked in front of the house for her to alight, she acted surprised and continued to mumble until she got off to get into the house, brushing Maria aside. I wonder what she expected.

"You know if you can just find a pocket in your bag to keep

your phone it will be easier for you to retrieve it any time it rings." I remind her, yet again.

"You're right, I'll do that." She does not attempt to re-arrange her bag.

"You won't do it now?" I shake my head, driving on. How many times have we had this conversation and I always get the feeling she would rather tell me it is none of my business how she arranges her bag?

"Alright, you don't have to make an issue of that."

"Sorry." The traffic moves a little, but I pause to let in the car hooting beside me. I wonder how I should ask her the question without upsetting her, since she has not referred to it. I turn towards her, but she turns her face the other way, looking out of the window. "That call, what was it about? I hope everything is all right."

She hisses. "It's nothing important, it's someone trying to be funny."

"Who, anyone I know? You sounded a bit uptight." I reach for her hand to assure her that I am asking because I care.

"It's one guy I met at Prime Bank, when I went for the interview. I don't know why he would call me on a Sunday if he is not trying to be mischievous. He asked if the bank has called me and if I wanted him to ask HR on my behalf. I told him not to worry."

A bunch of crawlies releases themselves all over my body with different ideas crowding my head about why this person would really call my wife. Why should he call her? How did he get her number? I swallow hard to keep the bile and my voice from rising. "Who is he and how did he get your number. Why should he call you if he's not the one hiring you?"

"It's nothing really. He was part of the interview panel. I've almost forgotten about him until he called now. I know he was kind of staring at me strangely that day. But I wouldn't take it to heart."

Her hand slips out of mine as beads of sweat break out from it. "So, he's not satisfied with just staring, he has to call you. Why did he call? You never even mentioned anything about him after your interview."

She pats my hand, which is still sweating profusely. "I should start reporting everyone I suspect of staring at me? I already told you what he said. He said he was calling to find out if I've heard from the bank. Truly, I didn't think anything of him beyond the interview, so it wasn't important to mention."

"He surely considered it important enough to call. You can't be so naïve as to tell me you don't know why he's calling you. Doesn't he know you're married?" All the fluid in my body is heating up and oozing out into the car, it is becoming uncomfortable in spite of the air-conditioning.

"Tokunbo, I don't know what he's up to beyond the fact that he called to find out if I've gotten my employment letter from their HR. Maybe he has it in his head to make a pass at me, but I can't help that. I can only tell you nothing is going to come out of it."

"So what if he's the one you're going to be reporting to? You said he was at the interview panel. What if you have to work with him?"

"We'll cross that bridge when we get there, but I think the world has moved beyond all that. What's the worst thing he can do, sack me?"

"You seem not to know how desperate these lecherous men can get. If he can sack you, why go and work there in the first place? You haven't gotten in and he's already pitching. What's going to happen when you start working with him?"

"This is not the first time a man will make a pass at me and I can assure you, I can handle it. Sometimes, I think you should be thrilled that other men find your wife attractive. Doesn't that confirm that you made a fantastic choice and taking good care of me?" She smiles at me, trying to inject some humour, but it is not funny to me at all.

"Really, you need to reconsider starting your own business. This is one of the reasons I don't fancy this bank idea at all and you know it."

Defiance rings from her voice. "What are you trying to say?"

I make the last turn into Mike's street. This was supposed to be a lovely Sunday afternoon with my wife, but that call has just about invaded my peace. Damn that man and whatever fascination he has with Tara. I hate it when she talks to me in that tone. "I'm not trying. I'm telling you I don't want you to work with this bank or any other bank for that matter. Look for something else to do that …"

"Don't even bother." She cuts in. "I shouldn't work because you think one stupid man somewhere can have his way with me? Is that how much confidence you have in your wife?"

"Definitely, you know I trust you." I reach for her hand, but she flinches. "Going to work with a man like that places you in a vulnerable position and I don't want to nurse the idea of someone wishing my wife was his girlfriend." I bring the car to a stop and turn to face her squarely.

She matches my stare and nods. "Right. Thank you for the trust." She turns immediately to open the door manually without waiting for me.

"Is there anything you want me to help you with?"

She pauses and leans into the back. "I'll manage. Unless you want to carry the cake." I am wise enough now to know there is no way I can carry the cake to her satisfaction. She is overly protective of her creations, but I keep that thought to myself as she picks up the cake with both hands. I pick her bag from the passenger's seat before joining her. She balances the cake in one hand and stretches her left hand to collect her heavy bag, which I carefully place on her shoulder. I slow down my pace to walk beside her. There are days we simply cannot carry on a reasonable conversation and this might become one of them. There has been Mama and her harangue for one, then the man who called a married woman on a Sunday afternoon. I wish I could retrieve his name from Tara and make an official report against him, but I know she will kick against that seriously.

I near the gate with Tara closely behind. Flora is by the door of her Toyota Corolla parked under the canopy. She calls the gateman to open the gate when she sees us and the lanky dark-skinned man with tribal marks all over his face like the impression of two sets of sharp claws at work, emerges from the gatehouse. He has a natural smile, which unavoidably includes the display of a brownish set of teeth, likely occasioned by an addictive consumption of *goro* or a lack of dental hygiene. He greets us with a cheerful diffidence and a glint of his chipping incisors.

The rate at which Flora bloomed out just one year after her marriage made it seem like she went to one of those fattening rooms in Akwa Ibom. She cuts the image of the settled homemaker with no cares in the world; light-skinned, hairy, average height, chubby cheeks and an aura of energetic assertiveness. She is casually dressed in *ankara* skirt and blouse, with flat flip-flops. With her natural aptitude for volubility, she comes towards us as we enter the granite-paved driveway to the elegant clay brown duplex.

"Hey my people, *how una dey*? Finally, you've arrived. I thought you weren't coming anymore. Tara, you won't kill me with these cakes, yet you won't eat half of it. The last one you brought for the thanksgiving is still in the fridge and you know I'm trying to get back to shape. If only I could catch up with you, I would have achieved something." She hugs me briefly. "Godfather, Amaka won't have forgiven you if you didn't come today again."

I smile. That is her tacit way of reminding me of my sin of not attending the thanksgiving party. "I will explain to her why I couldn't make the last time." When Flora was visibly pregnant and told Tara she was making us godparents, she whined to me that she suspected Flora was doing it out of pity, but she stepped into the role quite happily as the delivery date approached.

Tara warms up to her and hands over the cake to her outstretched hands with a smile. "Don't worry, this cake won't add much to you, it's carrot and almond. And it's for the children, so you can resist the temptation by restraining your hand."

"It's beautiful, I wish I could be this creative, but you know me." Flora shakes her head. Even though the cake is un-iced, topping it with some smarties makes it colourful. "Toks, my friend has been taking care of you. This stomach..." She chuckles without fully expressing her thoughts on my emerging potbelly. I grin self-consciously, although Mike and I seem to be on the same page with that. As if reading my mind, Flora goes on about the stomach issue while leading us into the marble-floored doorway. "I don't know if you men are trying to compete with Big Sam, but I've told Mike if that thing gets bigger than that, he has to substitute drinking with working out at the gym. Two of us can't be going about with pot bellies." One thing about her is that she can take a joke on herself as much as she can dish it. "Tara, we need to keep reminding them that there's also a gym at the club. By the way where's Mama, you said she'll come to see Amaka today."

"She changed her mind about coming out today. There was a bit of traffic jam on our way back from church caused by a soldier and a policeman fighting at Yaba. It will probably be on the news tonight, but then again, maybe not." I shrug, once again relieving the previous incident of the police and army clashing at Ojuelegba. It was yet another inglorious display of lawlessness by supposed law enforcement agents when the soldiers turned Ojuelegba into a battlefield against the police to the extent of setting buildings in the police barracks on fire. In a normal society, that should have been a source of national shame; but in Nigeria, some individuals and institutions live above the law. Till this day, I am not aware of any soldier or policeman charged with arson.

Tara picks the three-seater leather sofa and I join her there, she springs up almost immediately and goes to the baby's cot by the dining table. I follow suit when she beckons and we both peep in to see Amaka's peaceful smiley face. Tara holds her hand and pats it tenderly. I am almost sure she is saying a prayer to remind God about our own baby. That is what she does when she has an opportunity with new babies.

"Why did you go to Yaba?" Flora wonders. The natural route should have been the Third Mainland bridge.

"Oh, Mama said she wanted to see if the new Tejuosho Market has been completed." Tara winks discreetly at Flora.

"Toks, Toks." Mike cheers, descending the stairs, his chubby face filled with the outline of a smile. He is casually dressed in a polo shirt and shorts with flip-flops identical to Flora's. "Tara, how are you?"

We both get up to greet him, hugging him in turns. "I'm very fine, thank you. Happy Sunday." Tara answers cheerfully.

"Happy Sunday, how was church today?"

"Fun galore, you know today is thanksgiving." She enthuses. Flora takes the cake to the kitchen and yells out to announce she is bringing drinks for us.

"Look at you Tara, you're just *chopping* my brother's money.

My guy, well done." Mike pats me on the back before taking a seat.

"*Wetin I go do now*, it's because of her I go to work every day." I hold Tara's hand as I would a prized item. Her hand is cold and she unreceptively starts withdrawing it, but changes her mind. Flora comes in with the drinks, red wine for the boys and malt for the girls.

"Where are the twins?" Tara looks around.

"They've gone out with my sister and Amaka is sleeping now to make sure I don't sleep at night. I don't understand why she would rather sleep during the day and stay awake all night. Mike has moved to the spare room and left me to my destiny of sleepless nights. Sometimes I wish I had a nanny I could abandon her to and run away for some time, but she needs to be fed and I have to do vigil with her most times now." Flora laments.

"Good for you, I'm sure you were worse than that as a baby." Tara teases.

"Me? My mother said I was the most peaceful child anyone could pray for. I can't understand how some women are able to combine taking care of children with going to work." Flora shakes her head, making her way to a shelf to get Amaka's photo album. "I made special *banga* soup. Do you want pounded yam or *gari*?" She gives me the album.

"Pounded yam of course." With all her finesse, Flora is one of the remaining few who still pound yam with pestle and mortar, it amazes me. "Why would you ask me that question when you already know the answer? You know Mike's belly is not going down anytime soon if you've been feeding him with pounded yam."

Mike shakes his head. "Please don't be deceived, it's because you're visiting today. It's been a while she made pounded yam. Maybe you should come again tomorrow."

"Hmm, that 'a while' is last week." She brushes him aside. "Tara, you're in?"

"Definitely, but you know my portion." Tara confirms. Who can resist a taste of smooth traditionally-pounded yam?

Flora disappears into the kitchen. Mike looks at his phone after a beep. With his eyes still on the phone, a hiss from him catches our attention. He starts shaking his head and then chuckles. Still smiling, he narrates the mail he just read. One Hajia posing to be a relative of Gadhafi claims to have exclusive access to some millions of dollars left in one of the deceased leader's many accounts. She invited Mike to partner with her to move the money into his account until they can share it without a trace. The email ends with a request of Mike's full personal and bank details as an expression of interest.

We joke about the old antics scammers use to defraud people of their hard-earned money and how people's greed makes them prey to such plots. Tara recounts the experience of one of her former customers at the bank who acted on one of such mails from a CBN impostor and lost twenty thousand dollars in the process. We exchange views on how it would be difficult for the law enforcement agencies to hunt the criminals down without the right technology to match their activities. Mike asks Tara how she is getting on with the job market and she tells him she is still looking since she has not gotten any favourable response from the two interviews she has attended so far. He asks her why she is not considering going into private practice, so she can have control over her time. Her face turns my way briefly, then she responds to say that she will keep her options open.

"Toks, please I need you to give me a hand at the back, I want to get another cot for Amaka." Mike tugs my arm, heading towards the kitchen. "Madam, which one did you say I should bring?" He defers to Flora.

"What's wrong with that one?" Tara points at the cot in which Amaka sleeps. I wonder too. The last time we checked on her, the baby was sleeping peacefully without any problem in the light green carrycot with a doll tucked beside her; and Tara commented that the cot was beautiful with its rare cross shade of mint and lemon, whatever that meant.

"Don't you think it's boring? It looks very plain." Flora sits at the dining table close to Amaka. "It's in a Mothercare carton. My sister gave me a lovely pink one last week and I've been dying to use it." She winks at Tara as if there should be a conspiracy between them. Tara simply shakes her head.

"As bored as she is, one would expect her to get the cot herself." Mike pretends to whisper to me, but loud enough for everyone to hear. I get up from my seat and follow him through the side door to the one-room boy's quarter at the back; which Flora has apparently turned into a store, after their several failed attempts to get a live-in house help. According to Mike, the ones that have been lucky to pass the residential test never stayed beyond three months because Flora would not hesitate to wake them up in the middle of the night if she felt she had any need to be attended to. After the last maid left, she told Mike she would cope by herself, probably with an erroneous assumption that the non-residential cook and driver would lend a hand if she called them. However, the two of them mysteriously fell too sick to come to work for three days, after which Flora started whining Mike to get her another maid.

By some stroke of luck, Big Sam's mother in-law got one for her, who only agreed to work five days a week, so Flora makes sure Mike chips in his own bit into domestic affairs.

The room is an array of disorder like a hoarder's abode, with the only legroom limited to about two feet into the room.

Different items of no relationship, some in cartons, some unpacked and some gift-wrapped are strewn on top of one another without form; toys, kitchen utensils, books and suitcases. An intercom box is beside the door and anyone, except Mike of course, could easily trip on it when entering the room. Its cable has been stripped off the wall and lies on the floor in a disjointed circle.

"Don't you think it would be easier for you to arrange this place first?" I pick up an item and Mike picks another from the floor, placing them on others to create room to manoeuvre. "Where did all this stuff come from?" By my reckoning, they had a live-in help about a year ago.

He chuckles. "If I arrange it today, I can assure you that by your next visit it's going to be back this way, if not worse. Flora's definition of order revolves around someone else ensuring that it happens, not her." He hands me different items to set aside to help him locate his target cot. "Most of the recent ones are gifts from Amaka's christening."

"It seems you've overruled re-hiring a live-in maid."

"Would you recommend anyone to come and live with Flora?" He looks at me matter-of-factly.

"Well, you live with her and you're still here." I smile. Even at her best, Flora's pleasantness hovers on a borderline of cynicism.

"Yes, that's the cot, thank God." He reaches out for the Mothercare carton and in the process, knocks down some more. He hands the carton over to me and shakes his head. "I don't think it makes sense to leave this room like this. What do you think?"

"It's your call. You can use my services as long as the offer lasts." I put the carton outside.

He crouches to start unearthing some articles, pushing inwards little by little and I collect the ones he hands over to me, placing them somewhere behind me, so we can rearrange from the front. After a while, he lifts himself up to lock my eyes for a split second. "Have you considered IVF?"

"What?" I almost drop the small carton of porcelain. It has been over a year Mike and I made any allusion to the topic of trying for children.

"Well, I know it's not something we would usually talk about, but ..." Shifting his eyes now, he turns back to the pile. "One of my clients had a party last week for twin boys. They've been trying for twelve years and he said that was their third IVF. Who knows which one would be successful?"

"Hmm." I lament. "We've tried it, and I don't know really. I've been thinking about adopting and I thought it was a good idea, until I discussed it with Tara. She wouldn't even hear it. At the same time, I don't like the effect IVF has on her and our relationship. It runs her emotions haywire and she cries at any little thing. When it fails, she withdraws from everything except work. I'm always scared she'll run herself into a depression and sometimes, I think she blames herself for that. I'm asking myself if it's worth it."

"I can't blame her. Everyone's attention is usually on the wife when there are no children."

"But why should everyone's opinion bother her when I'm not complaining."

"Women take these things differently because they talk to each other. What about Mama, how does she take it?"

"Mama? Should anyone take my mother serious?" That would be like depending on a man who can't see to tell you how the sun sets. If she wasn't my mother, the pet name I would have given her since I became old enough is crapehanger. Mama complains about everything and everybody. Even Tara knows that by now. "If she wants to take it anyhow, let her produce the children herself. Seriously, I think we've done all a couple should do."

"Maybe one more time." He insists.

"When was the last time you masturbated?" I feel suddenly mischievous, not willing to take this IVF issue seriously. It is beginning to taste like a bitter bill.

Mike almost freezes midway as my question catches him. He straightens up and looks me straight in the eyes. His sudden awkwardness feels like I indeed caught him working on himself, but I stare back defiantly. "How does that help your wife conceive, Toks?"

I break into a laugh and Mike drops his shoulders in sheer relief as the tension eases out of the room. Still laughing, I pat him on the shoulder and shake my head at his embarrassing display of ignorance. "You mean you didn't know that's my only role in the IVF process?"

He smiles curiously. "Really? Wow! How?"

I nod. "What did you think?"

He shrugs and turns back to our task. "I've never given it much thought. You know, the word just flies around and you pick it up that that's what people need to do."

I wish I could tell him how awkward and distressing I have found it expressing sperm for the required tests and IVF procedures; but doing that would only make both of us uncomfortable again. One can argue I have only had to do it about five times, but it was not something I ever considered I would have to do and I hated it each time. Sure, Mike is my best friend, yet I cannot share my innermost thoughts with him. There are many things I wish I could tell him about my marriage and Tara.

However, beyond business, politics and football, every other thing we men discuss is superficial. The last time I heard any one complain about his wife was when the man was drunk, and then it was on TV. The only wives we ever talk about are those ones whose excesses are visible to the whole world. Should I tell him about Ameen? No, not yet.

CHAPTER FOURTEEN

Tara

Tokunbo's flight to London is around eleven o'clock, and he has to get to the airport at least two hours early. It is at times like this I envy people who live on the Mainland. Going to the airport from this side of town is fraught with so many traffic risks, so I hardly venture weekday-evening flights. Tokunbo is a victim of habits; any flight to London has to be with British Airways. Anytime he has a flight, he tries to schedule some meetings on the Mainland or go to the warehouse, but this trip seems different. He stayed home to pack his suitcase unlike his habit of getting everything ready three days ahead. He lingered around the house and made it seem like he would rather not go on the trip. When I asked him why he did not leave on time, his excuse was that he needed Ebi to complete some documents for him to take with him to London.

We have not talked much about the man my mother referred to as my father since she brought up the subject. I wanted to talk a bit about it yesterday after church and I mentioned that the man has returned to wherever he came from, according to my mother. She said he is likely coming back soon as if that should make any difference to me. After that, Tokunbo's two male cousins came in with their wives and children; the house went agog with activities thereafter. The twin boys – aged seven – of the older cousin were particularly restless and unruly, prancing and trampling all over; and knocking down food and drinks and any item that stood in their way of play. We all sat through their indolence without any word of admonition from either parent.

I have heard it said amongst family members that the children are spoilt rotten because it took their parents twelve years after marriage to have them. Witnessing their display of lawlessness and emotional blackmail against their parents made me wonder if the same will happen with my children when they are eventually born. I hoped not. Using the delay in conception to excuse instilling simple discipline is sheer irresponsibility. Even Mama's several threats of bringing out the cane was met with derisive laughter by the twins, so she turned to their parents and gave them a lesson in rearing godly children after all the children went to play at the back garden. Compared to the twins, the way the other three children of the younger cousin followed the adults' instructions to the letter made them look like compliant robots.

The twins' mother followed me to the kitchen to make small talk, but eventually got to the topic of asking about our attempt at having children. At least she was tactful enough to wait until Maria left the kitchen to join the children in the garden. This is the same reason I seldom attend functions with family or anyone that knows the history of my marriage. Sometimes, it makes me wonder if having children would solve all the problems couples have in their lives, otherwise why can people not look beyond the childless state and find something else to advise me on. No one bothers to ask me if I actually do want children, they just assume.

She went on to tell me about their several attempts to get her pregnant until she met a prophet who prayed with them for about two years. The prophet also warned them to take extreme care of the children and that is why it may appear she was over-indulgent sometimes. She said she knew the prophet was real because everything happened the way he foretold – twin boys. I was seething inside me, but smiled at her tales, gesticulating and interjecting appropriately with *hmms* and *haaas*, to assure her I was following. I should not compound my problems with a family gathering to discuss my disinterest in accepting an offer towards the big lottery. When she offered to take me to the prophet, I thanked her and told her I would discuss with Tokunbo, knowing fully well that even if I wanted to, he would not have a part in it. As if reading my mind, she confirmed that I may have to start the process alone, because her husband had also refused going with her initially, but with subtle persistence, she had won him over.

"You know these men are not so affected about these issues as much as we are. Some of them would even have a child with one stupid woman and you won't know, until ten years after." She eyed me and lifted her shoulders. Did she not know that I am one of such out-of-wedlock children? "Anyway, I'm sure you'll know how to convince your husband when the time comes. You just need to take this seriously." She rounded up. It is easy to assume someone is not serious simply because you have what they are striving to achieve.

When the visitors left and Mama resumed the topic of raising children, I was too physically and emotionally drained to bring up my own pressing issues with Tokunbo. Maybe, I should go and see my mother during the week. I have not really had much time to think structurally about my father. That trip back from my mother's had plagued me with a mix of inexplicable emotions. I wanted to hate him much more, yet I wanted him to tell me he loved me; to apologise for abandoning us at such a time; to tell me I would have been his favourite girl; to hold me; sit me on his lap; ruffle my hair; pat my back; and tell me I was a good girl. There are not many things I remember my father for, but sometimes life has a way of telling me my life is incomplete, like; once yearly on fathers' day or when my mother struggled to pay my school fees. There was the time the landlord's wife came to the house and called my mother *asewo* after accusing her of being too friendly with her husband, and so many other times when I caught uncles and aunties hushing up once my mother turned her back. Most of all was when big uncle walked me to the aisle on my wedding day. How can I ever forgive him?

Tokunbo comes out of the bathroom with the white towel tied loosely around his waist. When we newly got married, seeing him like this would have immediately turned me into a bundle of explosives, but now familiarity and the issues of life have detonated some of the oxytocic bombs. Yet, my body aches for him as my nipples stiffen at the sight of his broad hairy chest. I sit up and lean against the head of the bed.

"What are you smiling at?" His face puckers into a smile. I smiled? My face goes aglow with hot empty air. I am not sure if he is teasing or really wondering, but he turns to the dressing table to start creaming his body without waiting for an answer, backing me. "Has Ola come back?"

I wonder what he will say if I ask him to make love to me as I used to those early days, but the moment passes. "He's here, I heard him talking to Yisa."

"Good. Please don't forget to call Ebi about the party arrangement, although I've asked her to call you too. And when Ola comes back, remember to confirm from him if he dropped the envelope for Kunle. The documents are important." He picks a black pair of denim jeans from his wardrobe and starts putting them on.

"Yes sir." I mock.

He ignores my sarcasm. "I really wish I didn't have to travel today, I'm sorry. I promise I'll make up for it when I come back. There's a lot we need to talk about. I know you have many things to deal with right now. I wish you could come with me but…" He stops midway.

Really? Does a change of scene make people's problems vanish? "You told me about this trip two weeks ago, remember? Don't worry, I'll be fine I'm not going to do something stupid before you come back. You said you're back on Friday?"

"Definitely!" His voice is strained. "You know how to deal with Mama."

"I'll be fine." I reiterate as I yawn.

He is looking at me and tucking in his white striped shirt, briefly outlining the shape of his stomach. "Are you sure you won't need any money?"

Where is this sudden interest in my welfare coming from? "What do you think I'll need money for in four days that can't wait?" I cannot but wonder and a thought drops into my head. "Or do you think I'll want to give money to that man? Do you think that man came because he's desperate for money?"

"Which man, your father?" He asks in between putting on his blazer. "Believe me, he didn't cross my mind one bit." He comes to sit beside me on the bed. "Let me suggest something to you, which may not really make sense. Try not to think the worst of that man." He pauses. "Even if it's for your mum's sake."

"I hear you." I nod. "That's very easy for you to say because you can't imagine what I went through. What good is there for me to think about him?"

"That's the charitable thing for you to do."

"Oh, remind me."

"Tara, that's the right thing to do." He chuckles.

My face breathes and I smile reluctantly. "Thank you. I'll make sure not to forget."

"Good girl." He pats me on the back and nods. "And another thing you shouldn't forget is to call your mum to see how she's doing, I feel guilty that we haven't gone back to see her." I sigh and get up to follow him downstairs. He picks up his glasses, opens the door and goes on to the landing.

Downstairs, Maria's movement announces she is already in the kitchen. She comes into the living room. "Good morning sir, auntie good morning."

We both chorus. "Good morning."

She reaches for Tokunbo's small LV suitcase. "*I go carry am* sir." Tokunbo refuses as he always does.

A flicker of light seeps through Mama's door, an indication that she is awake. She knows Tokunbo is traveling today and I am sure she will expect him to bid her goodbye. Tokunbo glances at me, enquiring whether to peep in to see her or not. "Should I?"

I grimace, unsure. She is unpredictable. If she is asleep and he peeps, he may be greeted with what's-so-important-that-you-have-to-wake-me-up. If he does otherwise, she may accuse him of considering her unimportant. He looks at his watch, the same time I look at the wall clock; it is a few minutes to eleven. He tiptoes to her door, but stops and turns to head for the kitchen, shaking his head. I follow him to the car and watch them drive off without saying any other word, praying silently that Mama will not be waiting for me by the time I get back inside. She would not hesitate to make me the culprit. How do her daughters cope with her?

* * *

I try to keep a straight face once again as I drive past the Lilies Orphanage, even though I can still see the bold signs and the colourful drawings of children playing on the high wall. I cannot help but think about what is happening behind those gates. Since the day Tokunbo mentioned adoption, I have not been able to go past the orphanage without giving it a second thought. Now I see it every time and I wonder how those children ended up there. It must be a difficult life; abandoned, rejected, unloved with no hope of ever being able to meet either or both of their parents. With the benefit of having a mother to raise me, I still feel life has not been fair enough.

How do those children feel? Some of them may never get the opportunity to live in a proper home, know a mother or father's love or have a sense of belonging to a family. Hmm. How does it feel, waking up with strange people you do not have any blood relationship with every day of your life? You see new people come in and you see some leave. You wonder if it will ever be your turn and you envy them for going out to start a new life. How would it feel to be told to be at your best behaviour and be arraigned in line like stock on display for buyers to pick when adopters are scheduled to visit?

It may not be so bad for the babies, but how else will grown-up children get adopted? The only vivid account of orphanages I have is the one I read in Oliver Twist and my vague memory tells me it was not a good experience for the boy. I shake my head. No, it cannot ever feel good. I have never really taken any interest in how orphanages operate but I have heard mentioned that some orphanages have high standards and take care of the children even more than some families do. Yet, could it make up for the intimate touch of affection between a parent and a child; that simple look that communicates love without uttering a word; that harmless banter and struggle for trivial things between siblings? This God works in amazing ways sometimes.

I am here trying so hard to have at least one child and some women somewhere are having children they can afford to throw away. Even mad women on the streets are getting pregnant. How that happens I can never fathom. Why would God not just give each person what she needs per time? Why would you not just give one of them a home? Tokunbo's voice echoes as a whisper in my head despite being miles away from me. My phone rings.

"Hey girl, where are you?" Daisy's excited voice booms out. "I'm the one that usually keeps you waiting, and I've been here for over ten minutes. I'm getting frustrated."

"It's good to know how it feels on the other side." I laugh at her pretence. I am just round the corner but I try to rile her a little. "I'll be there in about ten minutes. I can't wait, I've got news for you."

"Please can you tell me now? You know I don't like suspense. "What's the gist?"

"Sorry girlfriend, you have to wait it out." I hang up to focus on getting a good parking space before she can protest. When Daisy called to say she had an urgent proposal for me, we agreed to meet at Terra Kulture to have lunch and probably catch a show if anything was going on, or at least wade through the arts gallery. She is seated at the left end corner of the food lounge and jumps up, almost knocking down her phone when I tap her shoulder. "What's so engrossing on that phone?"

"You! That wasn't up to five minutes."

I push her back to the seat. "Well, I'm here, so enjoy it." As if on cue, a waiter comes around to take our order. We make some small talk about her father' new found love, my mother-in-law and the news seeping in through our former colleagues. "What's been biting you? You can spew it all out on big sis now." I tease.

"I've got good news for you." She pauses for effect and I nudge her on. "I contacted Paul."

"Oh, you did?" I catch myself before getting overly excited for her. "So, so what did he say?"

She smiles with her face all beaming. "He was shocked and mad."

My enthusiasm drops. "I can't blame him."

"Mad that I didn't tell him as soon as I discovered." Daisy concludes, corking her head.

"Are you serious?"

She nods. "Yes. I was thrilled when he told me his fiancée called off their engagement shortly after we met. He said they'd been having issues but were sticking it out because of family pressures on him to get married. So don't blame me. And guess what? He wants me to consider if I want to get back together with him, but I made him understand it's not my intention to lure him into a relationship he doesn't want and he needs to go think about it properly and not do anything on the rebound." She stops for the waiter to set the food on the table. "He calls me almost every day now." Her smile is radiant.

"I'm happy you won't have his broken relationship on your conscience, but can you trust him not to bail again? You know how men can be. Well, I hope it works out well in the end, but like you said, don't rush into any decision you'll regret later. I don't know if it's right to get back together because of the baby although if we are honest, you guys were very good together."

"I know, I know, the other problem is he has to be serious

with God. I can't trade my faith for him now. Anyhow, that's not why I wanted us to meet. I've been doing some serious thinking."

"You, serious thinking?" I tease her with a chuckle. "Then I'm the first lady of Nigeria."

She ignores me. "I have an idea and I'm hoping we can work it out together." The enthusiasm searing out from her is infectious. She explains how it would be futile for her to continue looking for work in her pregnant state. She has come up with a business idea that she wants us to team up on. She is hoping to raise about fifteen million naira by selling her car and her shares, added to her pay-out by the bank. She does not know how much it will cost because she needs my consent to go ahead to start working on a business plan. "And that's one of the reasons I suggested coming here. This is a restaurant, but so much more. We can take inspiration from this and have a confectionary diner, but offering a different experience, depending on who we are catering to."

"Wow, this is a lot to take in."

"I know. You don't need to say anything now, just promise me you'll think about it. I'm not sure you get more fulfilment playing at law than at baking and you said Tokunbo wants you to start your own business." She raises her hand when I start to protest. "No, it's not about Tokunbo, but if you don't mind working with me, this might work. And you can sack me if you get tired of me. It's likely you have to put in more money than me, but I'm not scared, I trust you and I know we can do it. Together. You know I'm very creative, even if I say so myself." She winks. "I think, no, I know we can swing it."

She sounds very optimistic, but not me. At least not yet. Starting a business has crossed my mind randomly, but Tokunbo's insistence always made it an unattractive option; coupled with the security of having a regular income from work and the latent fear that he might abandon me for another woman who can give him a child. Besides, Prime Bank finally sent me a letter of employment.

I grumble. "You should have chosen a better time, I just received the provisional offer from Prime Bank this morning. They…"

"Hey, congrats. When were you going to tell me?"

"Yisa gave me the letter on my way to see you now. So this business idea of yours is …"

Daisy cuts in. "Confusing. I know. Don't say anything yet. It's good you have two options as of today. You're luckier than me because this is my only option right now." She tries to make light of it. "Go home and give it some serious thought. When do you have to get back to the bank?"

"Two weeks." I grunt. "You've surely given me something to think about for more than two weeks."

"I'll keep my fingers crossed. Let's go upstairs and catch some inspiration."

Terra Kulture is a dynamic entertainment centre. Its deceptively modest façade understates what lies inside the cultural hub that helps you stay in touch with the creative and artistic endowments of Nigeria. Apart from the food lounge that serves an array of well-presented Nigerian cuisine, it features an arts gallery, a bookstore, a crafts shop and a theatre. It continues to play host to the best of Nigerian Culture and its people. Sauntering through the gallery and gloating over beautiful collection of arts, several pictures of possibilities assail my mind about Daisy's idea. With each picture comes that affirmation that we can do it. If this is what Daisy intended, she has indeed succeeded in sowing the seed of constructive confusion in my mind. I suddenly turn around to the sound of a familiar voice behind me, instinctively pulling Daisy to a stop.

FG is talking through a painting with two other men. "FG?" I query with a raised eyebrow and a voice a tad louder than usual. Is this another co-incidence or what? He immediately excuses himself from the men.

"What are you ladies doing here?" I am not convinced at his surprised expression. He turns to Daisy with an outstretched arm. I'm Fola, I think we've met?"

"You're the one that bashed my friend's car, how could I forget?" She smiles with a harmless chirp and stretches her hand to FG. She can be quite mean when she wants to be. "Sorry, but that's the only way I can easily remember you."

"Delectable Daisy." He winks as if they have known each other for ages.

"I'm popular these days." She swings and moves aside for him to come between us, allowing him to face me.

His captivating eyes look into mine. "Are you buying anything?"

"Not really." My response is terse as I am still befuddled at this chance meeting. Again! Have we not been living on the same planet since?

"How is it going with you? One of my friends is travelling tomorrow and wants to get a Nigerian piece for his Brazilian girlfriend. You know we kind of share the same roots with Brazil."

Indeed, I have watched documentaries about some early Lagos settlers emigrating from Brazil. "Sure. By the way Prime Bank has given me an offer today." He probably knows since Amy is one of the signatories on the letter.

"Oh, congrats." I feel the weight of his arm around my shoulder as he hugs me. "It's well deserved. I learnt you dazzled them at the interview. "

I ignore the warmness flowing from his body to mine. "I don't know about dazzling them."

"Let me leave you ladies to enjoy your viewing. I shall take myself back to my friends." I am relieved to see him turn to leave, but he turns back after three steps. "Hey, can I invite you to a small party? Sorry, it's short notice, but…" He looks from Daisy to me and without waiting for an answer slides to his friends and comes back with two dainty red envelopes. Daisy, looking pleasantly bewildered, collects the small envelopes and hands me one. "It's the pre-launch of our new wine line – AfroGrand Merlot."

"Wow! This is beautiful. When is the party? What's pre-launch? She stares at the card without exactly reading.

FG humours her. "December fourteenth, Friday, Eko Hotel from six pm. The pre-launch is the wine tasting event for some selected high calibre potential clients. The public launch will be early next year, but that's for everybody. This is an exclusive one. I can send a car to pick you up."

"You will?" Her face lights up. "That's a new one for me." She is almost dancing but she catches herself. "Ha, you got me there. So that I don't arrive at your party looking harassed after jumping buses."

He grins. "Tara, you'll make it, won't you?" His voice is beseeching, but I am not as enthusiastic as Daisy; unlike her, I have Tokunbo to contend with. I know he does not usually object to my going out, but that was when I was working and had official or clients' events to attend.

"We'll see." I am unwilling to commit myself.

"Don't worry. We'll be there, even if I have to drag her. We do need some socialising now." Daisy winks at me.

"Is it okay if I call you to confirm the pick-up arrangement?" FG asks her. She looks at me with raised brows and I nod. She starts fishing in her bag and after a moment comes out with a business card.

"Of course, you know I don't work with the bank anymore,

but my number is still valid and I have your card too." She looks at me again. "On second thoughts, maybe you shouldn't bother, I'll come with Tara."

"Great, see you then. Congrats again, Tara. Enjoy yourselves ladies." With that, he whisks himself back to his friends and I can finally breathe properly.

"But this your guy is fine o." I roll my eyes and shift my gaze from her as she speaks. "All I know is that he's a fine boy. You can't deny you still find him attractive." She teases, poking me in the mid-section.

"Daisy! I think it's time to go." I pull her to the other side of the gallery towards the exit. Without saying any more word to FG or his friends, we make our way down the stairs.

"I miss VI, I must confess." Daisy looks like she would rather not leave just yet. As we get to the car park, we chat with an elderly lady we both knew from work. "I can't remember the last time I met a real human being in my area. One outing and I get an invite to an exclusive party. This is the life."

CHAPTER FIFTEEN

Tokunbo

When we were newly married, I looked forward to coming back home with much elation, because I could not have enough of Tara. She was highly intoxicating; pleasurable; and agreeable, so much that I could not stay away from her for over five days. No matter where I was in the world, I would find my way back home, even if only for a couple of days. I cannot now rationalise how those days passed us by. But they seem to be lost forever. I used to look forward to going home to the loving arms of my wife; now trepidation fills me at the prospect of having to tell her about Ameen.

For the first time in a long while, I was unable to shut my eyes for a minute on the seven hours flight to London. When we met at the airport, I graciously offered to upgrade Ada from Economy to Business Class, so she could sit beside me and fill me in on every detail she could about Ameen. By the time we got to London, I felt like I had always known the boy.

Expectedly Zainab was shocked to see me standing in front of her door beside Ada as early as seven in the morning. She was half-dressed and getting ready for work, but allowed us into her stylish compact flat all the same, grudgingly poised to listen to how Ada and I met. Surprisingly I still felt a stirring within me after all those years. Ada quickly apologised and explained that she acted with the best of intentions for Ameen.

Zainab was livid and accused Ada of treading where she had no business. Without saying a word to me, she thundered around the house and shouted at Ada to leave her house. But Ada was unyielding and kept saying she was sorry, pleading with her to calm down. When she finally let her guard down after placing a call to her office, we started talking freely about our lives without each other.

She had been excited to find out she was pregnant, but sad because she knew we could not be together and she was unable to offer me the stability I craved at that time. She mentioned that when she eventually persuaded herself to bring Ameen to me, she discovered I was about to get married and she could not bring herself to leave her son with a step-mother or cause a problem for me with my wife. Ameen was in a private secondary school in Kent and would be finishing in a year's time. He was a happy child, he knew his father lived somewhere in Nigeria and had been hoping to meet him one day if he ever visited Nigeria. Zainab was happy with her life as well and she hoped I was happy too.

Somewhere in the middle of the duologue, Ada excused herself and left us to our awkward selves. It was difficult not to drift off sometimes, thinking about what could have been with Zainab; but thankfully the distance between the sofas kept me glued to my seat and I was grateful she kept her distance too.

Then she posed the question I was hoping she would answer. "So now that you know about Ameen, what next?"

"I don't know. When Ada told me, I didn't know what to do. I still don't know what to do, but at least I would like to see him. I am hoping you'd tell me what we can do. I haven't told my wife anything."

"I'm not the one who got on the plane and had seven hours to think about it. Why did you come? Definitely you know you can't take him from me." She grumbled, still feigning to be upset.

I wrote and rehearsed a list of things I would discuss with Zainab when I saw her, but everything flew out of my head as I sat under her probing eyes. "When can I see him, can you work something out with the school? I'm not leaving until Friday. That's the only mission I've got here and I'm open to whatever you can arrange."

"And after that?"

I sighed and the only thing I could do was tell her about Tara and how she never got to know her father which had left a massive gap in her life. "As long as I'm alive, I'll hold myself responsible for him. I want to be part of his life as much as you both can allow me. I feel terrible that I've missed out much of his life already and I hope we can somehow make up for lost time. Please, just give me a chance, if I had known all this time..."

"I'm sorry to say this, but are you sure it's not because you don't have any children with your wife now?" She eyed me suspiciously. "Look, Ameen is doing okay. I've always told him he'll meet his dad one day when I can take him to Nigeria. You're one of the reasons he's never been to Nigeria with me."

Afterwards, she agreed to arrange with the school and I joined her to pick Ameen home early the following morning. He was very happy to see Zainab and confessed that he has missed her.

When we got back to her house and she introduced me to

him, he went quiet and avoided my eyes totally. I reached for his shoulder and he lifted his eyes. "You are my dad?" His voice quivered and his hands were shaking when I touched him. I carefully moved close to embrace him but his body was stiff. I did not know what to say. Thankfully, Zainab came to the rescue and sincerely explained what had happened between us, putting all the blame on herself. I felt pained that I could not read what was going through his mind as he listened to Zainab. Was he mad at her or me? He was impassive, only adjusting his glasses intermittently.

She asked him if she could leave him with me and he nodded. There was a long uneasy silence when she left, until I took the courage to start asking him questions. His favourite food was *eba*, which he never got to eat in school; he wanted to be a software engineer; and like me, he loved football. He was captain of his school team, but a Man City fan. I latched on to football and we were both able to talk freely from then.

After that, he asked me what my plan was. "Is it going to be like once in five years or are you planning to stay?"

Zainab and I had agreed that he was mature enough to understand the dynamics of both our situations and I should be as honest as possible. So I told him about my life in Lagos and that we would all need to agree what was best. She suggested that he should take me out and he took me to the London Museum and a boat ride on the Thames, where Zainab joined us and we took several pictures. In the evening Ada came along with us and we went bowling. By the time I left the first night, I was highly fulfilled. He was a good lad and did his best to be cordial with me. We had even laughed occasionally.

On Thursday, I got to Zainab's house around ten to pick Ameen. She followed us to the technology fair at the Excel London before leaving us to attend to her business. The excitement on his face over computer games and tools revealed his love for technology; he was simply lost in that world. Zainab joined us later for dinner and by ten o'clock, it was time for me to say goodbye, until such a time none of us agreed on. Those three days were very gratifying for me, despite the initial uneasiness. When I told him I would be back soon, I was not sure if he believed me, but he shook my hands all the same and called me dad for the first time.

Now here I am, on my way to the airport to catch a flight to take me home to my dear Tara without a clue of what I am going to tell her.

* * *

Tara

The gentle knock on the door distracts me from the clothes I am trying to sort to take to church for the compassionate ministry. It is unbelievable how many clothes and shoes I have not worn in ages, yet I continue to buy more and extend my wardrobe to the other rooms. The pastor's sermon last month that any piece of clothing that has not been used in one year should be given out caused a comedic uproar in church as many husbands laughed and poked their wives. That was enough to remind me that there were plenty of people out there whose nakedness needed to be covered.

"Auntie Daisy *dey ask of you ma.*" Maria peeps in.

"Daisy?" She nods. Daisy did not tell me she was coming. "What of Mama, is she in the living room?" After returning from the dry-cleaners earlier, I turned to my wardrobe and got caught up in the sorting task. Since Mama abandoned the TV in her room and decided to spend more time with me in the living room, I have watched less and less TV. Our commentaries on films and issues are usually divergent, and she must have the last say. Her excuse was that she did not come to stay with us to spend all day by herself, so after saying her prayers and reading the bible, she comes out for my company or watch TV.

"Mama never comot her room after she chop."

"Is she sleeping?" That is rather unusual.

"I no know ma, I knock softly to tell am make she come chop afternoon food but she no answer." I push past her as she starts explaining. *"So I leave am, say make I no wake am if she dey sleep."*

Daisy is at the dining room by the time I got downstairs. "Daisy, Daisy." I give her a hug. "I'll be with you, let me quickly check on Mama." I head towards the room and I almost bump into her as I reach to open the door the same time she opens it, but I swiftly regain my balance. "Mama!"

"Haha, *kilode*, you want to kill me?" She bursts out. "Why are you surprised, you don't expect me to be alive?"

My hand remains on my chest as my breathing gradually slows down and I move aside to give her room. "Good afternoon ma."

"Good afternoon to you too." She sniffs and saunters into the living room, all dressed up in her boubou. I follow closely behind, beckoning to Daisy who moves close enough to greet her.

"Good afternoon ma. How are you ma?" Daisy exudes with a curtsy.

"Mama, you remember my friend Daisy." I introduced her to Mama as my only friend about two years ago on one of her unwarranted visits.

"My daughter good afternoon. You didn't go to work?"

Daisy glances at me. "No ma, I'm not working now. I will be starting a business soon."

"That's good. At least you know what you're doing. Maybe

you should advise your friend to find something to do too."

"Yes ma. Thank you ma." Daisy retains her cheerfulness.

"*Iyawo*, what are we eating today?" Mama turns to me as she goes to the sofa. *Iyawo* is the title reserved for newly wedded wives or old ones that have no children.

"Maria." I call out and lead Daisy back to the dining room.

"Maria again?" Is it only when your husband is home that you'll cook? Please I don't want Maria's cooking again this afternoon." Mama whines ignoring Maria who is by the kitchen entrance.

"What do you want for lunch? There's plantain, beans, yam flour. And if it's your favourite pap again, I can quickly make *moinmoin* or *akara to go with it.*"

"Isn't it the same pap I had this morning? We can have yam porridge, but not the one you'll cook with sugar as sweetener. Or maybe rice and beans. And I want fresh vegetable soup, not that frozen spinach. Simple *efo riro* with just a pinch of oil."

"That will take some time ma, because Maria has to go to the market for fresh vegetables."

"It's okay, I'm not in a hurry. Or maybe I should go to the market myself so I can get what I like." She faces me squarely. I am not sure about the look on her face, maybe it is a bait or a sincere suggestion. Daisy shakes her head.

"Don't worry ma, I'll go. Ola has gone to the office with Tokunbo's car. I'll get my bag." I head for the staircase, but she gets up immediately.

"Am I an invalid that I can't walk to the bus stop or you don't know how boring it is to stay at home all day? I'll go to the market with Maria. In London, nobody monitors me, but anytime I come to Lagos, you and your husband won't let me go out. It's not like you have any task for me here."

"But Mama…" I look to Daisy for support. She smirks undecidedly. My phone rings as she disappears into her room. I grab the phone from the dining table in a quick reflex. "Hello."

"Babe, I'm close to your house."

"Flora?"

"Yes, it's no other. What's wrong, don't you have my number?" In my hurry, I did not bother to check who the caller was.

I exhale. "Sorry, I didn't check. *How you dey*? Where are you?"

"I'm at Second Roundabout. I just want to know if you're home and I can drop by to say hello. But if you're busy, maybe…"

"No, no, I'm home. It's okay if you want to stop by. Thanks. I'll see you when you come then."

"Okay."

I drop the phone and rub my hand on my temple to ease out the looming head throbs. "Sorry Daisy, where was I? Ah yes, I need to get my purse." I hiss, not sure if I want to climb the stairs. "Maria." She comes in as I pull out the chair opposite Daisy. "Please get my purse. I don't think you've met Flora. She's on her way here. Did you guys decide to meet at my place today?"

Daisy smiles and twirls in her seat. "It seems you need some of us after all, a good distraction from all this." She stretches her hands towards Mama's room and whispers in my face. "I hope you know we are going for FG's launch this evening." FG's launch? I had totally forgotten, although I did not intend to attend. My phone rings again. This time I check the caller and shake my head, hissing. "You won't answer it?"

"It's that silly guy from Prime Bank that has been pestering me. He sent me a text to ask when I'll be resuming and I've told him I'll send a response to HR."

"How is it that I'm single and can't attract a single guy to say hello, and someone is pestering you? And as your friend I'm not supposed to be jealous of you." Daisy jeers. "This life is so unfair, I can't understand."

"My dear, be careful what you wish for. The guy is not your type."

"No be when dem plenty person dey get choice?"

"At least you've succeeded in dragging Paul back."

Mama comes out in a change of clothes and her small leather handbag the same time Maria gives me the purse. I get up. "Are you sure about this? Or should I come with you?" I bring out some money from the purse; unsure who to give the money to, I hesitate.

"Was I not brought up in this same Lagos, ever before you were born?" She corks her head towards Daisy and sniggers. "And I know you want to be with your friend, so I shouldn't bother you."

I give the money to Maria and whisper to her. "Get one of the cabs from the gate. I hope your phone is charged. Call me if there's any problem. Take a bottle of water with you, in case Mama is thirsty."

She curtsies. "Yes ma."

"Daisy, I'll be back in a minute."

"Bye ma, I may have gone by the time you come back. I'll come back and see you some other time." Daisy stoops as I escort them outside.

Yisa comes out from his post immediately we reach the front of the house. "Madam, *you wan comot?*" He makes for the gates, but I stop him.

The noise of the generator was drowned a bit by the air-conditioners in the house, but now that we are outside, we have to pitch our voices louder. "No, don't worry, I'm not taking the car." Flora's Benz pulls up in front of the house as Maria opens the small gate. "It's Flora parking ma. She called that she'd stop by." I volunteer to avoid any probing question from Mama.

"Hmm, and you wanted me to stay in the house with all your friends around. I hope you're not forming an association of bored housewives? Who else is coming today?"

What will I do with this woman? I stop myself from responding that Daisy is not married. Who knows, she may have noticed she is pregnant.

Flora joins us in front of the gate and greets Mama with a wide smile all over her face. *"Epele ma."* She makes an effort with her Ibo accent.

Mama reaches out to embrace her. "My daughter, welcome. How are my children?"

"They're fine ma. How is Lagos treating you?"

Mama flails her hands. "There's nothing for me to do, except now that your friend will allow me to go out."

"But you should come and see your children. Those twins are growing up fast and you haven't come to see Amaka too?"

"I wanted to come the other day, but your people left me behind. Maybe tomorrow or after church on Sunday. I was also planning to see Tara's mum on Sunday since I'm leaving next week."

"That will be fine. I can come and pick you or if Tara can drop you." Flora glances at me.

"Sure, I'll bring her."

"Okay, Maria let's go. This sun is not getting any friendlier. Greet your husband."

"Don't stay too long ma. You can call me if you want me to come and pick you up too." I volunteer. Yisa shuts the pedestrian gate behind us.

"Wetin she *dey go buy?"* Flora's tone is mischievous.

"Why didn't you ask her? *She say I no give am work. Short of say I no give am pikin to play with.* You can have her all to yourself from today *sef.* My task is to drop her at yours."

"Yes, I'll call her once I'm free. Okay, thanks." Daisy hangs up the phone as we enter.

"So sorry Daisy, this is Flora, she is the one that recently had my god-daughter. Daisy is my personal person from work."

"I've heard so much about you." Flora switches to her edgy smile. Only God knows what she is thinking as she sizes Daisy up.

"Really?"

"Definitely." Flora winks mischievously. "Some good and some not so good. How are you?"

"I'm doing very well. I could do better though."

"I feel you my sister."

We sit around the dining table. "Anything to drink or eat Flora? Daisy, you too? Should I fix something for us? I was going to make rice and beans for Mama, so maybe…"

"I already had a meal at home, but if you have any cake, it's …"

I spring to my feet while Flora hesitates, heading for the kitchen. Daisy opens her mouth, then closes it almost immediately. Anyone meeting Flora for the first time will not expect her to be friendly with anything pastry, but Flora has never cared about what anyone thinks of her weight. "Definitely, I made some *zobo* too."

"*Zobo?*" Daisy is surprised. "It's been a long time I saw that around. I'll take some. I hope it's not too sugary. Anyhow I'll take it over any of those packed acidic fruit juices?"

I come back with a big chunk of orange ginger cake and the *zobo* in a big tray. "You guys help yourself. I have more bottles and you can take home a bottle each if you want. Flora, when are you resuming church, since you've started going out now?"

"I don't know. These house maids are just lazy and not ready to do anything. The one I got now says she has to have a break on Saturdays and Sundays. Times have really changed."

Flora grumbles, pinching her nose. "Or Daisy, do you know any agent?"

Daisy shakes her head with her gap-toothed smile. "Maybe you can employ me."

"*Ehen*, Flora, did you know Laraba was pregnant? She came with her baby for child dedication the last thanksgiving. Even Tokunbo was surprised." I butt into the conversation. If anybody would know, it is Flora.

"Laraba, pregnant?" Flora gabbles with a mouthful of cake. "She adopted a two-month old baby girl. The process took her about two years."

"Are you serious? Her marriage is just about three years old, what's she adopting for?" That bit of news is somewhat stunning.

"The doctors said it was impossible for her to have children. She had some issues in the past that they needed to remove her womb, so she and her husband decided to get along with it. She says they're still hoping for a miracle though." She smiles with a glint of pride in knowing the intimate details.

"Wow, that's wonderful." Flora and I give Daisy the quizzing look. "I mean it's wonderful that she has her husband's support. You know the way it is in with some of our men and their beliefs." She swallows, pauses for a few minutes and turns to me. "Tara, couldn't you consider adopting too?"

I clench my lips and shake my head, but stay mute, trying to digest Laraba's action and motivation. I would not have thought someone will bring an adopted baby to church for dedication. How could she? I am sure if Tokunbo hears this, he will mock me. How can anyone be comfortable with adoption? Does that not appear to be an admission of failure?

Flora also stares at me now, raising her brows. "It's true. It doesn't stop you from still having yours." I continue to shake my head. Flora shrugs. "Just think about it. Once you have a child frisking around the house, even Mama will let you be." I sniff at Flora. It is because Mama is not her mother in law. Though, she is the least of my problems since I am already used to her antics. It is really this burden of everyone believing that I cannot have children. Maybe I should give up and accept my fate. God, I know you are not wicked and you have given children to those who have done worse than me. Why not me?

Flora tears from the roll of paper napkins and wipes her hand, clutching her bag with her. "I need to go now. I don't want to miss the appointment with the hairdresser. Daisy, it was nice meeting you. I hope to see you again. Babe, bring my *zobo* and let me leave you girls to it."

I lead her out and as soon as we get to her car, she asks me to get in for a short discussion. It was an issue she did not want to broach in Daisy's presence. She asks if I knew a Zainab, to which I shake my head.

"Zainab Mustafa, she's a property dealer, living in London. You don't know her?" I shake my head again. "When was the last time you were on Facebook?"

"Facebook? It's been a while. I logged out from my phone after the bank sack. What business would I have on Facebook if I have nothing to boast about? What's the gist *abeg*?" My ears are twitching for some exciting rumours. Anything Flora says is authentic, but she is not forthcoming.

"You need to find her yourself on Facebook. The gist is there. Zainab Mustafa. That's Mustafa with an F. Although, there are a few of them, she's on top of the list and the only one living in London. You can't miss her."

I am more curious. "You're serious, you won't even give me a clue?" She shakes her head. "Okay, no *wahala*, I open the door to get out. "Call me when you get home." I poke my head back at her. "This gist had better be worth it, otherwise you have Mama to yourself for one week."

"We'll talk." She smirks and zooms off.

* * *

Daisy

Tara returns inside and rushes to the guest room to bring her laptop bag to the dining table. With a flow of optimistic energy, she explains that Flora told her to look up someone on Facebook.

"Or do you know Zainab Mustafa?"

I ponder and shake my head. "Never heard of her."

"We shall soon meet her." She exudes excitement, pressing the keyboard as she hums.

"The dealer called me yesterday that they've sold my car. That is one piece of good news I've heard in a long time, and the broker has been able to sell some shares too. Now, I feel like I'm ready to storm the world with our world-class diner. I'm definitely on my way to raising the fifteen million naira, maybe it will be more, but I don't want to be too optimistic. I hope you've given it some thoughts because I'm not doing it without you. I've mandated an estate agent to start looking around for old warehouses that we can touch up or vacant land and I'm sure we should have some leads by next week. That will give us an idea of the actual going rate for the long-term lease. I've been thinking of different names that will be suitable. You know, something romantic. At least, that will prove to you that I've been busy. How would you like Aurora? It's the name for the Roman Goddess of sunrise and we can have a sunny logo with …"

The look on her face stops my monologue. Her eyes have gone bloodshot and misty and her hand is shaking "What is it?" She heaves and puts her left hand under her chin pensively, pushing the laptop towards me. I can feel the pulse of her trembling body. "What is it?" I repeat, even though she must have heard me the first time. On the screen is the Facebook page of a lady that looks almost like me, but a version that makes me wish I was more glamorous with more money backing me up.

Several pictures splash Zainab's page, reflecting lots of adventure and happy times at different phases of her life. A picture of Zainab with a boy and someone that looks like Tokunbo on a boat deck stands out. There is another one with Tokunbo and the boy. I scroll to see other pictures; constantly with Zainab is the boy, whom I can now assume is her son; nothing more of Tokunbo. There are pictures of birthdays, school events, beaches, trips, and parties of all kinds. I go back to Tokunbo's picture. The boy looks very much like him, with his Afro and can easily pass for his brother or son. Knowing that Tokunbo has no junior brother, the possibility of what this means suddenly dawns on me. I look intently before turning to Tara. "Can this be your husband?" She nods. "So what does it mean? You said he's not on Facebook." I look back at the pictures and except for a few likes, there is no comment or description for the pictures. Something about this portends bad news. The only logical picture forming in my head is that Tokunbo is the father of the boy, who could be anything from fourteen to eighteen years old. There is no mention of Tokunbo's name; only the pictures, and he is just as stern looking. Could it be? Tokunbo? My mind refuses to process it. The same no-nonsense bespectacled Tara's husband that I know. No, it cannot be. I unglue my eyes from the laptop and turn to Tara. "Do you think... is it possible?" The complete words will not come out from my mouth.

"I always knew this would happen." She mutters in between

her tearful sniffs as she gets up.

"But you can't conclude with these pictures. It doesn't confirm anything."

"This boy is a teenager, Daisy. Did you see his tenth birthday pictures? How long could this have been going on and I didn't have an inkling?" She disregards my response. "This is where he goes, when he goes on those London business trips. Do you know he left for London again this Monday? I thought he was acting strangely. I just bought this shirt for him last month." She points at the laptop again. "All men are the same. I told you, I always tell you. You can see now. And he keeps pretending he wants a child from me." Tara rants on, pacing back and forth, and I let her. "How could he do this to me? Why? Because I can't give him the children he wants. But I've tried all that I know to do. What else can I do?" Her voice begins to rise as tears flow from her eyes in an irrepressible torrent. I lead her to the sofa and place my hand around her shoulder.

I continue patting her in silence, buying time to think of what to say. "Please don't work yourself up unnecessarily. Those pictures don't tell anything for certain. Why don't you wait to discuss with him? We can also ask his mother when she returns. For all we know, it may not be what we think." I cannot say I believe those words myself, but I have to say something. "Why don't you give him a call now?"

She gives me an incredulous look. "He should be airborne, but who knows? What's there to discuss with him? If he has kept it away from me for God knows how many years, do you expect him to now tell the truth?" She reaches for her bag and I help her get it. She brings out a tissue and wipes her eyes in between sobs. "I always feared this would happen. How could I have trusted him? No wonder he was taking sides with my father, they are all…"

"Tara!" I cut her, anticipating where her thoughts are heading. One belief she has not been able to get out of her head is that men are not reliable because of how her father treated her mother. Yet how can you hold all men accountable for one man's deed. "All men are not the same, Tokunbo is ..."

"How?" She sobs. "Tell me how men are not the same. Which one of them is different? Look at Paul. You said he was engaged, yet he got you pregnant."

My hand drops from her shoulder sharply. Waves of mixed emotions sweep over me: embarrassment, sickness, shock and empathy all rolled together. "Why would you say that? I told you I take absolute responsibility for what happened between Paul and I, I'm as much to blame as him."

"I know." She sobers a little. "But the difference is he was engaged, you were not. He already made a commitment to someone to be her husband. What if they hadn't called off the wedding? Would he have told his wife when you eventually show up with your baby? Isn't that what this is about?" She pauses and taps her head. "I'm sorry, I'm not thinking straight, my head is exploding."

Sometimes I wish life was plain black and white. When I had that one-time escapade with Paul, it was to purely appease my consuming passion and for physical gratification. I did not give any thought to unfaithfulness on his part and causing one woman heartache as it is causing Tara now was not in the plan. There was no plan in the first place. Definitely, in Tara's mind, I am simply another Zainab; a home-breaker; the other woman. How many times have I questioned my resolution not to have an abortion and face life as an unmarried mother? How many times have I asked God for forgiveness, hoping fervently that I would have a miscarriage and for the pregnancy to miraculously implant itself in Tara, who is the one that needs a child now? How many times will I have to face this stigma in my life? Over what? A piece of cheap porridge! I am not sure if Paul's broken engagement gives me any consolation other than that I am not the cause of it.

"Well…" I start, but Mama's voice interrupts mine.

"Is that not how they all do, cheating everyone?" She is deep in conversation with Maria. "*Ekule o.*" She yells from the kitchen. Tara wipes her face once more for any trace of tears; draws a huge sniff as if it is her last; and clears her throat while I take in a huff of air.

"Welcome ma." Tara's voice is still a bit croaky. She gets up to welcome her mother in-law. I follow her, ready to leave, to go and continue reflecting on my life.

Mama meets us in the dining room. "What's wrong with your voice? Are you okay? Why are your eyes red?" The sincerity with which she asks the questions shocks me as she inspects Tara and looks from her to me. "My daughter, what's wrong with your friend?"

"It's her head ma, she's okay." I hope that is the correct response.

"Nothing Mama, just a slight headache." She holds her palm to her forehead. Did you get what you wanted from the market?"

"Hmm, everything is expensive in this town, but I was able to get some things. In fact I'm going to cook for everyone now." Mama announces, heading for her room. "I'll change and cook after saying my prayers."

"Should we ask her about it? I whisper, but Tara declines with a shake of her head. I reach for my bag. "I'm so sorry for what happened but God…"

"Where are you going?" She snatches the bag from me. "I'm the one that should apologise. Please don't go now." She shakes her head and gives me a very weak smile. "I thought we had a party to attend."

"Party? Who's in the mood for a party now?"

"I am. Better than any other thing I can think of." She squeezes my hand. "Please, I don't know what to do with myself if you leave."

I eye her quaintly. If she wants to go and let off steam, I need that too after this unpleasant event with Tara. Life is too short.

CHAPTER SIXTEEN

Daisy

"Oh Jesus!" Tara grabs my hand, almost bringing us to a halt as we climb the walkway to the lobby.

"What is it?" I look around but cannot find any item that should cause her distress.

"It's that woman. I hate her so much." She seethes, her body tensing and heating up."

"Which woman?" There is more than one woman moving in and out of the lobby. A woman steps out of a car ahead of us before the driver zooms off. She goes towards the hotel reception. Another car soon pulls up and a man, the Commissioner for Finance alights. Then I see the woman Tara was referring to as she embraces the Commissioner with a peck on both cheeks. They pose for a camera and head into the hallway. I lift my hand to point to them, but Tara slaps it down. It is Mrs. Gomez, looking like the queen of the night. She is playing hostess, flanked by two figure-eight ladies in peach skirt suits. I never knew peach could look lovely as a suit. We also look gorgeous enough to fit well into the event. After much ado, Tara eventually settled for a purple lacy dress with low cut back to contrast my black jumpsuit.

"Get over yourself Tara, do you think she remembers you? How many years ago and you're still hung up on her?" How much of this girl do I actually know? Her body temperature has gone suddenly venomous. She urges me to go in through the side entrance on the left, in order to avoid Mrs. Gomez; thwarting my dream of standing shoulder to shoulder with one of society's celebrity tycoons and the potential of appearing in one of those glossy magazines. I follow her leading towards the side entrance where an usher welcomes us and asks if we want to go through the lobby for the red carpet and pictures. Tara shakes her head slowly, but firmly. She holds me down in case I have any contrary idea, making it impossible to sneak a pose with the Commissioner as well. The usher checks our invitation cards and looks up the names on a list before beckoning to another usher, widening her pleasant smile.

"Please take them to VIP Two." Hmm, that sounds like we are some important people.

"I hope we won't be seated close to FG's mother." Tara cowers behind me as if I am the main guest and she is the *waka pass*.

"I don't care. I came here to enjoy myself and neither you nor that woman will stand in my way. You should thank your stars that you're now married. If you couldn't get a husband after FG, would you have killed his mother?" As we wade through the half-filled hall of elegant and vibrant people, I wonder how she can still harbour such deep feelings against the woman. Could she possibly think that she may have been better off with FG? We women and our delusions! As if by magic, FG appears in my face from nowhere, taking over from the usher to lead us to a table with four vacant chairs.

"Hey ladies, welcome to the exotic world of AfroGrand Merlot. I'm sorry I wasn't out to welcome you. I'm so glad you made it." He tactfully ogles Tara from bottom to top. "You really look good girl. This colour suits you. Daisy, you look great too." He pulls out a chair for me, and then Tara. I must admit, plus his money, the guy is a charmer. How he is still single is a big puzzle. There are already finger-foods and open bottles of different drinks on the table, most of which I have never seen. "Unfortunately, we can't serve any red wine here, except AfroGrand Merlot. So you have to wait just a little bit for the unveiling, if you don't mind. Make yourselves comfortable. I'll be back soon. I promise. I need to be in front of the cameras, or will you join me?" He is off and my eyes and Tara's follow him into the crowd. The red room lightning gives the atmosphere some sensuality, but also makes it difficult to see anyone not close by. I can still make out the faces of MDs of Zenith and GT Bank. This is high society.

Tara reads the label on a bottle of champagne and fills her glass. I ask her not to fill mine and instead I fish out a bottle of sparkling wine. I have renewed my pledge never to touch alcohol again since that night with Paul. I am still pouring my wine when she reaches for the bottle a second time for a refill after gulping down the first glass.

"Have you looked at what you're drinking?" 12% is boldly written on the bottle.

"I don't care. I just want to forget about my past and that terrible woman. I shouldn't have come." She slurps on the second one.

"What's so bad about your past that you can't live with?" We should be making small talk, but if she is in the mood to un-bottle herself, I can listen.

"I've told you what she did to me, but…"

"Good evening glamorous ladies and great gentlemen." The MC's voice booms out over the fading volume of jazz music as the hall lights dim further into almost complete darkness with the spotlight focused on the stage. It draws all attention to the MC and the veiled structure beside him. "Welcome to the unveiling of our lovely new bride. If you see what I'm talking about, you'll agree with me that she's an outstanding bride." The audience acquiesces with laughter. "I have the permission of the wonder woman herself Mrs. Gomez to appreciate you for turning up on time, especially with the traffic on the Island today. This should be a lesson to you all, that you need to confirm the President's itinerary when you want to pick a date for your event. Please don't ask me how you'll achieve that." On our way out, there was a heated conversation about people spending an average of two to three hours coming from the Mainland to the Island caused by a traffic build up because of road blockages for the president's planned visit to Lagos. "So if you see anyone walk through those doors after seven thirty, you don't need to ask if they're coming from the Mainland or Island. Just pardon them." Another round of applause and laughter blares out. The MC goes on to talk about the reason for the gathering, chipping in random jokes and riddles to engage the audience. Then he starts adulating Mrs. Gomez and Tara's smiley face suddenly stiffens without any logical transition. "Ladies and gentlemen, with a standing ovation, please welcome the respectable, creative, beautiful, fashionable, effervescent, industrious Lady Gomez."

We break out into a roar of applause and excited hoots as the spotlight trails a small, encased podium descending with Lady Gomez hanging onto FG's hand. Clad in a shimmering but flattering royal blue lace and chiffon dress, she steps out in measured pace towards the main stage as one of the ushers gathers the train of her dress to the podium. The woman sparks of gracefulness and makes lavishness look ordinary. Although Tara stands with the rest of us, she does not join in the applause, rather she holds on to her champagne glass as if her life depends on it. Whatever grudge she has against this charming woman must be eating her up. If the MC did not start by interrupting me, maybe I would have been able to make her talk. Unfortunately, that moment has passed; or maybe not.

A lady taps me on the shoulder. "Daisy?"

"Sure, I'm the one." She looks familiar, but I can't recall where from. I force out a smile.

"I knew it. I saw you two walk in. You don't remember me?" She seems excited, in spite of the continuous shaking of my head. "At the bank. You helped me with my accounts when my husband died. Mrs. Agbe-Davies."

Now I remember her. "I'm so sorry ma. It's been quite long. Four years ago? I hope you're okay now and business has picked up." She was a distributor for top breweries with a chain of retail stores at Oke-Arin, backed by a credit facility with the bank. Then her husband died in a car accident, leaving her with three children and a four-month old pregnancy. It was one of those times Central Bank was raging on banks to comply with loan provisioning and recovery policies. She had suffered a nervous breakdown, lost the pregnancy and her staff looted the stores. Her business nose-dived and her loan mounted with unpaid cumulative interests, which led her to the brink of losing their mortgaged home. When she came into the office to sign off some documents, she looked lost and had simply given up on holding on to any remaining asset. After I heard her story, I discussed with her account officer and I wrote a two-paged proposal to management. It was a real miracle that we got the exceptional approval for the write-off of the accumulated interest and restructuring of the loan. I never saw her after that, but she looks very bubbly and self-assured now.

Unexpectedly, she hugs me. "Thank you so much. I was so eaten up during that period, I couldn't come back to say thank you. You can't imagine what you did for me."

"Thank God ma, it's nothing. I couldn't have done otherwise."

"That God will bless you too. Are you still at the bank? I know they've been sacking people since, but I'm sure you were not touched. You're too good."

I shake my head with a smile. "I left." I use that opportunity to introduce Tara, who has continued drinking. "We left in the last shake-up exercise. This is Tara, we used to work together."

"Good evening ma." Tara acknowledges her, but sits down immediately.

I pre-empt her next question. "I haven't gotten another job yet. I think I will be moving away from banking for now and I'm seriously considering starting a business of my own."

"Oh dear, I'm so sorry to hear that. Can I ask for a favour?" She brings out her business card from her gold clutch purse. "Do you mind if we stay in touch. I'm very much back in business now and who knows?"

I bring out a pen and a stack of post-it notes from my purse to write my name and phone number for her. I have swapped my old business cards for the post-it paper to give out my contact. Truly, one never knows where the right opportunity would present itself, but if she really wants us to stay in touch, she had better be the one calling me first. "It's good to know that you're okay. And the children?"

"They are doing great too. Thank you once again, my little angel." She hugs me for the second time and returns to her seat.

I sit and join the subsequent applause for the captivating

Mrs. Gomez who now has the mic and has begun talking about the journey to the birth of AfroGrand Merlot. Meeting Mrs. Agbe-Davies looking very well-recovered at such a gathering gladdens my heart in no small measure. It gives me hope that I can also build a business. I just need Tara to make up her mind and give me a positive answer because that voice in my head keeps telling me I need her. FG greets and cheers people around the hall and eventually makes his way to our table with a wide grin on his face.

"Hey ladies, sorry, I've been away. I had to make sure mum is all good." He sits beside Tara, patting her bare back.

"What could possibly go wrong with her majesty Lady Gomez?" Tara responds sarcastically, jostling her head towards the stage. Her words come out muffled, crispy and a bit louder than normal. She picks one of the brochures on the table and starts fanning herself, despite the coolness of the room. "She's got it all together."

FG does not seem to mind the sarcasm. "You'd be shocked how many people put on a tough façade to do what they need to do. Mumsie is a tough one."

"Sure, she looks like she's got the world under control. Your MC is doing a very good job too." I feel obliged to say something nice. "Are you sure you shouldn't still be on the stage with her."

"There's only one thing I need to do tonight apart from making sure you girls are okay, and that's the vote of thanks. She succeeded in hijacking the programme from me."

"That's because you still let her control you. Don't you think you should stand up to her?" Tara challenges, her eyes darting back and forth between FG and the stage.

"Some things will never change girl, and I love my peace of mind." His hand returns to Tara's back. She seems to be rocking in her chair. "Are you okay, sugar?" The romantic inflection in his voice matches the longing looks in his eyes. When did Tara become his sugar?

She drawls now. "Definitely, but it's kind of stuffy in here."

"We can go outside if you want, the poolside should be quiet and cool."

"I don't think that's necessary." I counter, although it seems neither of them is listening as Tara is already pushing herself up. FG gets up to help her to her feet, so I get up as well. "You have an event going on here. I can take Tara out if she wants, but it's not right for you to leave." I protest.

"Hey Daisy, sit down and enjoy yourself." She pushes me down gently. "I want this guy to myself." She purses her lips and draws closer to FG. I have never seen her drink; until now I would have sworn she never touches alcohol. I guess finding out that your husband has fathered a child with someone else is enough to make anyone drink. I am hesitant to leave her alone with FG though. But what could go wrong?

"Don't worry, I'll take care of her." FG winks and I watch him lead her out in a cuddle, before returning my attention to the affairs on the stage.

* * *

Tokunbo

With only my hand luggage, I am one of the first to get out of the airport to meet Ola waiting patiently by the car. Big Sam's call rings through immediately I switched on my phone. I cut it short so I can send a text to Zainab and Ameen that I arrived safely. I place a call to Tara, but the call rings out. My call log shows Big Sam has actually called twice earlier, so I call him back.

"Hey Toks. I've called you several times. Your trip was fine?"

"My trip was okay." Conscious that Ola is in the car, I am guarded about volunteering any information about Ameen and Zainab. "But we need to tie some loose ends, I still don't have a clue how to handle it without anyone getting hurt. Traffic is light, so I should get to the club in about thirty minutes. What's up at your end?"

"I called earlier to let you know I'm working late in the office and I also don't have a car in case I don't make it to the club."

"What happened to your car?" The likelihood of not being able to rub minds with Big Sam before I go home to Tara does not sound like a viable option.

"It got stuck in the floods two days ago. The mechanics said it will be ready today. As you can already guess, they failed." Big Sam hisses. "You know nothing seems to work in your absence. I don't know why I refuse to close shop anytime you're away."

"Sorry boss, I'll pick you up from the office. I'll be there soon, we really need to sort me out."

After hanging up, I call Tara again but she still does not pick up. Should I call Mama? No. She may want to compel me to come home immediately. I send Tara a text that I have landed safely and will stop by to see Big Sam. Can she possibly be asleep? I rule that out, because she usually waits for me to get home anytime I go on a trip. She is probably engrossed in her home videos. A croaky voice on the radio catches my attention, especially because it is a man's voice; sniffing while narrating his predicament to the presenter. I ask Ola to increase the volume a bit. The man goes on to explain how he has never cheated on his wife despite being exposed daily to alluring ladies at the bank where he works, to the extent that his friends make fun of him regularly. Two months ago, one of his three daughters fell sick and they discovered she had sickle cell. However, no one could explain to him how that happened since both his wife's and his genotype were AA. That was what prompted him to have a DNA done. The results came back last week to reveal that he fathered only one of the girls, leaving him to wonder who fathered the other two.

Sometimes, knowing what is happening in other people's lives gives you a fresh perspective and consolation that your life is not as complicated after all. Though, the presenter had started the programme with a different subject, he graciously asked listeners to call in to help deal with the caller's pain. The conversation goes on between the presenter and the caller, until the phone calls start coming in. Callers offer a range of ideas empathy and advice; some reasonable and some utterly stupid. One woman calls to say she feels good that finally, someone is bold enough to pay back a man with what all men deserve. People really have issues.

Big Sam is a block away from the office, hands in pocket, chatting animatedly with Abba, his girlfriend who owns a shop downstairs. They are both leaning on Abba's car with the driver's door open and a comfortable gap between them. Ola finds a parking space and as if on cue for my arrival, Abba jumps into her car and drives off before I reach Big Sam.

"Do I scare ladies even from afar?" I grab Big Sam's hand. "I thought I'd have to drag you from your desk."

"They switched off the *gen* at seven for emergency servicing, so I got chased out of my office?" He feigns sulking.

"They did you or Abba a favour then. Which one?"

"She was trying to convince me to take her out, but my loyalty to you prevailed. Truthfully, I was almost tempted to go with her." He grins ruefully. "Not that…" His phone rings and he stops to pick the call. "Hello. Yes. Oh, I totally forgot. Toks is here with me. Okay, no problems. We'll be there. Yes, I still have the IV. Later." He pockets his phone. "That's Kunle. I forgot he asked me to join him for an event this evening. He's left the club and is heading there now. He'll wait for us to go in together. Should we go? Mike is not at the club either."

"Sure, why not. I just need us to talk this issue over before I mess things up with Tara or Zainab."

"You're a big man with a big problem now." Big Sam teases before getting into the car."

* * *

Daisy

The President of the Lagos State Chamber of Commerce supported by a lady representing the US Ambassador, lifts the veil covering the wine as Mrs. Gomez watches on. She wears that bubbly smile permanently on her face. How does one become this successful? I muse about what lies ahead of us in the unknown terrain of business. Definitely, she must have faced some challenges too on her way up. The thought of approaching her for mentoring crosses my mind and causes me to remember Tara, who left for the pool with FG almost thirty minutes ago. It has crossed my mind to go and find them, but I told myself that they are both adults and should not need a chaperone to make them behave appropriately. One of the reasons I came to the event was to start learning about protocols in the world of business that I am planning on entering soon, and to take advantage of networking opportunities. Obviously, Tara and I are not on the same page yet about my business idea, so I cannot blame her.

The MC returns to the stage, while the ushers serve

AfroGrand Merlot to the tables. Once they finish, he asks everyone to fill their glasses for a toast. Since I am alone on my table, I turn around to a table on my left and I am lucky to find someone to click glasses with. The touch of the wine on my tongue reveals a lush bittersweet taste, but as I am now a sworn enemy to alcohol, I decide that one sip is sufficient for me. The MC invites two well-known restaurateurs to share their opinions of AfroGrand Merlot and they speak glowingly about it. The Lebanese man speaks his language, gesticulating by doffing his hat and interpreting himself. Done with the crux of the night, the MC closes the event by urging people to get up and enjoy the cocktail. With my glass of non-alcoholic wine, I walk to Mrs. Agbe-Davies' table to thank her for coming over to me earlier and she introduces me to two people on her table, speaking highly of me. To my utmost shock, she practically drags me to meet Mrs. Gomez, who extricates herself from her circle when she sees Mrs. Agbe-Davies approaching.

"Congratulations ma." I am self-conscious to my very being and unsure of how to conduct myself around her. She pecks me on both cheeks. Was she trained for this?

"Thank you my dear. Thank you for coming. I hope you liked the wine and will be spreading the word."

"It's wonderful ma and the event too. Well done."

The photographer stands in front of us and Mrs. Gomez turns us round to face the camera. Finally, I get to take a picture with her. Dreams do come true. Two other people are waiting already to talk to the charming hostess, so I quickly excuse myself to in order to share the good news with Tara. Hopefully, she will not murder me for dancing with the enemy. I push my way through the main lobby and head for the swimming pool, but stop abruptly. Right ahead of me are three men entering the hall; one of whom is Tokunbo, Tara's husband. My heart thumps so loudly I feel it is going to burst out of my chest and I hold my hand to it.

Several questions jump at me. What are they doing here? What is he doing here? Does he know FG? How come? Does he know Tara is here? And where in the name of God is she? I should not have allowed her leave the hall with FG. Tokunbo stops to talk to someone and disappears from my sight while his two companions enter the hall, scanning around. I move towards the door and realise that Tokunbo is heading towards the pool as some people leave; others converge to listen and dance to the highlife music from the band. I make a sign of the cross on my forehead and mutter a prayer. Discreetly following Tokunbo, my eyes dart back and forth in search of Tara. I descend the stairs to the pool and locate Tara by her dress at an extreme corner of the pool, almost shielded from the spotlights.

They are both seated, facing each other, hand in hand as if removed from the rest of the world. With his hands in his pocket, Tokunbo strolls along the pool, shaking his head slowly to the rhythm of the music. It is inevitable that if he keeps walking on, he will eventually see the two people snuggling like lovebirds. I wish there is a way to stop that from happening. But I cannot see how. Oh God, why does this have to happen today that I am here?

FG lifts Tara's face with his hand and it looks like they are about to kiss

"Tara!" Tokunbo and I shout at the same time, but he trots towards them while I stay rooted to the spot praying that this is not happening. Luckily, we are about the only ones in that area of the pool. They both look in our direction and FG gets up.

Tokunbo pushes him roughly and pulls Tara up. "What are you doing?" He turns to FG, who is straightening his shirt.

"Are you mad? This is my wife." Tara prises her arm from Tokunbo. I move quickly to join them, fearing what may further ensue. When FG sees me, he nods and graciously leaves without uttering a word. "Daisy? You're in on this. Tara, what's this?"

"Just leave me alone, you lying, two-timing cheat." She spits out ferociously, moving away unsteadily.

"Tokunbo, please relax." I manage to mumble.

"Relax? Can you explain what all this is about?" I start to say something, but he shuts me up. "I knew it. I knew it would come to this one day. I always tell her to steer clear of you, but she'd never listen."

"Tokunbo…"

"And you parade yourself about like a saint." He rants on, shaking. "Now, you've brought her to your level. That's what you've always wanted?" He reaches for his wife again. "You, let's go home."

She moves back in a snap. "Never, I'm not going home with you. You can go and bring your bastard son home now, so you can stop hiding him." She hisses and Tokunbo's jaw drops with his eyes betraying his shock at what his wife said. Tara walks past him, leaving us standing and staring at each other.

"Daisy?" He shoots his hands out in front of him, pleading for an explanation. I almost retort good for you, but I feel sorry for him already and I am not the type to kick a man that is down on his luck. Unsure of anything reasonable to say that will not worsen the situation, I shake my head. He squeezes his mouth with one hand and shakes his head in shock before turning around to leave. I follow from a safe distance.

CHAPTER SEVENTEEN

Tokunbo

Yisa opens the gate for Tara about fifteen minutes after I got home and I rush down the stairs to meet her outside. I stop and turn back to the living room when I got to the kitchen, cautioning myself not to create a scene and wake Mama up. What will I tell her? What will she tell me?

After she walked out on me at the party, I went inside the hall to look for either Kunle or Big Sam. I found myself scanning the room for that worthless Fola, who thankfully did not fall in my line of vision. Tara seemed to be talking to a woman in a corner and did not as much as give me a glance. I hurried through the hall and found Kunle talking to someone. He excused himself and asked me if I knew Fola, pointing him out. He mentioned he had seen him with Tara at a restaurant; I got more infuriated. I had no answer for him, but I told him I had to leave and he should drop Big Sam off. Waiting for her to come back home felt like waiting for a court sentence, unsure if the outcome would be positive or negative. My mind was afflicted with images of her cavorting with that stupid boy, making me doubt that I did the right thing by leaving her behind.

What if she decided to lodge at the hotel and not come back home? What if she went back to Fola after I left? Have they been having an affair? If not, how could she have been so close up with him? I wished I had stayed to ask Kunle for more information. Could she? How long could this have been going on? I had many questions with no one to answer. Where did I go wrong? How could she do this to me, to us?

She walks in, shoes in hand and heads straight for the stairs without saying a word to me.

"Tara, what's wrong with you?" She stops only for me to finish my question, hisses and continues upstairs. I feel like strangling her, I clench my paws instead and follow her, telling my body to relax. She drops her bag on the bed, goes to the guest room and returns with a suitcase, triggering me to pant violently. "What are you doing?"

She corks her head defiantly. "Watch me. What does it look like I'm doing?" She goes to the wardrobe and brings out a pile of clothes to arrange in the suitcase. Not knowing what to do or say, my hands jut out involuntarily, I want to be angry, but I am overwhelmingly calm.

"Is this your plan? To go to that wretched boy? How long has this been going on?"

"What does it matter to you where I go?" Her voice is icy cold and she comes to confront me squarely with the great fury in her eyes, tipsily swaying a little. "Don't stand here and play double standards with me. I know about the boy, your son. I don't want to stand in your way, so you can go back to your lover. You should be grateful for that." Her look makes me feel diminished, as if I mean nothing to her. "I should have known better than to trust you."

Every one of her words feels like a whip lashing against my body. "My lover? If you just relax a little, we can talk about the boy, it's not what you think, I can…" I am suddenly on the defensive.

She shakes her head and raises her hand to interrupt me. "It's never going to be what I think. Should I expect the truth from you? There's no explanation that will be good enough Tokunbo. I saw your picture exactly where you want the whole world to see it. How long has it been going on? That boy must be at least thirteen, yet you come home every day and mock me that we don't have children. Now, there's no confusion over who is barren. It was easy to find someone else to give you a child since you got rid of that pregnancy with me. Is it because …"

"How dare you?" Suddenly, a rush of rage wells up within me and I snap. "How dare you try to turn this against me? If you're so concerned about being barren, why would you go running to that coward who got you pregnant in the first place? Don't you think he's the one you should be angry with?" She stops folding the clothes, turning pale; but I am not done, as I regurgitate their image together by the poolside. "You want to justify your adultery by blaming me for your woes? You wanted that abortion Tara. You were consumed with yourself and the shame of being rejected with your unwanted baby. How is it my problem if you can't come to terms with the consequences of your action? I've never accused you of being barren. It's always been in your head, so really you don't need my help and you don't need to pin your guilt on my." I stare intently at her to drive home my message and our heavy breathing magnifies the uncomfortable silence that lingers in the room.

After a moment, she turns away from me, closes the suitcase

and carries it. "I always knew it would come out of you one day. I'm sorry I've not been able to give you a child, but I did what I did because … never mind. I'll save you the details."

"Where do you think you're going now?" This has definitely gone out of hand and we are both losing the battle.

"It's none of your business." She smirks and heads down the stairs.

It is on my lips to plead with her to stay and sort things out; but pride surges within me like a fountain; and I shout after her, following when she gets to the landing. "Fine with me. I'm equally tired, tired of your miserable self-pity and emotional blackmail. It's been chocking me for far too long."

By the time I reached downstairs, Mama, with her wrapper tied over her chest is standing in front of the kitchen door, tactfully blocking Tara's way. She eyes me as if to make me disappear and I shrink back. "What is wrong with the two of you? I'm in this house and this nonsense is going on."

"Please, let me pass. I can't live with this betrayal, I don't want him to wake up one day and kill me." Tara starts sobbing. "And don't even pretend like you know nothing about it."

"Don't you dare insult my mother!" I point a finger at her.

Mama's voice is curiously calm and she gawks at me again. "Did I tell you I can't speak for myself?" She turns to Tara and gently lowers the suitcase from her, ushering her to the dining table as her sobs increase in intensity. "Sit down my daughter. Tokunbo, what is this about?"

Tara does not let me answer. "How can he keep such a secret for this long and pretend that he cares about having children with me? Yet, he already has another family with a full-grown son somewhere."

"Which son, *ngbo* Tokunbo, you have a son?" Mama looks from her to me, bewildered.

The tide has indeed turned against me. I cannot even

mention to my mother that I found my wife with another man now and I feel cheated. "It's not like that, I can explain. I didn't know that..."

"Explain? It's a simple yes or no. Is your wife telling the truth?"

"Yes." I feel like a child caught with a stolen piece of meat from the pot.

Tara springs up again with her phone and gives it to Mama. "That is your son and grandson and his other wife. I'm sure you're happy too."

Mama looks from the phone to me, thwacks her hands three times and sighs. "Ah! But this does not warrant you leaving. Where are you going? He's still your husband and he's here with you. Let's talk about it, Tokunbo..." That mention of my name implies I should beg Tara, but I shake my head and take a step backward. This is the woman I caught romancing another man a few hours ago shedding shallow tears to make me look bad.

"*Lailai,* I can't spend a minute longer with him. Mama, please leave the way. I'm not staying in this house with him."

Mama sighs again. "I know you're upset, but sit down. I can't let you walk out of here." Mama pushes her back to the chair. "Tokunbo, I didn't train you to treat women like this, especially not your wife. I won't take that from you. So if you can't resolve this like a man, then you'll be the one to leave."

"No!" Tara and I chorus.

"I'll go, I'll be fine." Tara sniffles as Mama sits beside her on the chair, such that she will have to give Mama a good push to get past her.

"Tokunbo." Mama calls me again. Just as well. At least if I leave I will be safe from committing murder. Without saying a word to either of them, I head up the stairs to pack a few clothes.

Daisy

Yesterday's incident weighed so heavily on my mind that I could not sleep. Instead I prayed for God to save my friend's marriage; and the only thing impressed on my mind was to head straight to Tara's house once it was day, despite not knowing what I would find there. After several calls, which she did not pick up, I am now close to her house. I silently ask God to give me wisdom and favour with Tokunbo, so he does not throw me out. I cannot recall the last time I came that close to seeing a man brimming fire with fury like I saw in his eyes yesterday, when he saw Tara with FG and accused me of connivance. Yisa comes to open the gate with just one bang at the gate and thankfully, Tokunbo's X5 is not in front of the house.

"Oga dey?" I thank him for opening the gate. He shakes his head and points me to the kitchen door. It is a good sign if Yisa can still trust me to go in unannounced. Maria drops the broom from sweeping the compound when she sees me and offers to carry my handbag, which I refuse. She goes ahead of me into the house and goes upstairs to get Tara, but Tara asks me to come to her bedroom.

There are clothes lying all around the bedroom as if someone pushed a pile from the bed to litter the floor. An open suitcase lies upside down with clothes underneath it. Tara, still in her nightgown, crouches up knee high in a corner of the bed, clutching a pillow close to her chest and rocking intermittently. Her swollen face tells me she has done more crying than of sleeping overnight. Wading my way to the bed, I turn the small suitcase side up and put some clothes inside it.

"How are you?" It is obvious she is not fine. I sit and inch close to her on the bed. Her body temperature is a bit warmer than usual.

"I'm sorry about last night." She blurts out. "I don't know what got into me. I should have called to find out if you got home safely after dropping me off. I'm so sorry for the way Tokunbo talked to you and me making a blatant fool of myself. Will you ever forgive me?"

"I'm not offended my dear, otherwise I won't be here. I've been worried all night, not knowing what would happen between you and Tokunbo. Where is he?"

"He left." She bursts into a gale of tears with her eyes, nose and mouth altogether.

"Left?" I knew something bad would definitely have happened, but not this. I pat Tara on the back and let her cry on me as she lets go of herself. After drenching my shirt with her hot tears, she musters enough breath to raise her head and talk.

"He left because Mama wouldn't let me. I wanted to leave, I wanted to be as far away from him as much as possible."

It is not exactly as I have imagined it. "You wanted to leave? Why? Did he ask you to leave, did he hit you because of FG?"

"I felt like a fool, he must have been mocking me all these time, yet pretending we were trying for our own children."

"But didn't he say anything about FG or why you were with him?"

She sniffles and squeezes her nose with her hand. "No, what's there to say about FG?"

Really? I straighten up a little. "Your husband didn't make an issue about FG and you think there's nothing to be said about that? What were you thinking getting that intimate with him? You don't seem to appreciate the enormity of how Tokunbo found you yesterday."

"I don't justify it, I was tipsy, but that's nothing compared to what he has done. And before you ask me if I listened to his explanation, he already admitted to his mother that the boy is his."

"And the boy's mother?"

Her voice is steady now. "I don't care."

I suspire. God, please speak to this girl. "Listen, yesterday I saw a part of you that I've never seen when you saw FG's mother. I don't care what that woman did for you to hate her that much. How many years ago, ten, fifteen? And you still have her in your system as if it happened yesterday. You're carrying too much garbage about, it's hurting you but you can't see. Hatred and bitterness don't do anyone any good and it seems you've pitched your tent with them for a long time. You need to stop playing church and let God truly reach you to heal your heart. That woman probably won't remember your name, but you…"

"It's easy for you to say because you don't know what she did. That woman ruined my life." She starts sniffing again, and goes on to tell me the story behind her abortion. After Mrs. Gomez walked her out of FG's life, she discovered she was already carrying his baby and she did not tell him because she knew they had no future together. When she confided in Tokunbo, she had already made up her mind to terminate the pregnancy because she did not want to end up like her mother. Although Tokunbo offered to marry her then, not minding that she was pregnant, she refused because she could not handle running from the arms of one man to another. "If not for that wicked woman, I wouldn't have lost my baby and be in this childless situation."

"And you would have been married to FG." I conclude for her. She doesn't respond. "Do you think you would have been happier with FG or you think Tokunbo doesn't love you as much?"

She shrugs. "At least I wouldn't be taunted for want of a

child."

"That's what you think, but life never goes on in a straight line and there are so many ifs that we can never fathom. What is definite is that you can't alter your past, it's done. But you can choose to live a happy life, no matter where you find yourself and be grateful for the things you have. You've been killing yourself over not having a child. Has it occurred to you that you've been favoured to even find someone else to marry? What should I do? I didn't have an abortion, but guess who got a husband. You! All the time I was dating Paul, until we broke up, I never got pregnant and then one night of unguarded emotions, I end up with this." I point to my bulging belly. "But, I'm still thankful and I know God is faithful to..."

"Which God is faithful? Do you know how many times I've pleaded with him to forgive me and give me a child?"

"And you think he hasn't forgiven you?" She looks at me with derision in her eyes. "The evidence of forgiveness is not necessarily in you having what you desire. It's in you being at peace with yourself and God, and trusting that he's got greater plans for you. For you to qualify for that forgiveness, Tara, you have to forgive yourself and forgive others. That's the only way to go. As far as I can see, you are far off that mark."

"What's the point?"

"The point is the people you begrudge may have found their peace with God, but you've allowed echoes from the past to colour the way you live your life in the present. You hold men against your father's standard, you blame your mother and FG's mother for your misfortune, and Tokunbo, you don't even know how much you've pushed him away. I..."

Mama's head peeps in after one knock on the door. "Is everything okay here?"

While Tara adjusts herself to sit upright, I get up to greet her with a curtsy. "Good morning ma."

Mama comes in and looks fleetingly around with no effort to sit down. "My daughter, it's you, good morning. I heard voices and wondered who it was. Has your friend told you what happened?" I nod. "Tara, I hope you're feeling better."

"Yes ma. Thank you." At Tara's response, I wonder if Mama's interest in her is genuine because this is different from the brusque, unimpressionable behaviour Tara describes to me.

She pauses for a moment as if pondering what to do and then she sits on the edge of the dressing table, entwining her hands intermittently. "I just finished talking to Tokunbo and he's told me his side of the story, but I don't want to be his mouthpiece so that no one will say I scattered everything. You two will have to find a way to cool off and talk to each other. I think he has wronged you as much as you have wronged him. You've both come a long way and sometimes you need to recognise that God allows some things to happen to us so we can find our way to him. Maybe this is the case, I can only ask you to use this time to seek God's face rather than let the devil come in between you." Tara stays quiet and continues to stare at her feet. "Have you thought about what you are doing next?" Tara shakes her head. "Has Tokunbo called you?"

"My phone is off ma."

"Hmm." Mama sighs and pauses again. "Are you going to call him then?" She does not respond. "Okay, let me give you space with your friend. *Iyabeji* is coming to pick me later today." Mama gets up to leave. When she gets to the door she turns back. "I hope you remember I'm going back to London on Monday."

"I remember ma." Tara starts rubbing the side of her head.

"Okay, do you want Maria to get anything for you?"

"No ma, thank you."

"I will check in to see you when I'm leaving ma." I chip in before Mama disappears from the room. "I don't think there is much else to say. What are you thinking?"

She shuts her eyes as she continues rubbing the two sides of her head. When she is like that, she has reached a dead end and I am wise enough not to push.

* * *

Tara

My head hurts so bad I can see two midgets hammering walls at the sides of my head. As I try to will them away, Daisy asks me what I am thinking and my thought goes to my body lying on that dingy hospital bed with blurred images of Tokunbo, my mother and FG. The one I remember vividly was FG wagging his finger at me. He tried to tell me something before I dozed off for the doctor to perform the surgery.

Three years after marrying Tokunbo without children, the images came back to me and always ended with FG telling me *'Don't do it.'* But I could not rewind time. When three years became five, then eight and no child came I knew it was karma. It did not help that Tokunbo knew about the abortion and I could read all the signs that he blamed me for not being able to conceive or carry one to full term. Sometimes I convince myself that it serves him right, because it seems God decided to punish the two of us for our complicity in snuffing that life out of me.

When I saw his picture with that boy yesterday, it reminded me of my failure at becoming a mother and brought the images to the surface again. Running into Mrs. Gomez yesterday, all I could do was blame my mother for her indiscretion and for not giving me a self-assured heritage, enough to challenge back someone like FG's mother. After all, if I had been a rich girl and born legitimately, she would not have disdained me as she did and FG and I would have lived happily with our children. I started drinking the champagne to help me forget my heartache over my losses and when FG offered to take me out, it felt like he was taking his rightful place. It triggered the idea of how sweet revenge against Tokunbo would be. From the first time I met him, he had made me know he had deep feelings for me and assured me he would take care of me. I never fully trusted him, but he was the only other man who showed any real interest in me and did not care about my background. I started suspecting that he was dissatisfied with our marriage after my third miscarriage, and it always crossed my mind that he would find another way to sort himself out; leaving me like my father left my mother. That one even had the effrontery to venture back into our lives. Does he think it is only sperm that qualifies him to be a father?

"Tara." Daisy shakes me by the arm. "Are you going to stay in bed all day? Why don't you take a bath and let's go get some fresh air?"

"Do you really believe Mama doesn't know about that boy?" I am not exactly interested in Daisy's response. "I don't know why she's being nice, but I'm not fooled. I'm sure she was happy when she finally got a grandson. Maybe that's why she spends more time in London. All this while. I don't think Tokunbo could have kept it away from her. You see what..."

"Why don't you ask her?" Daisy butts in. "She came to talk to you, but you weren't ready to talk. Why do you shut yourself in? Why don't you talk to her? Why don't you talk to Tokunbo, rather than providing answers for them to justify what you want to do? The world may not always be as you see it, so you need to look beyond your feelings sometimes and ask why people do what they do."

"So that they can lie to me or make me feel good about

myself?" I hiss and shake my head. "I don't need any man to make a fool of me anymore. Thank you."

She soughs and the room quietens as if the world has stopped working suddenly. "So what do you want to do with yourself now?"

"I don't know." I burst into another round of delirious tears. Daisy embraces me and starts praying under her breath; her voice rises against my erratic sobs; until her praying voice subdues the room; and I succumb by responding to her prayer of peace, forgiveness, redemption, love and restoration.

CHAPTER EIGHTEEN

Tokunbo

"Hey Toks." Big Sam peeps in after two taps on the door. He pauses to wait for me to ask him either to come in or to come back later. Ordinarily, I would have elected to go and see him later rather than early this morning, but I have been itching to see him since I got in. I headed straight to his office when I arrived but had to leave him a message to see me. Ebi is half-way into her brief, and I believe she should have noticed that my mind is pre-occupied with other matters than the ones she wants to discuss with me.

"Come on in." I beckon to Big Sam. "Ebi, I'll look through the remaining documents, but remember to send the draft of the annual reports to the chairman." She reluctantly gets up, greets Big Sam with a forced smile and exits my office.

"You didn't show up at the club yesterday. Your team won, you know, and you could have made loads of money. Mike doesn't have to pay for his drinks for the next one month." Big

Sam gloats over Arsenal's victory. "I'm off to Abuja around noon. What's up? My secretary said you popped in."

"Tara found out about Ameen before I could tell her and she's sent me packing from the house." I try to make fun of myself.

He moves closer as I go round to his side to lean on the table. "You're joking. Why would you leave the house because of that? It's not like you cheated on her. Didn't this happen before your wedding? Since when did she have the right over your stay in the house?"

"She was also at that party on Friday and everything happened so fast after we got home. Before I could even explain, she threatened to leave the house. Unfortunately, Mama was there and asked me to leave rather than Tara leaving in the middle of the night. When I spoke to Mama on Saturday, she said she feared if Tara left, that may be the end of us and she knew I could always go back home. I've tried reaching Tara, but she isn't picking up my calls."

"That's tough man." Big Sam's incredulous eyes are probing, but I cannot tell him about the other issues that caused the eruption on Friday night. How do I talk about the abortion she had ages ago that has become a cloud over our lives? Will I talk about my suspicion that she is having an affair or about her liaison with that ex-boyfriend of hers? No, there is nobody close enough to me to know my deepest agonies. "Where have you been hanging out?" He shakes his head, pitifully. "Does she know that's a sure way of chasing you into the arms of another woman?"

"Another woman? Do I need that to compound my woes? I was lucky to get a room at The Palmview Manor."

"Tara is lucky you know. I wonder why my wife won't make that mistake to send me packing. She probably know she'd have to appeal to all of you to drag me back home. Seriously, what's the plan now? You can't allow this to drag on and become a real issue. Should I ask my wife to speak with her, or Flora?"

I shake my head. "Thanks, but I believe she would have had enough time to reflect and simmer down a bit. I'm going to the house later today to pick Mama for the airport and we should be able to talk definitely."

"These women." Big Sam smirks and pats me, ready to leave. "Anyway, I'll see you when I get back. Maybe we can all have an outing with the girls next weekend. It's been a while since we did that."

Truly, it seems like ages since we all went out together, except for parties. About five years ago, the four of us started a tradition of going out on the last Sunday of every month with the wives and children, but after about two years, interest started waning. To be fair, the others used to make an effort, but my dear wife always came up with some last minute excuses, which traced back to the fact that we were the only ones without children. I am not hopeful, but it is definitely a good idea.

"We'll see how it goes, first I need to be sure I will be granted asylum back home." I try at humour again, walking him to the door. "I hope your meeting goes well."

* * *

Ola turns the car into our street and Zainab's call rings through. I promised to call them both on Saturday. With the stress of finding a hotel late Friday night and the anguish rippling in my insides, I totally forgot. I did not wake up until late Saturday evening, after speaking with Mama in the morning. I ask Ola to let me out of the car, so he can go ahead while I walk to the house.

"I'm so sorry I've had a situation since Saturday."

No courtesy of a greeting as Zainab purrs out her disappointment. "This is exactly why I didn't want you to see Ameen. I don't want anyone, least of all you to start toying with his emotions. By the way, he was doing fine without a father before you came along. I need you to be really sure about what you want to do with him. I don't want him to lean on promises that won't be kept or a relationship you don't intend to nourish. Just a phone call, and you can't deliver on that. The poor boy called to ask if I've spoken with you. Why would you do that to him?" I wish I could tell her to get off the phone, but I keep quiet. "Hello, Tokunbo, are you there? Can you hear me?"

"Yes, I'm here. I can hear you."

"Won't you respond?" She mellows her voice.

"You didn't ask me a question." I stop myself from laughing aloud. If she can talk civilly, why have a tirade in the first place? I am about two blocks away from the house, so I stop to finish the call, lest I go and wake my sleeping lion of a wife.

"Okay, I'm sorry. You promised to call on Saturday and you didn't. I don't want Ameen to get mixed up about whether you are a good father or not, now that you've shown up."

"I'm sorry, it wasn't deliberate. I've not had any iota of rest or peace since I got back. I don't want to start this by sneaking around to call you, but I haven't been able to talk to Tara. We had some issues, but…"

"I hope you're okay. Please don't feel pressured if you think you can't tell her now. It's okay, after all, we've managed without you thus far."

"It's nothing like that. We'll be fine. Anyhow, please tell Ameen I'll call him tomorrow. I'm dropping my mum off at the airport and would need to go now if that's okay with you?"

She pitches her voice high again. "You can go anywhere you like, but I'm not telling him anything to avoid another disappointment. If you don't call by the end of the week, be guaranteed that you might not see him anytime soon. That's enough rope for you to sort out your issues." The phone goes dead at the other end.

It seems like I am facing a double-pronged road of life now. Tara's car is not in the driveway; but I cannot imagine that she is not in. Mama is in the living room with the TV on. "Good afternoon, ma. You look all set to go." I flap my hands. "Where is Tara?"

"You're asking me. Is she not your wife?" She ogles as if I have committed a crime. "Anyway, she went out with Maria and left me to myself. Although she said she would come back soon, but this is three hours after. Maybe she's still trying to avoid you. Have you two not spoken? No one has mentioned your name in this house since I came back yesterday?"

I can only shake my head to her question. Is Tara not taking this too far? I should be the one acting out here, not her. I am not the one caught in a situation unbecoming of a married woman. Unless she has been planning this for some time, why should she be eager to leave without listening to my version of the story about Ameen? Where has she gone? I hope not to that Fola boy. Why is she doing this to our marriage? And what if I did not show up today; would she have left Mama stranded or asked her to get a cab to the airport or what? She must really want out of this relationship. Maybe I should give her the space she so much craves and see how far she intends to go.

"Are your bags all ready, ma?" There is no reason to discuss Tara with Mama any further; the thought of her is already riling me up. I call Ola to pick Mama's suitcases while she insists on carrying her handbag. I may not be coming back to this house in a hurry. Maybe I should go and spend some more time with Zainab and Ameen. I may find some joy there.

* * *

Tara

It is early hours of Saturday and a week since Tokunbo left. Despite the sound of the generator, the house is very quiet. It seems suddenly too big, empty and cold. For someone threatening to leave her husband a week ago, I should have been able to fool myself that I had my life planned out. However, after one trip to the market with Maria, followed by a visit to the drycleaners, my mum's, the bank, the spa and to the car wash, I ran out of anything worthwhile to do. Unsure about my desire to work with Prime Bank anymore, I tried to think about Daisy's business proposal; but I could not think clearly. I have avoided calls from Tokunbo, Flora and FG, and even the TV has lost its allure. The overpowering presence and sound of Christmas everywhere in the atmosphere only made me feel emptier.

A day before I got married, I was filled with apprehension, afraid of the future and unable to sleep. I thought about the many possibilities of what could go wrong in my marriage and tried unsuccessfully to conjure a reason not to go ahead with the wedding. For the first and only time, I told my mother about my insecurities and fear of trusting a man. She calmed me down and said it was natural for people to develop cold feet ahead of their wedding. Then she prayed for me and it was as if a heavy weight of steel lifted off my soul. I slept soundly and my mother had to wake me up when the make-up artist arrived in the morning.

When I visited her during the week, I did not mention any issue between Tokunbo and I. Rather, I sat through her monologue about how I should not squander the lifetime chance of meeting with my father as if it was a favour from God. Then she started probing me to find out if I was okay and asked why I looked bereft of joy. That is the way she put it and I think she is right. I am seated on my bed, bereft of joy; again afraid of the future and unable to sleep. Instead of calling my mother like I did before, I call Daisy.

She picks on the second call, sounding drowsy as she whispers into the phone. "Omotara, are you alright? You should be asleep." She yawns into the phone.

"I am not asleep, I am, I am..." I stutter and erupt into tears. "I can't sleep."

"You can't sleep? Other than that, are you okay?"

I nod instinctively, no minding the fact that Daisy is not in the room with me. "No, I'm not okay. I have a serious headache and I don't know what to do. I think I'm messing up my life, but I don't know what I can do about it."

"Listen, it's okay. We're going to clean the mess. I'll pray with you now and you'll sleep soundly, okay?"

I nod again, still sobbing. "Okay."

"Father, your word says that you give your beloved sleep. I lift up Tara to you and ask that you soothe her to sleep now in Jesus name." I say amen in my blubbering voice while she carries on, until gradually my hand starts to drop.

* * *

Daisy

Maria returns without Tara. *"She say make you come up* auntie.*"* I leave my bag on one of the sofas and head for Tara's room. After she dozed off while we were praying in the middle of the night, I decided it was time to have another talk with her. Since last Saturday, I have deliberately refrained from calling or coming to see her, hoping she would come to some kind of resolution with her husband by herself. Apparently, that has not happened.

On my part, I have focused on gathering more information and visiting some settings towards developing a fool-proof business plan so that I can pick up with her where we left off. On Tuesday, Paul and I went for counselling with my pastor, who told me that I had to step down from my deacon position, and from leading the treasury team. That did not surprise me. Since I decided to keep the pregnancy, I have also decided that I will stolidly face up whatever the consequences would be rather than hide my head in shame.

I catch Tara with a yawn while trying to sit up. "I didn't know you'll come over. You're such an angel, I don't know what I'll do without you. Thank you."

"For?" I shrug and smile. "Sleepless nights come with the friendship package, the last time I checked." This time I sit at the dressing table.

She smiles and pulls herself up. "I don't know why you put up with me, but I promise you, I'll pull through." She excuses herself to go into the bathroom. I pick up the magazine on the dresser. Flipping through pictures and randomly reading bits of articles, I stop at the pictures of Mrs. Gomez at the centrespread. The woman is definitely beautiful. Beside the pictures, I start reading the article captioned - My Story. From a very poor home, she grew up in a remote village in Ondo State and followed her aunt to Lagos at the age of twelve to start secondary school. After school, she had to work at her aunt's textile shop until late in the evening and continue with household chores when they returned home. On a typical day, she would wake up at five and sleep at twelve midnight. After secondary school, her aunt stopped her from going to university despite exceeding the requirements; rather, she continued to work at the shop. Two years after, she left her aunt to work with another textile dealer, and from there she saved money to start her own business. She was already successful by the time she met FG's father and she only complemented his success. She concluded that she had no grudge against her aunt and that it was through her she first learnt resilience, diligence and entrepreneurship.

I find her story inspiring and it makes me admire her more; but I cannot help wondering why she would not give someone like Tara a chance, since she also came from a poor family. Maybe it was a test. Maybe not. Maybe she wanted to sift the gold diggers from true lovers. That does not explain why FG should still be a bachelor. The afflictions of the rich! How do rich people know friends from pests? It is a precarious situation, where what should be a source of blessing could become a disadvantage. I thank God for what I am. Tara comes back in, bathed and half dressed. We go out into the small living room and I wonder when last anyone sat here in its spick-and-span state.

"Have you reached out to Tokunbo?" She shakes her head. "So what have you been up to?"

"Do you want a drink?" She stares at the blank TV, avoiding my eyes and my question; but I go to sit on the centre table in front of her, lifting her chin for eye contact. She exhales resignedly. "I must confess. Not much. After Mama left, I went to see my Mum and I thought she could brighten me up, but she started harassing me again about making peace with my father."

"I'm worried about you Tara, you need to move out from

this bubble building up around you. Are you happy?"

"I don't know what to do. Apart from that…" I raise up my hand to hush her up before I lose track of my thoughts and prepared speech.

"It's obvious you don't know what to do and unfortunately, I can't tell you what to do." I try not to sound too serious. She gawks at me. "I can tell you what I'd do though. I would open my heart to anyone that needs my forgiveness and love. I would forgive them and embrace them. Not because they are right or good, but because I want to live right with God. You know what the bible says?" She shakes her head. "If you are about to place your gift on the altar and remember that someone is angry with you, leave your gift there in front of the altar; make peace with that person, then come back and offer your gift to God.' How much more your husband and your father? You need to set them free to set yourself free, my dear. There's no other way." She sighs again, head bowed in her hand. "Listen carefully, family is not only for when the going is good, because there may come a time when family will be all that is left for you and if you've turned your back on them, then you are stranded. Trust me, I've been there. If someone knocks on my door, my brother, sister, in-law, father or cousin and says, 'I'm in trouble, I've committed a crime, and I've done what I shouldn't have done. Do you know what I'll do? I will open my door for them to come in and I'll hold their hands to walk through their challenges with them. Why? Because God has placed you in your family for a reason and your responsibility is to take care of your own, no matter how far gone they are. Open your heart and let God help you."

She wipes the tears rolling down her face. "Ever since I was a child, I prayed to God to bring my father back, but he never came and I thought he must hate me so much. I was a mistake, the one that shouldn't have been born. I envied other children when I saw them with their parents and I hated him the more. I vowed never to trust any man, until I met FG. Then his mother…" She swallows.

"Maybe God answered your prayers and that's why your father came back. You know he was father to some other children too, but now he's here. You can't afford to hate him. When you recognise that no one is perfect, least of all you, then you should try to understand their motives before you take a stand. It's not doing you any good. If you want God to forgive you, you need to forgive others. Life is too short and transient to live in bitterness."

"So what do I do now?"

"Put your heart back with God and share your burdens with him. He's the only one that can heal you and make you whole again. This season should not be lost on you. Don't spend Christmas alone, make it meaningful and embrace the love of God."

CHAPTER NINETEEN

Tara

As the pastor brings his message to a close, I reflect on how this setting is different from my regular church. I have not attended my church for two Sundays in a row to avoid lying when people ask me about Tokunbo. I am also unwilling to discuss my affairs with anyone. The keyboardist joins the pastor on the Christmas-themed platform and slowly interjects with some tunes; until it flows into a consistent, soothing melody, accompanying the pastor's words and piercing through my soul.

"It doesn't matter that you've been in church for ten, twenty years. It doesn't matter that you've been a Christian for as long as you remember. If you know you're not in right standing with God, there is no better time than now. Please stand to your feet and ask God to forgive you and take you from where you are to where he wants you to be."

A tiny voice repeats Daisy's words, '*stop playing church*', and it suddenly feels like someone has poured cactus on my chair; while another pulls me up to rescue me. Oblivious to my environment, my arms lift in tune to the rhythm of the keyboard and my body follows immediately. The tears flow freely as my contrite heart swells almost to the point of eruption, and my body shivers. With my quivering voice, I cry to God, asking Jesus to mend my broken heart and soul. I ask for forgiveness; for the grace to get over the bitterness eating me up; for his joy to fill me up; and I ask him to free me from the noisy shackles of the echoes from my past. Surrendering my whole being, I feel someone touch my heart and pour fresh blood on it. It stops swelling and starts pumping normally. An overwhelming peace permeates my entirety.

I am in no hurry to leave after another pastor closes the service after making some announcements. While people throng out of the church, I stay behind, praising God and subconsciously appreciating the fact that I did not go to my regular church today otherwise. Otherwise, I would have been distracted. I feel excited and energised and it feels like I have moved into a new body and spirit. I blow my nose into my hankie, which is now totally wet and stained from my tears and makeup, I throw it into a bin at the exit, telling myself it is a relic of my past. I am now a new creature.

It takes me only about twenty minutes to drive to my mother's house, but she is not at home. I send her a text and drive to the newly-opened diner close to the house, to give her time to get home. If her routine is anything to go by, she will come back home straight from church, unless she has some meetings. I order a plate of salad to avoid looking odd sitting there alone, but I am too excited to eat as I play different possible scenes of meeting my father in my mind. My phone beeps to announce a text. *'Maria has gone home, but come and meet me at your big uncle's place,'* it reads from my mum. Why Big

Uncle's place on a Sunday? She goes there only if it is exceptionally urgent. I hope there is no crisis.

My big uncle is one of my mother's favourite uncles who secretly supported her through school when she became pregnant. He was the one that played my father's part at my wedding and he lives about twenty minutes away in Palmgrove estate. He is a lawyer with a huge sense of humour and a sanguine outlook towards life. He is one of the non-conforming fellows in the family, but respected all the same, probably because he is wealthy enough to call anyone's bluff.

My stomach churns slowly and gradually drains my excitement away to replace it with apprehension as I make my way to the house. Big Uncle lives alone with a live-in steward, since his three children moved abroad. His wife divides her time between him and the children, which explains why the massive house looks deserted, even from the outside. This house holds some of my happiest childhood memories. The steward ushers me past the abandoned big living room into the well-furnished functional lounge with a homely smile. Big Uncle is seated, facing the open doorway. They have made good efforts to infuse some life in the house with the chiming Christmas tree at a corner of the room. I stopped the Christmas tree ritual after five years of marriage.

"Good afternoon sir." With a big smile, I kneel fully in front of him.

He hugs me and pulls me up. "Omotara." He drawls my name as he usually does. *"O ma to ojo meta ke."* That is always his first line of attack, but in a fondly way.

"You know how it is in Lagos sir." I respond with my usual line as well, and make my way to my mother. I stop suddenly, when I see a man unexpectedly on the sofa opposite Big Uncle behind the doorway. My heart skips at the instinct that this is the man, my father. He is bald, looks deceptively youthful, but with tiny wrinkles across his fresh clean-shaven face. He seems to have a permanent smile etched on his face, clouding the tiredness behind his weary eyes. His dark frame fills the chair and without a doubt, I can tell that he is tall. His smile widens when he locks eyes with me for a few seconds before I quickly look back to my mother.

She thumps the space beside her for me to sit and I gladly sink into the well-padded sofa. "Sit down." She pats me on the knee as I look everywhere in the room except at the old man in front of me. "How was church today?" I want to answer but no words come.

"Your mother and I have been talking about this for about a month now. Since you're here today, I don't think there's any appropriate way to say this without offending you, but you should try to understand." Big Uncle pauses, waiting for a response from me, but I am too unsettled to say anything. "This is your father." He stretches his hand towards the man I think I somewhat resemble.

As much as I was excited after the church service earlier today, I suddenly realise nothing prepares one for a moment like this and I am at a loss for words or reaction. I want to rush to him and hug him as a small child would cling on to her father; but I am numb and confused with a million questions jamming in my mind, and an indescribable loop in my stomach. The only thing I am sure of is that there is no feeling of any hurt, hatred, anger or condemnation. He does not fit the image of the cruel, uncaring, masquerading old man I kept in my mind over the years; rather, he looks graceful and demure. I look at my absentee father who missed the most important aspects of my life without any defined emotion. He did not have the opportunity to give me, his child a name. He missed out my first smile, my first baby steps, my first day at school, and my prize day when I won a medal for interschool debate.

He did not witness my graduation and my wedding day and he would probably never know that my favourite colour is red, nor that I hated sciences because I did not want to be a doctor like him. It could not have been easy for him either, could it?

He gets up, I get up and Big Uncle gets up to leave the room without saying another word. He is indeed tall and unbent like an oak tree. He quickly sits down again; maybe his knees are failing him just as mine are. "The only thing I can say to you Omotara is I'm very sorry." There is a shiver in his voice. "I've rehearsed this day over and again in my mind since that day I left. I always hoped this day would come but I don't have the right words. I am sorry. If I ever live again, I'll never do what I did to the two of you." I start muttering something, but he lifts his hand and goes on talking. "I had a wife back in London then and we were about to separate because of the turbulence in our marriage. When I returned from Nigeria and she saw a letter I wrote to your mother, she threatened to kill herself. She was depressed, erratically suicidal and always on the edge, and I couldn't afford to find out if it was mere blackmail or not. It was a tough choice I had to make and I didn't think I could live with her killing herself over me. I always wanted to come back, but time went by and it seemed too late to disrupt your lives if I couldn't offer any hope of permanence. Please, can you find it in your heart to forgive me?" He leans on the edge of his seat and wipes the dripping tears from his face.

Through my sobs, I tell him I have forgiven him and God has forgiven him as well. My mother tries to hold back her tears as she pats my lap, muttering inaudibly. We snivel quietly and awkwardly for a while, until I muster enough breath to ask him about his life. His wife died five years ago; he has three other children by her, who are all married and keen to meet me whenever we can arrange it. He is considering relocating to his hometown, Ekiti, where he plans to build a hospital and diagnostic centre. He tells me about his other relatives and his father who is alive and living in Ekiti. In between, the steward brings some drinks and hot pepper soup. I tell him about Tokunbo and how we met, and suddenly realise that there is almost nothing else of my life to talk about. How is it that our job defines us? Then I mention that I like baking and may be starting business with my closest friend soon since I am not fully persuaded about going back into paid employment anymore. Big Uncle returns with his own pepper soup bowl and asks us to get started on ours before it gets cold. We all join in cautiously.

In this short time, I have learnt that I have a grandfather, some uncles and aunties who all live in Ekiti. I wonder why he never asked them to make contact with us, but I soon chide myself considering, that only he knew what was best for the situation at the time. To break the huge silence, Big Uncle starts talking about football and I soon learn that my father is also an Arsenal fan, same as Tokunbo. The two men tease each other about Arsenal and Chelsea and the atmosphere is a bit lively. While my father's demeanour is somewhat guarded, Big Uncle is at ease with himself, gesticulating and laughing without restrain. I glance at my mother who has been quiet throughout and it seems some years have fallen off her face and the accumulated pain of her life experiences is almost wiped away. I can practically say there is a new sparkle in her eyes.

It is soon time to go and Big Uncle thanks everyone for coming and thanks me for my maturity and understanding. My mother prays and we all go out into the compound to our cars without any solid plan of reunion, just promises to keep in touch. I hug my mother before she enters her car and hesitate when I reach my father, but he extends his hand for a handshake. After they both leave, Big Uncle hugs me and ruffles my hair as he used to do to all of us when we were young, assuring me of his love and support. I look up to his face with my teary eyes and thank him for making it possible. It is one of my happiest days.

* * *

Tokunbo

My phone has not stopped ringing since I got into the office this morning. It is as if everyone was waiting for the weekend to be over to bombard me with their requests on Monday morning. Within two hours, I received four calls. The chairman called to have a meeting on Thursday, Mike called to meet up later in the day for a property viewing, a client called to know if they could reduce their order as they had over-estimated and my sister in London called to complain that Tara has still not picked her calls and they were worried about me.

I am about to call Ebi to keep the phone when a message comes in. It is a picture sent to my mail by Zainab, with Ameen in sportswear, brandishing a trophy above an explanatory note that he and his team won a big match yesterday. That is cheering news. At least my son is succeeding at something I can only run commentary on. Good boy. I finally call Ebi to give her my phone and bury myself in the pile of documents in my in-tray.

I am unaware of how much time passes before the door opens. I start complaining that Ebi should have answered the call, until I lift up my head. I should have guessed by the scent of her perfume, but Tara's appearance is the last thing I expected this morning. She is dressed in red peplum top and white skirt, which both accentuate her killer-figure. Her face is radiant, briefly reminding me of our early days as husband and wife, when she was my sunshine. I am stuck to my seat, apprehensive. She walks straight to my desk and I turn my swivel chair sideways to receive whatever attack she has for me. To my utter shock, she kneels down in front of me, totally disarming me.

"*Oko mi, Olowo ori mi,* I am sorry." She clasps her hands on my knees. "I've acted foolishly and I'm here to say I'm sorry. Please, will you forgive me and come back home? I can't spend Christmas without you."

"Tara." Still unsure of where this is going, I lift her up and go to lock my office door to stop anyone from entering, in case our discussion turns unpleasant. She is standing right in front of me, as soon as I turn back to face her; and I am assaulted with intense desire as I inhale her sweet fragrance. She moves in to embrace me and I shut my eyes, kissing her and enjoying the warmth of her body as I sprout to life. When she starts unbuttoning her blouse, I half-heartedly hold her hands to stop her, but she frees herself and starts on my own shirt too. Soon, we are making love as two young lovers, afraid that the moment to steal this sensual pleasure will pass.

It is not perfect, but it is the first time we have been mutually intimate in a very long time and it is satisfying.

* * *

Tara

Before going home, I drive to Jakande market to get some fresh vegetables, pepper, meat and snails. My energy level is so high that I just have to find something to do. And what better than to make Tokunbo his favourite dish? I could have bought frozen snail at the supermarket, but I feel that will take away from labouring in love over this dish. I refrain from haggling when the woman looks at me expectantly, knowing fully well that she is overcharging me. She is lucky I am in a good mood. When I ask her to pack the snails, she hesitates; then quickly catches herself and prays for me. Driving back home, I dance along with my head to the music booming out from Classic FM.

Maria is not back from her hairdressing apprenticeship, enabling me to set myself up to work by myself in the kitchen. I plug on my earphones before selecting a song from my phone's playlist and I start singing along as I begin my cooking spree. Not long after, my phone beeps to announce a text and then another beep. I ignore the phone until I finished washing the snails and put them in a pot. The two texts are from Tokunbo. The first one says *'Thank you for being my sunshine'* and the second one says *'I love you'*. My inside heats up and I respond *'I love you too, very much,'* and resume my chores with a smile. I did not hear the car drive in because of the high pitch of the blender coupled with the music playing straight to my head and I am surprised to see Ola carrying his compact suitcase with Tokunbo behind him.

"Hey, what happened?" He does not respond, but waits until Ola leaves after dropping the suitcase."

"Are you alone?" I nod in response to his question, after which he smiles and bolts the door. I am amused, unsure of what he wants to do. "Just the two of us." He twirls me around, removes my apron and my phone, and leads me into the living room. Thankfully, the cooker is off.

"What about your meeting?" He told me about his scheduled meeting with Mike before I left his office self-consciously, but unapologetically.

"I've cancelled the meeting. Mike understands. I couldn't

stop thinking about you."

"Me too." I confess, touching his face. "And I'm making your favourite *edikainkong* soup." I beam with excitement and he responds by drawing me closer to him and saying thank you. "But, first we need to talk, no more secrets."

"Yes we do." He acquiesces. "Me first." He reminds me of who Zainab was, with the expectation that I should remember. He goes on to narrate how Ada called to tell him about Ameen. He did not know Zainab was pregnant when she left him and he only wanted to be sure about Ameen and Zainab's plan before he told me anything. He takes my hand in his. "I'm sorry sunshine, I never meant for you to hear it from someone else. You know we've been having our issues and I didn't want to push you further away. But I was so confused I didn't know what I could do until I spoke with Zainab and ascertained Ameen is indeed my son. No woman can ever take your place Omotara, if I've never told you before, I'm telling you now."

With his explanation now, I feel very stupid over my reaction. "I must confess I feel like an idiot, but I thought you've been having an affair for that long with her. I should have listened to you, I should have trusted you, but I allowed my insecurities to get the better of me. And that almost pushed me to do something stupid with FG." He corks his head and adjusts his position at the mention of FG. "Don't worry, nothing happened and I can assure you nothing will ever happen. But I was tempted. I ran into him the day we got sacked. In fact he was the one that hit my car. Remember?"

His face contorts in a frown but he releases it almost immediately, enunciating my name. "Omotara."

"Well, the secret is out now." I smile. "Anyway, he tried to help me get a job with Prime Bank, but I've rejected the offer. He kept turning up when I least expected and it made me sometimes wonder if he wanted more. But I didn't plan to go to that party when Daisy showed up, until Flora came and told me about Zainab. I wanted to get drunk to dull the pain, then FG showed up beside me and I guess I got carried away. Thankfully, my husband and friend came to rescue me." Now I can talk about it remorsefully, but when Tokunbo found me that night, I wanted to punch his face.

"I felt like killing that guy, you know. And I've warned you about Daisy, but..."

I rise up to Daisy's defence. "That's one person you've always been wrong about. In fact, we both owe her a great deal for talking sense into me and making me see my folly by leading me where we are today. You know, I never forgave myself about that abortion and I always hated FG's mum. But now I have peace like I haven't had in a long time. I'm free from all condemnation and bitterness." I go on to tell him about rededicating my life to God and ridding myself of all the baggage I had been dragging about with me. Then I tell him about my meeting with my father.

"Come here." He pulls me close up once more. "I'm very proud of you and I love you more." He kisses me, slowly at first, then with increased intensity and in anticipation of what he will do with me eventually, I leisurely urge him on with my response.

It is the start of a new life together, a second chance to a loving future.

CHAPTER TWENTY

Six Months After

Tokunbo

Tomorrow is the open house party of Sweetest Arena, the confectionary outfit that Tara and Daisy birthed and we are lounging in the living room. Tara jokes that she hopes Daisy will not give birth at the event. Then we start arguing over what she should wear and she stylishly chips in that we can dash to town to shop for a new dress. She starts cat-walking in front of me, but screams suddenly, squeezing her face while clutching her stomach.

I jump up and lower her onto the sofa. She moans that her stomach is hurting. I try to think about what she could have eaten yesterday to cause her food poisoning but nothing comes to mind as we both ate the same coconut rice she made earlier.

She cries out, complaining that the pain is worsening, so I dash to the kitchen to mix some salt with water. She clutches her stomach, moaning out in pain while I struggle to remain calm and try to force her to take the salt mixture. The only thing that really gets her sick is her migraine attack but this looks serious.

"Can I get you some paracetamol?" She nods and I rush to the kitchen again, but turn back when I hear her agonising scream. "I think we should go to the hospital." I manage to say in my muddled state, unsure of what else to do. I yell out to Maria who dashes in quickly as if she was waiting on me. I ask her to go upstairs to bring Tara's shoes, but Tara shakes her head mumbling. I lift her up and realise her dress is soaked with blood. Confused and embarrassed that Maria is seeing her in this demeaning state, I ask her to get the car keys and open the door. Before driving out of the gate, Maria, more composed than me, brings a towel to wrap around Tara. I head straight for the hospital, which is about fifteen minutes away. Thankfully, a few minutes from the house, she says the cramps and bleeding have stopped. She chides herself for being unmindful of her menstrual cycle and suggests that we go back home, but I insist on getting her to the hospital.

I support her inside and a nurse offers her a seat to get her temperature checked. I am tempted to tell the nurse she does not have a fever, but restrain myself. The nurse leads us to a room and asks Tara to give her a urine sample before lying down to rest, to which I want to scream. Sensing my agitation, Tara squeezes my hand and nods. The nurse takes the sample, gives Tara a hospital gown and assures us that the doctor will be with us in a few minutes before leaving the room. Tara reassures me that she is okay and says she will take a shower before changing. She asks me to send a text to Daisy that she may be unable to meet her as they were to meet up at the Sweetest Arena later in the day for last minute planning.

It beats me how they achieved it, but within five months, they have been able get the Sweetest Arena operational. This included securing a long term lease on a house with a big compound at Ikoyi, purchasing equipment from overseas, furnishing it and hiring four employees. All with Daisy's burgeoning stomach. Apart from serving different kinds of exotic cakes, beverages and ice-creams I never knew existed, the Sweetest Arena also has two games room. The room for adults has table tennis, snookers and board games: scrabble, draughts, monopoly and *ayo*. The children's games room contains an array of picture books and many interactive and educational toys. They also have two meeting rooms to hire out for meetings or seminars depending on the crowd size.

They have succeeded in creating a relaxing atmosphere as an escape from the stresses of everyday domains. Apart from helping them with negotiating the lease, Tara made me promise not to come around during the renovation unless she invited me. I never got invited until she told me they were ready for operations. When I got there, I was humbled by the level of detail invested in the place and the splendour they produced. I complimented them that I was honoured to be associated with them, and I meant it.

In between all that, a lot has happened, but the most important is the fact that I have my beautiful sunshine back. I love our life now, just as it was when we got married before, the cares about not having children overtook our lives. Tara volunteered to give her body some rest and stop the fertility treatments for a while. I could not care less, as long as she was happy. About five months ago, on our way out, she suggested that we should visit the orphanage when we drove past. She confessed she had been burdened about it since I mentioned adoption, but she had not been able to come to terms with not having her own children.

It was an experience filled with mixed-emotions and reflection for us and by the time we left, Tara already decided she would do all she could to try to give at least one child a loving home he deserved. She asked God to forgive her for complaining about growing up with only one parent, when most of those children never knew both parents. It is quite easy to be removed from the realities of the world when all you focus on is yourself.

There were children who had grown up in the orphanage and who would probably never know what it means to live with a father and mother, or with other children they can call siblings, because they were no longer adoptable. The social worker explained that once a child was over four years old, the likelihood of adoption was very slim. There was a girl, a law student at the University of Lagos, who had spent all of her eighteen years at the orphanage. Tara offered to mentor her and pay her school fees. When we got into the car, I teased her about how she intended to pay someone's school fees when she did not have an income yet. That was when she realised she had not thought about it before making the commitment; though she was hopeful that the business would pick up once they started. Of course, I assured her I would pay the fees.

The office Christmas party was held on New Year's Eve; Tara supported Ebi to organise a fun-packed event and we eventually met her boyfriend. In the New Year, I joined Tara and her mother to visit Tara's father in Ekiti, where we also met her grandfather who has frail from old age. The man intermittently prayed for Tara and thanked God for allowing him to live to see his long lost grandchild. Tara's father and I had a connection with our Arsenal ties and it was easy to converse with him. When he started talking about his practice and life back in the UK, his feelings oscillated between a sense of accomplishment against all odds and regret for his lost years.

It would have been too much to expect a filial bond between him and Tara, but they were cordial with each other and managed to talk about peripheral issues. I saw Ameen and me in how their interactions played out and I was grateful that I did not have to wait another thirty years to find my son. During our visit, it seemed I was the only one who sensed Tara's mum was still enamoured by the man, but I did not mention it; I decided to keep my fingers crossed and watch events unfold. When she went to Europe to shop for the business, she scheduled to meet her three siblings in London. She said they were all excited to meet her and they agreed to have a re-union once every year.

I have been to see Ameen in school three times after we first met and our relationship is definitely improving, slowly, but progressively. I promised him and Zainab that I would always stop by anytime I visited London. Tara has assured me that Ameen can come to visit or stay and Zainab agreed to think about it. I am very keen for Tara to meet my son, although I am yet to figure out how that will work out, if it will be with or without Zainab, but there is no rush or pressure from either side.

The doctor comes in after two taps on the door. Despite being a new face, he greets us as if he is a friend. "I'm Doctor Bassey." He looks young and confident in his white coat and his smile gives me some comfort that nothing serious is wrong with Tara. But it is possible that he wants to cajole her for further tests.

"What's wrong with my wife?"

"We'll get to it soon Mr. Akande, but I need to ask her a few questions." He goes to the bed and touches her forehead. "How are you feeling now madam?" Tara says she is fine and he makes a note before he starts asking her other questions. Does she feel feverish? How is the pain? Has it ever happened? Does she have dizzy spells? When was her last period? Tara draws a blank, because the only time she monitored her period was when she was going through the IVF treatments; and since the last one, her period has been somewhat erratic. The doctor is indifferent and goes on with the questioning. Are her periods usually painful? Is there a possibility that she is pregnant? I almost snicker and wish this young doctor will simply ask us to leave if he cannot diagnose her without these silly questions. She patiently says no and he asks another question. Does she normally spot in between her period? Has it happened before? No. I thought he asked these questions already. "Are you sure the pain has stopped?"

Tara nods. "Yes, I can breathe now." He updates his notes.

"Maybe it's something she ate."

He ignores me and addresses her. "Mrs. Akande, your urine sample reveals that your HCG level is high. It's a bit on the borderline, and I'd like to do a scan to confirm if you are pregnant and hopefully to rule out that you've had a miscarriage." Have you ever been to a hospital and had to listen to a doctor trying to tell you things about yourself that you know he knows nothing about? Yet, you sit through it, because you know he is too arrogant to listen to you.

Doctor Bassey excuses himself to bring the ultrasound machine. His face is impassive and I show little interest when he starts the scan by rubbing some gel on Tara's stomach. Tara raises her head reluctantly when he asks me to move close to see the screen. Within a short moment, he points at the screen and asks if we can make out the shapes in the sac. For some inexplicable reasons, I start to sweat as I struggle to focus on the fuzzy lines and circles in black and white. He practically touches the defined beings lying beside each other, with a thin line separating them. "There are two foetuses, twins. Can you see them now?" Too afraid to speak, I nod. "Your babies are intact, but we need to stabilise you and put a stitch in."

Tara exhales a tiny sob. The doctor continues to talk, but I cannot hear a single word. I can only see my children behind his hand on the screen. A tear drops and I bite my lip when he hands me the print-outs of the scan and tells me my wife is about three months pregnant. I have waited six odd years to hear those words.

GLOSSARY

Abeg – Please
Abeg siddon make we watch game – Please sit down, let's watch the game
Abi – Right
Aboki – Friend or vendor
Akara – Fried beans cake
AMCON – Asset Management Corporation of Nigeria
Ankara – African print fabric
Area boys – Street hoodlums
Asewo – Prostitute
Arike – Pet name
Asaro – Yam porridge
Asun – Cooked goat in pepper sauce
Ayo – Nigerian Mancala game
Banga – Palm fruit
Boli – Grilled plantain
Chopping – Winning
Chop tire – Eaten too much
CIB – Chartered Institute of Bankers
Danfos – Vans used for commercial transport
Dey – Within different contexts: At home, present, are
Dey ask of you – Wants to see you
Dey talk – Are talking
Eba – Cassava flour swallow
Edikainkong – Mixed vegetable
Efo riro – Vegetable soup
Elemimeje – Assorted ingredients

Ema binu – Don't be annoyed

Even if person take one day old pass you, senior na senior – Even if someone is older by one day, the person is still your senior

Ewo – Look

Eyin lemo – It's your problem

Gen – Generator

Gonna – Going to

Goro – Kolanut

Haba – How, why

How una dey – How are you

How you dey – How are you

I don chop tire – I've eaten too much

I go carry am – I will take that

I no know ma, I knock softly to ask am make she come chop afternoon food but she no answer – I don't know ma, I knocked softly to ask about lunch, but she didn't answer

I never see this kain before – I've never seen this type before

Iya-Ibeji / Iyabeji – Twins' mother

Iyawo – Wife

Jeje – Simply

Kilode – What is it

Lailai – Never

LASTMA – Lagos State Traffic Management Authority

Make I pack am for you? – Should I pack it for you?

Make I serve your food? – Should I serve your food?

Mama never comot her room after she chop – Mama has not left her room since she has eaten

Moinmoin – Steamed beans pudding

Mon ami – My friend

Ngbo – Is it true?

No be when dem plenty person dey get choice – It's when they are many that someone has a choice

No get – Doesn't have

NUGA – Nigeria University Games Association

NYSC – National Youth Service Corps

Oga – Boss

Oga dey – Is the boss in

Ogbanje – Evil spirit

Okada man – Motor bike rider

Okadas – Motor bikes used for commercial transport

Oko mi, olowo ori mi – My husband, my crown

Oma to ojo meta ke – It's been a while

Omo mama – Mama's child

Ore – Friend

Oya – Come on

Pele – Sorry

Sha – Anyway

Sebi – You know

Sef – Even

Settling – A local term for giving bribe

She say I no give am work – She said I didn't pre-occupy her.

She say make you come up – She said you should come upstairs

Short of say I no give am pikin to play with - That's short of saying I don't have children she can play with

So I leave am, say make I no wake am if she dey sleep – I left her, so I don't wake her in case she is sleeping

Suya – Grilled peppered meat

Today na today – Today is the day

Wahala – Stress / trouble

Waka pass – Stage extra

Wetin I go do now – What will I do

Wetin she dey go buy – What is she going to buy

Yabis – Taunts

Yankeed – Americanised

You wan comot – Are you going out
Zobo – Homemade hibiscus drink

ACKNOWLEDGEMENTS

I am grateful to a lot of people, especially those who give me a reason to write, to share part of their stories and to help others find real value in their relationships. I thank my family and friends for their support and endurance at reading multiple versions of my manuscript.

To my readers, I say a big thank you for reading this book and my other books. I sincerely hope you find this interesting enough to want to read the next one.

I raised some questions to aid book club discussions if you are a member of a book club or if you generally enjoy good teasers.

I would like to hear from you. Please, let me know your thoughts by leaving a comment at www.tayoemmanuel.co.uk.

BOOK CLUB DISCUSSION

1. Echoes from the past is narrated by three characters. How does this help you relate to each of the main characters?
2. The book starts with a prologue. How does this opening relate to the story and why is it important?
3. Are you able to identify with any of the characters? Which one and why?
4. Tara knew she had a father who didn't want her and whom she couldn't contact. In what way do you think this affected Tara?
5. What do you think is the underlying problem between Tara and Tokunbo?
6. Do you think Mama was fair to ask Tokunbo to leave the house? Is there something else she could have done?
7. FG continually runs into Tara, do you think this is coincidental or deliberate? Why do you think so?
8. If you were Tara, how would you react to her father's request to meet her?
9. If you were Daisy's friend, how would you respond to the news that she got pregnant?
10. Why do you think Tokunbo doesn't want Tara to work in the bank?
11. How do you think the past has affected Tara's relationship?
12. How would you describe Tokunbo's mother?
13. How would you describe Tara's father?
14. Would you agree with Tokunbo that Daisy is a bad influence on Tara?

15. Why do you think Daisy initially wanted to have an abortion?
16. How would you describe the relationship between Mike and his wife?
17. Why do you think Tokunbo was interested in Ebi's relationship?
18. Do you think Zainab and Ameen pose a threat to Tokunbo's relationship with Tara?
19. What is your opinion about Daisy as a Christian?
20. What else would you have loved to read in the book?

"Good girls don't mix with bad boys." That's what they told young conservative Tobi when she's smitten by alluring playboy Richard. Will their love defy the sceptics?

TAYO EMMANUEL-UTOMI

Tayo has worked in financial services for over two decades, with professional competencies in Business Development, Corporate Communications, Brand Management and Business Analysis.

An incurable romantic, she is often found setting up or trying to fix relationships. She is a passionate speaker on relationship and family life matters; and she writes engaging experiential articles on her website www.tayoemmanuel.co.uk.

She finds the interplays and unpredictability of human relationships intriguing and beautiful, and she continually strives to capture real life issues.

She lives in London with her unconventional family.